What People Are Saying on Twitter...

"IN MONTE CARLO WAITING FOR RAIN TO STOP. JUST FINISHED VERY GOOD FIRST NOVEL BY ADELLE WALDMAN, *THE LOVE AFFAIRS OF NATHANIEL P.*" —JAY McINERNEY

"SERIOUSLY ENJOYING THE HIGHLY QUOTABLE & SMART *THE LOVE AFFAIRS OF NATHANIEL P.*" —EMILY NUSSBAUM

"@EMILYNUSSBAUM WHY DID SHE MAKE IT SO SHORT? THERE BETTER BE A SEQUEL." —GARY SHTEYNGART

"BRIGHT YOUNG MEN, ADELLE WALDMAN HAS VIVISECTED YOU IN *LOVE AFFAIRS OF NATHANIEL P.*" —RON CHARLES

"*THE LOVE AFFAIRS OF NATHANIEL P.* SUPER SMART, WELL OBSERVED, FUNNY, SAD. @ADELLEWALDMAN WRITES ABOUT MEN BETTER THAN MOST MEN." —JOSH RADNOR

"@ADELLEWALDMAN GETS OFF SO MANY GOOD LINES IN *THE LOVE AFFAIRS OF NATHANIEL P.*" —REBECCA MEAD

"FINISHED READING *THE LOVE AFFAIRS OF NATHANIEL P.* & I'M STILL IN SHOCK THAT A WOMAN WROTE IT. EVERY GIRL SHOULD READ THIS BOOK." —ASHLEY SPIVEY, CONTESTANT ON *THE BACHELOR*

"@ADELLEWALDMAN P＿＿＿＿＿＿NEXT REPRINT: 'ADELLE FLAT＿＿＿＿＿＿A DUDE

"Nate is almost too real. Mark my words:
This book will inspire laughter, chills of recognition,
and flights into lesbianism." —**LENA DUNHAM**

"Incisive and very funny." —*THE ECONOMIST*

"A sharp and assured tale about a sharp and
assured young man, who often acts like a dog." —**NPR**

"Adelle Waldman just may be this generation's Jane Austen."
—*THE BOSTON GLOBE*

LOS ANGELES TIMES BESTSELLER

WASHINGTON POST NOTABLE BOOK

NEW YORK TIMES BOOK REVIEW EDITORS' CHOICE

GQ's Best Debut Novel of the Summer

Maureen Corrigan of *Fresh Air*'s
Debut Novel of the Year

A *People* Great Summer Read

Lou Rouse

ADELLE WALDMAN worked as a reporter at the *New Haven Register* and *The Cleveland Plain Dealer*. Her articles have also appeared in *The New York Times Book Review*, *Slate*, and *The Wall Street Journal*, among other national publications. She lives in Brooklyn, New York, with her husband.

Additional Praise for *The Love Affairs of Nathaniel P.*

"Adelle Waldman may just be this generation's Jane Austen, as she skewers the mating mores of today's aristocrats, the young literary elite of Brooklyn, New York, in her funny and at times painfully acute debut novel."   —*The Boston Globe*

"My daughter just graduated from college, but her education won't be complete till she's studied Waldman's brilliant taxonomy of *Homo erectus brooklynitis*. I'm making her read *The Love Affairs of Nathaniel P.* in exchange for paying off her student loans. . . . Waldman offers a delectable analysis of contemporary dating among literary wannabes. You might think it'd be easier to find a parking space in Manhattan than to say anything new about that subject, but this dark comedy delivers one prickling insight after another. . . . Waldman attains something like the universal truths an older female writer articulated by recording the antics of a group of genteel folk in early nineteenth-century Bath."
                                                     —Ron Charles, *The Washington Post*

"Brilliant . . . Waldman has written such a crisp, comic novel of manners *and* ideas that I was completely won over. I inhaled this slim novel; now I want to go back and read it again."
                                                     —Maureen Corrigan, NPR's *Fresh Air*

"Waldman has done the heretofore impossible: Get at the core of the modern female state through the roiling inner monologue of a man. . . . Her protagonist is well-meaning, and that may be the most sobering part. Nate is almost too real. Mark my words: This book will inspire laughter, chills of recognition, and desperate flights into lesbianism."
                                                     —Lena Dunham

"Ms. Waldman has sorted and cross-categorized the inhabitants of Nate's world with a witty, often breathtaking precision. . . . This book takes seriously the question of romantic compatibility—of why we end up with one person and not another—and foregrounds the question of whether it's a subject even worth paying attention to. (Nate thinks it isn't, but of course it is.) There is something beguiling about the very project of teasing out the thought processes of someone like Nate, who so often cuts and runs, avoiding spelling things out when feelings get complicated."   —Maria Russo, *The New York Times*

"A smart, engaging twenty-first-century comedy of manners . . . Waldman is terrific at describing the halting miscommunications of a relationship. Nate's self-destructive moodiness and reverse-engineered justifications are especially well drawn; his shallow pick-a-fight thoughts may even be painfully familiar. (But really, why does she keep wearing those jeans?)"
                      —Jess Walter, *The New York Times Book Review*

"One of the most realistic, wrenching, and wise depictions of single life I've ever read."   —Nara Schoenberg, *Chicago Tribune*

"[A] pitch-perfect debut . . . In the demure tradition of the comedy of manners, Ms. Waldman is rarely mocking or mean-spirited. . . . Even if you find hipster Brooklyn alien territory, Ms. Waldman's surgical skewering of its pretensions and hang-ups is a comic performance you shouldn't miss."   —Sam Sacks, *The Wall Street Journal*

"Adelle Waldman's *The Love Affairs of Nathaniel P.* is that most unusual and wondrous of things: a novel that wants to educate our hearts. Beneath her highly graceful and entertaining prose, Waldman has a moral project in mind: she seeks to extend our sympathies and (with great charm) shame us into becoming better versions of ourselves. Her novel is constantly witty and profound. It is also a reminder that novels can be far more than pleasant diversions, they can be highly sophisticated tools that help us to grow up."   —Alain de Botton

"Incisive and very funny . . . This is an impressive book, full of sharp and amusing observations about urban life, liberal pieties, and modern dating. [Nate] is a man of his age, though his strengths and weaknesses are timeless."   —*The Economist*

"Does America need another novel about bookish young New Yorkers falling into and out of one another's beds? Probably not. So I thought until I read Adelle Waldman's debut novel, *The Love Affairs of Nathaniel P.* . . . Without a trace of cant, Waldman imagines her way into the mind of a talented, callow young man as he slides from one romantic possibility to another, and with equal acuity she imagines a reasonable young woman's righteous response."   —Tom Bissell, *Harper's Magazine*

"Waldman writes with great acuity about the hazards and rewards of dating in an age when thirty is the new twenty."   —*The New Yorker*

"[Nate] is an outrageously well-observed stand-in for a generation of indecisive and conceited millennial man-children. But Waldman keeps him from becoming a straw man by giving him real emotional depth: He is self-aware, rueful, and still somehow unable to change. *Love Affairs* is the comedy of manners we need to understand what ails modern romance."   —Adam Kushner, *National Journal*

"*The Love Affairs of Nathaniel P.* is as good as everyone says."
                              —Lucas Wittmann, *The Daily Beast*

"Although the novel is about his love affairs in Brooklyn, this is really a novel that reveals—astutely—how Nate thinks. . . . The book is an exacting character study and Waldman an excellent prose stylist. . . . [Nate] is a frog in a wax tray, sliced open and pinned back, his innermost private thoughts on display. . . . One must read the magical ending to understand that although his thoughts on women will leave many outraged, his dissected frog's heart still beats."   —Jennifer Gilmore, *Los Angeles Times*

"The best debut novel of the summer . . . Waldman's gift is to give voice to the minute calculations and fickle desires of modern manhood as we cringe and read just one more chapter, and then another, and then another." —GQ

"I have told everyone I know to read this book, and now I'm telling you to buy this book. Nathaniel is a guy who considers himself one of the good ones—sensitive, smart, caring. He went to Harvard. He lives in Brooklyn. He has a book deal. He thinks nasty things about his girl-friend Hannah's arms. In short, he makes me insane. Hannah's attempts to be fun, cool, super laid-back, and easygoing also kill me. We've all been in relationships like this, and please, read this book!"
—Laura Kostelny, *D Magazine* (Dallas)

"Fiendishly readable . . . Waldman gets the big detail right: When it comes to women, Nate's 'clamorous conscience' comes into conflict with the exercise of his natural advantages as a single, successful, attractive hetero-sexual man in a sexual economy that, for him, is very much a buyer's market." —Marc Tracy, *The New Republic*

"Psychologically astute, subtle, funny, and whip-smart, this is a novel that anyone interested in how we live now should read. . . . On every page of *The Love Affairs of Nathaniel P.* there is something that gives pleasure—the prose is razor-sharp, the characters in all their preten-tions are lovingly skewered. This month's hot novel it may be, but this is a book that will bear repeated readings; funny, angry, subtle, and sad, it is the debut of a novelist who's already achieved the real thing. Highly recommended." —*The Sunday Business Post* (London)

"Hilariously astute." —Megan O'Grady, *Vogue Magazine*

"While Lena Duham's TV series *Girls* and Noah Baumbach's film *Frances Ha* have reaffirmed Brooklyn's status as the capital of hipster cool, Waldman's debut novel offers a more critical look at the district's arty milieu. . . . Beneath the protagonist's liberal veneer we glimpse

both political incorrectness and a preening self-regard. . . . Brilliantly observed."
                              —David Evans, *Financial Times* (London)

"We have lately heard ad infinitum the new sensitive literary man's account of his life and times. . . . What we haven't yet heard enough of is the smart literary woman's view of him. . . . Waldman deftly skewers the new literary man . . . with his stylish torment, his self-seriousness, his dangerous admixture of grandiosity and insecurity, and old-fashioned condescension toward women gussied up as sensitivity, his maddening irony, his very specific way of treating people badly while worrying about liberal politics. . . . [An] excellent funny novel."
                              —Katie Roiphe, *Slate*

"An enormously enjoyable debut . . . [This] elegant book is quaveringly attuned to the mores of our times. . . . Engagingly self-aware and pitiably self-involved, Nate is a triumphant creation."
                              —*The Telegraph* (London)

"The way Waldman structures Nate and Hannah's arguments feels akin to fight choreography: vicious and violent, yet almost beautiful in its meticulousness. This is Waldman's debut, but she brings Franzen-level domestic chaos . . . a magnificent trick of making distant experiences feel like familiar heartaches."   —*Grantland*

"Waldman has written a book of stately revenge, exposing all that is shallow and oblivious about Nate and men like him. But it's also a book of beautifully modulated sympathy—for men as well as women. . . . With her eye for social folly in the streets and restaurants of New York, Waldman resembles Edith Wharton."   —Sasha Weiss, *NewYorker.com*

"In the tradition of writers from Austen to Tolstoy, Ms. Waldman delights in showing us the way we rationalize our treatment of others."
                              —Zoë Lescaze, *New York Observer*

"A discomfitingly thrilling read."   —L. V. Anderson, *Slate*

"Sometimes it's more complicated than 'He's just not that into you.' A delightful comedy of manners told from the point of view of one bookish Brooklyn hipster."   —*People*

"A fabulous book . . . This is such a modern portrait. This guy will be so utterly recognizable to all of us."

—Hanna Rosin, *Slate* DoubleX Gabfest (July 11, 2013)

"[Written] with courage and determination and more than a little bit of moxie."   —*The Baltimore Sun*

"Like a contemporary Jane Austen, Adelle Waldman unpacks every nuance of modern mating mores in her debut novel. . . . Bravo to Adelle Waldman for getting inside the psyche of *Homo erectus literaticus*, and for not making it as easy as it should be to hate him."

—Marion Winik, *Newsday*

"Those who pass on *Nathaniel P.* will . . . likely be dating themselves, especially if they're still using Nick Hornby or, worse, John Updike, as a guide to the modern male psyche."   —*The Cleveland Plain Dealer*

"Early readers of this novel have already started arguing about how unlikable Piven is, but there's no debating Waldman's success in etching such a fine portrait."   —*Milwaukee Journal Sentinel*

"A fizzlingly witty debut novel that manages to skewer the new Brooklyn scene and the baffling business that is male sexuality."

—*Daily Mail* (London)

"There's so much truth in *Nathaniel P.* that I just can't stop reading it. Oh, it's one hot book. . . . This is a guy's book. You might classify it as chick lit. You might think it's too narrow, about the Brooklyn literary scene. But the personal is universal. And there's a lot of personal in *Nathaniel P.* . . . Read this book."   —Bob Lefsetz, *The Lefsetz Letter*

"It makes the social life of a twentysomething New York literary up-and-comer feel fresh."   —*Time Out* (New York), Critics' Pick

"Deliciously infuriating . . . a compelling, brilliant satire of modern love: think *Girls* meets *Pride and Prejudice* meets *Annie Hall*."

—Elissa Goldstein, *Lilith*

"I started to read the book and was immediately struck by Waldman's brilliance as a novelist of manners, a sort of Edith Wharton of our own Gilded Age 2.0."   —Baynard Woods, *Baltimore City Paper*

"Waldman is a staggeringly talented prose stylist, easy and elegant in every particular, learned, undeceived, and with a dash of sly, quiet humor in nearly every line that irresistibly recalls Jane Austen."

—Maria Bustillos, *The Awl*

"I basically stayed on the couch for an entire day reading it; I was that riveted."   —Mary Pols, MSN Page-Turner

"One of the things that stands out most about this novel is that characters of both sexes are completely realized, something that just doesn't happen as often as you'd like."   —*Brooklyn Magazine*

"[This] lovable antihero quickly becomes irresistible to us. . . . The upshot: a thoroughly, hilariously of-the-moment tale that marvelously captures what it's really like to be young, smart, and looking for love in the big city."   —*Elle*

"A must-read if you've ever dated."   —*Glamour*

"This bighearted yet brutally honest novel about finding love in the big city is a major eye-opener." —*Cosmopolitan*

"If you ever wondered what that guy could have possibly been thinking (or been that guy and still found yourself without a clue), you'll probably laugh, scowl, and hide your eyes in equal measure as you page through this hilarious, smart-as-hell debut." —Emily Temple, *Flavorwire*

"Waldman takes a cliché and turns it on its ear."
—Julie Elliott, *Library Journal*

"*The Love Affairs of Nathaniel P.* is one of the most nuanced and precise portraits of the muddled male mind since Nick Hornby's *High Fidelity*."
—Teddy Wayne, author of
The Love Song of Jonny Valentine: A Novel

"Adelle Waldman writes about very twenty-first-century manners and sexual mores with a deep fluency of psychological intelligence reminiscent of a nineteenth-century classic."
—Benjamin Kunkel, author of *Indecision*

"Wow. What a psychologically astute and very, very witty novel."
—Rivka Galchen, author of *Atmospheric Disturbances* and *American Innovations*

"This former young-literary-man-in-Brooklyn found himself cringing in recognition." —William Deresiewicz, author of *A Jane Austen Education*

The Love Affairs

— of —

Nathaniel P.

{ *a novel* }

Adelle Waldman

PICADOR HENRY HOLT AND COMPANY NEW YORK

This is a work of fiction. All of the characters, organizations, and events portrayed in this novel are either products of the author's imagination or are used fictitiously.

www.picadorusa.com
www.twitter.com/picadorusa • www.facebook.com/picadorusa
picadorbookroom.tumblr.com

Picador® is a U.S. registered trademark and is used by Henry Holt and Company under license from Pan Books Limited.

For book club information, please visit www.facebook.com/picadorbookclub or e-mail marketing@picadorusa.com.

Designed by Kelly S. Too

The Library of Congress has cataloged the Henry Holt edition as follows:

Waldman, Adelle.
    The Love Affairs of Nathaniel P. : A Novel / Adelle Waldman. — 1st ed.
        p. cm.
    ISBN 978-0-8050-9745-0 (hardcover)
    ISBN 978-0-8050-9746-7 (e-book)
    1. Young men—New York (State)—New York—Fiction.   2. Authors—
New York (State)—New York—Fiction.   3. Man-woman relationships—
Fiction.   4. Self-realization—Fiction.   5. Brooklyn (New York, N.Y.)—Fiction.
I. Title.
    PS3623.A35674L68 2013
    813'.6—dc23

                                                                2012040366

Picador ISBN 978-1-250-05045-8

Picador books may be purchased for educational, business, or promotional use. For information on bulk purchases, please contact Macmillan Corporate and Premium Sales Department at 1-800-221-7945, extension 5442, or write specialmarkets@macmillan.com.

First published in the United States by Henry Holt and Company

First Picador Edition: May 2014

10   9   8   7   6   5   4

To my parents, Edward and Jacqueline Waldman

To give a true account of what passes within us, something else is necessary besides sincerity.

—George Eliot, *Romola*

It was too late to pretend he hadn't seen her. Juliet was already squinting with recognition. For an instant she looked pleased to make out a familiar face on a crowded street. Then she realized who it was.

"Nate."

"Juliet! *Hi.* How *are* you?"

At the sound of his voice, a tight little grimace passed over Juliet's eyes and mouth. Nate smiled uneasily.

"You look terrific," he said. "How's the *Journal?*"

Juliet shut her eyes briefly. "It's fine, Nate. I'm fine, the *Journal's* fine. Everything's fine."

She crossed her arms in front of her and began gazing meditatively at a point just above and to the left of his forehead. Her dark hair was loose, and she wore a belted blue dress and a black blazer whose sleeves were bunched up near her elbows. Nate glanced from Juliet to a cluster of passersby and back to Juliet.

"Are you headed to the train?" he asked, pointing with his chin to the subway entrance on the corner.

"*Really?*" Juliet's voice became throaty and animated. "Really, Nate? That's all you have to say to me?"

"Jesus, Juliet!" Nate took a small step back. "I just thought you might be in a hurry."

In fact, he was worried about the time. He was already late to Elisa's dinner party. He touched a hand to his hair—it always reassured him a little, the thick abundance of his hair.

"Come on, Juliet," he said. "It doesn't have to be this way."

"Oh?" Juliet's posture grew rigid. "How should it be, Nate?"

"Juliet—" he began. She cut him off.

"You could have at least—" She shook her head. "Oh, never mind. It's not worth it."

Could have at least what? Nate wanted to know. But he pictured Elisa's wounded, withering look if he showed up so late that all her guests had to wait on him to start dinner, heard her slightly nasal voice brushing off his apology with a "whatever," as if she had long since ceased to be surprised by any new bad thing he did.

"Look, Juliet, it was great to see you. And you do look great. But I've really got to go."

Juliet's head jerked back. She seemed almost to wince. Nate could see—it was obvious—that she took his words as a rejection. Immediately, he was sorry. He saw her suddenly not as an adversary but as a vulnerable, unhappy young—youngish—woman. He wanted to do something for her, say something earnest and truthful and kind.

"You're an asshole," she said before he had the chance.

She looked at him for a fraction of a second and then turned away, began walking quickly toward the river and the adjacent strip of restaurants and bars. Nate nearly called after her. He wanted to try, at least, to put things on a better footing. But what would he say? And there was no time.

Juliet's strides, as she receded into the distance, were long and determined, but she moved stiffly, like a person determined not to let on that her shoes hurt her feet. Reluctantly, Nate started walking in the opposite direction. In the deepening twilight, the packed street no longer seemed festive but seedy and carnival-like. He got stuck behind a trio of young women with sunglasses pushed up on their heads and purses flapping against their hips. As he maneuvered around them, the one closest twisted her wavy blonde hair around her neck and spoke to her companions in a Queen Bee–ish twang. Her glance flickered in his direction. Nate didn't know if the disdain on her face was real or imagined. He felt conspicuous, as if Juliet's insult had marked him.

After a few blocks, the sidewalks became less congested. Nate began moving faster. And he began to feel irritated with himself for being so rattled. So Juliet didn't like him. So what? It wasn't as if she were being fair.

Could have at least *what*? He had only been out with her three or four times when it happened. *It* was no one's fault. As soon as he realized the condom had broken, he'd pulled out. Not quite in time, it turned out. He knew that because he was not the kind of guy who disappeared after sleeping with a woman—and certainly not after the condom broke. On the contrary: Nathaniel Piven was a product of a postfeminist, 1980s childhood and politically correct, 1990s college education. He had learned all about male privilege. Moreover he was in possession of a functional and frankly rather clamorous conscience.

Consider, though, what it had been for *him*. (Walking briskly now, Nate imagined he was defending himself before an audience.) The party line—he told his listeners—is that she, as the woman, had the worst of it. And she did, of course. But it wasn't a cakewalk for him, either. There he was, thirty years old, his career finally taking off—an outcome that had not seemed at all inevitable, or even particularly likely, in his twenties—when suddenly there erupted the question of whether he would become a father, which would obviously change everything. Yet it *was not in his hands*. It was in the hands of a person he barely knew, a woman whom, yes, he'd slept with, but who was by no means his girlfriend. He felt like he had woken up in one of those after-school specials he watched as a kid on Thursday afternoons, whose moral was not to have sex with a girl unless you were ready to raise a child with her. This had always seemed like bullshit. What self-respecting middle-class teenage girl—soon-to-be college student, future affluent young professional, a person who could go on to do anything at all (run a multinational corporation, win a Nobel Prize, get elected first woman president)—what such young woman would decide to have a baby and thus become, in the vacuous, public service announcement jargon of the day, "a statistic"?

When Juliet broke the news, Nate realized how much had changed in the years since he'd hashed this out. An already affluent, thirty-four-year-old professional like Juliet might view her situation differently than a teenager with nothing before her but possibility. Maybe she was no longer so optimistic about what fate held in store for her (first woman president, for example, probably seemed unlikely). Maybe she had become pessimistic about men and dating. She might view this as her last chance to become a mother.

Nate's future hinged on Juliet's decision, and yet not only was it not his to make, he couldn't even seem to be unduly influencing her. Talking to Juliet, sitting on the blue-and-white-striped sofa in her living room with a cup of tea—*tea!*—in his hand, discussing the "situation," it seemed he'd be branded a monster if he so much as implied that his preference was to abort the baby or fetus or whatever you wanted to call it. (Nate was all for a woman's right to choose and all the lingo that went with it.) He'd sat there, and he'd said the right things—that it was her decision, that whatever she wanted he'd support, et cetera, et cetera. But who could blame him if he felt only relief when she said—in her "I'm a smart-ass, brook-no-bullshit newspaper reporter" tone of voice—that, obviously, abortion was the natural solution? Even then he didn't allow himself to show any emotion. He spoke in a deliberate and measured tone. He said that she should think hard about it. Who could blame him for any of it?

Well, she could. Obviously, she did.

A livery cab idled past, its driver eying Nate to see if he was a potential fare. Nate waved the car on.

As he crossed an empty street, he began to feel certain that what Juliet actually blamed him for was that his reaction, however decent, had made abundantly clear that he didn't want to be her boyfriend, let alone the father of her child. The whole thing was so *personal*. You were deciding whether you wanted to say yes to this potential person, literally a commingling of your two selves, or stamp out all trace of its existence. Of course it made you think about how different it would be if the circumstances were different—especially, he imagined, if you were a woman and on some level you wanted a baby. Sitting in Juliet's living room, Nate had been surprised by just how awful he felt, how sad, how disgusted by the weak, wanton libidinousness (as it seemed to him then) that had brought him to this uncomfortable, dissembling place.

But did any of it make him an asshole? He had never promised her anything. He'd met her at a party, found her attractive, liked her enough to want to get to know her better. He'd been careful not to imply more than that. He'd told her that he wasn't looking for anything serious, that he was focused on his career. She'd nodded, agreed. Yet he felt sure the whole thing would have played out differently if he could have said to her, Look, Juliet, let's not have this baby, but maybe some other, at some future point . . . But while he admired Juliet's sleek, no-nonsense demeanor, that brisk, confident air, he admired it with dispassionate fascination, as a fine example of type, rather than with warmth. In truth he found her a bit dull.

Nevertheless, he had done everything that could have been expected of him. Even though he had less money than she did, he paid for the abortion. He went with her to the clinic and waited while it was being performed, sitting on a stain-resistant, dormitory lounge–style couch with a rotating cast of teenage girls who typed frenetically on their cell phones' tiny keyboards. When it was over, he took her home in a taxi. They spent a pleasant, strangely companionable day together, at her place, watching movies and drinking wine. He left the apartment only to pick up her prescription and bring her a few groceries. When, finally, around nine, he got up to go home, she followed him to the door.

She looked at him intently. "Today was . . . well, it wasn't as bad as it could have been."

He, too, felt particularly tender at that moment. He brushed some hair from her cheek with his thumb and let it linger for a moment. "I'm really sorry for what you had to go through," he said.

A few days later, he called to see how she was feeling.

"A little sore, but okay," she said.

He said he was glad to hear it. There was a long pause. Nate knew he should say something chatty and diverting. He opened his mouth to speak. But a panicky premonition came over him: this phone call would lead to an endless string of others, the day at Juliet's apartment to a regular movie date, all tinged with a sense of obligation and an almost creepy quasi flirtation.

"I've got to run," he said. "I'm glad you're feeling better."

"Oh." Juliet drew in her breath. "Okay . . . Bye, then."

He probably should have followed up after that. As he turned the corner onto Elisa's street, Nate conceded that he should have called or e-mailed a few weeks later. But, at the time, he hadn't known if a call from him would have been welcome. It might have been a painful reminder of something she would rather put behind her. Nor did he know what he would have said. And he'd gotten distracted, caught up in other things—in life. She could have called him.

He'd done more than many guys would have. Was it his fault if he just didn't feel that way about her? *Could have at least what?*

The front door of Elisa's building was propped open with a large rock. Light from the hallway made a yellow arc on the concrete stoop. Nate paused before entering, taking a breath and running a hand through his hair. Inside, the stairs sagged and groaned under his feet. Elisa's landing smelled of sautéed onions. After a moment, the door swung open.

"Natty!" she cried, throwing her arms around him.

Though he and Elisa had broken up more than a year ago, her apartment, on the top floor of a row house in gentrifying Greenpoint, still felt almost as familiar to Nate as his own.

Before she moved in, its brick walls had been plastered over and covered with floral wallpaper. The thick, irregular beams of the wood floor were hidden under carpet. Elisa's landlord, Joe Jr., once showed Nate and Elisa photos. After more than twenty years, its elderly Polish occupant had left to live with a daughter in New Jersey. Joe Jr. had torn up the carpet and ripped the plaster off the exterior walls. His father, who had bought the house in the 1940s and had since moved to Florida, said he was crazy. Joe Sr. thought adding a dishwasher or replacing the old bathtub would have been a better investment. "But I told him that that wasn't the way to attract high-class tenants," Joe Jr. explained to Nate and Elisa one afternoon, while he repaired some tiles in the bathroom. "I told him the kind of people who pay the big bucks go wild for clawfoot tubs. It's a matter of taste, I told him." Joe Jr. turned to face them, a jar of spackle dangling from his fleshy fingers. "And was I right or was I right?" he asked jovially, a big grin lighting up his face. Nate and Elisa, holding hands, nodded uneasily, unsure of the appropriate response to being so openly—and aptly—characterized as a certain kind of dupe.

Nate had helped Elisa paint the two nonbrick walls a beige that contrasted with the dark brick and the cream-colored rug under her couch. The dining room table they had purchased together at Ikea, but the chairs and a long cabinet by the door had belonged to her grandparents. (Or was it her great-grandparents?) Her bookcases reached nearly to the ceiling.

The apartment's familiarity now felt to him like a reproach.

Elisa had insisted on his presence tonight. "If we really are friends, why can't I have you over for dinner with a few people?" she'd asked. What could he say?

On the couch, Nate's friend Jason, a magazine editor who, to Nate's alternating irritation and amusement, had long wanted to get into Elisa's pants, leaned back regally, cradling the back of his head in his palms. Jason's knees were stretched absurdly far apart, as if he were trying to bore the largest possible impression of himself into Elisa's furniture. Next to Jason sat Aurit, another good friend of Nate's, who had recently returned from a research trip to Europe. Aurit was talking to a girl named Hannah, whom Nate had met before here and there—a thin, pert-breasted writer, pleasant-looking in spite of rather angular features. She was almost universally regarded as nice and smart, or smart and nice. Seated on the loveseat was a woman Elisa knew from college. Nate couldn't remember her name and had met her too many times to ask. He knew she was a lawyer. The weak-chinned suit with his arm draped over her shoulder was, presumably, the banker she was hot to marry.

"We've been wondering when you were going to grace us with your company," Jason said as soon as Nate had both feet in the door.

Nate set his messenger bag on the floor. "I ran into some trouble on the way."

"The G?" Aurit asked sympathetically.

There followed murmurs of agreement that the G, among all the New York subway lines, was especially unreliable.

Nate took the only available seat, next to Elisa's college friend. "It's good to see you," he said, with as much warmth as he could conjure. "It's been a while."

She looked at him levelly. "You and Elisa were still going out."

Nate thought he detected an accusation in her voice—as in "it was before you trampled all over her self-esteem and ruined her happiness."

He forced himself to hold his smile. "In any case, it's been too long."

Nate introduced himself to her banker boyfriend and tried to get the guy talking. If he'd just refer to her by name, Nate would at least be relieved of one anxiety. But the ex-frat boy mostly let her answer for him (equity research, Bank of America, former Merrill Lynch, transition stressful). His preferred means of communication appeared to be nonverbal: a fixed smile and benign, fatherly nods of his head.

Soon—though not necessarily soon enough—Elisa beckoned them to a table crowded with platters and bowls.

"Everything looks delicious," someone said, as they circled the table, smiling beatifically at the spread and at each other. Elisa returned from the other side of the room, carrying a butter dish. Frowning, she scanned the room one last time. A self-satisfied sigh escaped her mouth as she sank gracefully into her seat, the billowy yellow fabric of her skirt fluttering on her descent.

"Go ahead and start," she said, without making any move to start herself. "The chicken will get cold."

While he ate his chicken cacciatore—which, as it happened, was quite good—Nate studied Elisa's heart-shaped face: those big, limpid eyes and dramatic cheekbones, the pretty, bow-shaped lips and profusion of white teeth. Each time Nate saw her, Elisa's beauty struck him anew, as if in the interval the memory of what she actually looked like had been distorted by the tortured emotions she elicited since they'd broken up: in his mind, she took on the dimensions of an abject creature. What a shock when she opened the door, bursting with vibrant, almost aggressive good health. The power of her beauty, Nate had once decided, came from its ability to constantly reconfigure itself. When he thought he'd accounted for it, filed it away as a dead fact—*pretty girl*—she turned her head or bit her lip, and like a children's toy you shake to reset, her prettiness changed shape, its coordinates altered: now it flashed from the elegant contours of her sloping brow and flaring cheekbone, now from her shyly smiling lips. "Elisa the Beautiful," Nate had said without thinking when she hugged him at the door. She'd beamed, breezily overlooking his lateness.

Yet only a short while later, he'd acclimated. Hannah had complimented her apartment. "I hate it," Elisa responded. "It's small, and it's laid out poorly. The fixtures are *incredibly* cheap." Then a quick smile: "Thank you, though."

The familiar hint of whine in Elisa's voice brought back to Nate an equally familiar cocktail of guilt and pity and dread. Also sheer annoyance—that spoiled, ill-tempered quality about her. Her prettiness became an irritant, a Calypso-like lure to entrap him, *again*.

Besides, as he poked at his chicken with his fork, Nate noticed the pores on Elisa's nose and a bit of acne atop her forehead, near her hairline, flaws so minor that it would be ungentlemanly to notice them on most women. But on Elisa, whose prettiness seemed to demand that she be judged on some Olympian scale of perfect beauty, these imperfections seemed, irrationally, like failures of will or judgment on her part.

"What are you working on these days?" she asked him as a bowl of potatoes was passed around for the second time.

Nate dabbed his mouth with a napkin. "Just an essay."

Elisa's round eyes and cocked head implored him to elaborate.

"It's about how one of the privileges of being elite is that we outsource the act of exploitation," he said, glancing at Jason, seated diagonally from him.

The idea for this essay was a bit hazy, and Nate dreaded sounding naive, like the person he'd been in his early twenties, before he'd learned that writing ambitiously, about big or serious subjects, was a privilege magazines granted only to people who'd already made it. But he had recently written a book. He had received a significant advance for it, and even though publication was still many months away, the book had already generated quite a bit of publicity. If he hadn't yet made it, he was getting closer.

"We get other people to do things that we're too morally thin-skinned to do ourselves," he said with more conviction. "Conscience is the ultimate luxury."

"You mean that it's almost entirely working-class people who join the army and that sort of thing?" Jason said loudly enough that all other conversation ceased. He reached for a slice of baguette from a butcher block. "Can you pass the butter?" he asked Hannah, before turning back to Nate expectantly.

Jason's curls were tamped down with a glistening ointment. He had the aspect of a diabolical cherub.

"That's not exactly what I had in mind," Nate said. "I mean—"

"I think you're absolutely right, Nate," Aurit broke in, wielding her fork like a pointer. "I think Americans in general are too removed from all the ugliness that goes into safeguarding so-called normal life."

"That's the Israeli perspective, of course—" Jason began.

"That's offensive, Jason," Aurit said. "It's not only reductive but racialist—"

"It *is* offensive," Nate agreed. "But I'm actually not so much interested in security issues as day-to-day life, the ways we protect ourselves from feeling complicit in the economic exploitation that goes on all around us. Take Whole Foods. Half of what you pay for when you shop there is the privilege of feeling ethically pure." He set his wine glass on the table and began gesturing with his arms. "Or consider the Mexican guy the landlord pays to put the trash in front of our buildings twice a week. We wouldn't exploit him ourselves, but on some level we know the guy is an illegal immigrant who doesn't even get minimum wage."

"Joe Jr. does the trash himself," Elisa said. "But he's really cheap."

"Is there a difference between being 'racialist' and 'racist'?" Elisa's college friend asked.

"Same with the guys who deliver our pizza and make our sandwiches," Nate continued. He knew that he was violating an implicit rule of dinner party etiquette. Conversation was supposed to be ornamental, aimed to amuse. One wasn't supposed to be invested in the content of what was said, only the tone. But for the moment he didn't care. "We don't exploit them ourselves," he said. "No, we hire someone, a middleman, usually a small business owner, to do it, so we don't have to feel bad. But we still take advantage of their cheap labor, even as we prattle on about our liberalism—how great the New Deal was, the eight-hour workday, the minimum wage. Our only complaint—in theory—is that it didn't go far enough."

"Excuse me, Nate." Aurit held up an empty wine bottle. "Should we open another?"

"Joe does hire Mexicans to renovate," Elisa said in a tipsily thoughtful voice as she walked to the cabinet by the door. Atop it stood several wine bottles whose necks poked out of colorful plastic bags. They had of course been brought by the other guests. Nate recognized the lime-green packaging of the Tangled Vine, his own neighborhood wine store. This seemed to make his failure worse. He had meant to pick up a bottle on the way over.

Elisa selected a red and returned to her seat. "Can someone open it?" she asked before turning to Nate. "Sorry, Nate. Go on."

Nate had lost the thread of his argument.

Hannah took the bottle from Elisa. "You were saying that we benefit from exploitation but pretend our hands are clean," she said helpfully as Elisa handed her a tarnished copper corkscrew that looked old enough to have accompanied Lewis and Clark on their westward journey. One of Elisa's "heirlooms," no doubt. "I think—" Hannah started to say.

"Right," Nate said. "*Right*."

His argument came back to him at once. "You know how you read a Dickens novel where these eight-year-old boys work in factories or beg on the streets? And you wonder why didn't anyone give a fuck? Well, we aren't so different. We've just gotten better at hiding it—from ourselves most of all. People back then at least justified their behavior by admitting to their contempt for the poor."

Jason addressed the banker. "If you haven't already noticed, young Nate here suffers from a particularly acute case of liberal guilt."

Jason was currently working on an article about the obesity epidemic, to be called "Don't Let Them Eat Cake."

Before Nate could respond, Hannah turned to him. She was cradling the wine bottle in one arm and gingerly twisting the ludicrous corkscrew with the other. "When people voluntarily pay more to shop at Whole Foods, aren't they, by your logic, trying to be responsible?" she asked. "Aren't they paying more so as *not* to take advantage of cheap labor?"

"Absolutely," Nate said appreciatively. (Someone, it seemed, was actually listening.) "But do those marked-up prices really benefit anyone other than Whole Foods shareholders? All they have to do is put some picture of an earnest lesbian couple on a cereal box and we just assume it comes from some free-love workers' paradise. It's in our self-interest to think so because it allows us to buy good conscience, just like we buy everything else." He paused before concluding. "It's basically a Marxian argument, about the inexorability of exploitation under capitalism."

Aurit frowned. "Who's this essay for, Nate?"

"I don't know yet," Nate said. "I want to write it before I start worrying about whether it will advance my career."

Aurit scrutinized him the way a doctor studies a protuberance he suspects is malignant. "Also, don't people shop at Whole Foods because the food is healthier?"

The wine bottle whooshed as Hannah removed the cork.

"*I* think your idea sounds interesting," Elisa said.

Elisa, Nate thought, was being extremely, even uncharacteristically, nice to him. Maybe they really were, as she had said, turning a corner?

"I think it sounds interesting as well," said the guy half of the couple, whose name, Kevin or Devon, Nate had by now also forgotten but who had, Nate noticed, found his voice as the wine began flowing more freely. "I haven't heard anyone call an idea Marxist and mean it as a good thing in a long time," he said as Elisa "refreshed" his glass. "Not since college."

Nate nudged his own glass into Elisa's line of sight.

While she poured, chair legs scraped the floorboards, ice cubes cracked between molars, and silverware clattered against plates. Nate scanned the books on Elisa's shelf. Her collection was impressive, suggestive of seriousness and good taste. The chick lit and the women's magazines, she kept in the bedroom.

"So, what *is* the difference between racialism and racism?" Kevin/Devon's girlfriend finally asked.

"Racialism," Aurit began enthusiastically, "is not so much dislike or prejudice against a group but the—"

"Hey, guess who I heard got a four-hundred-thousand-dollar book advance?" Jason interrupted. Out of courtesy to Aurit, no one responded.

"—attribution of personal qualities or"—Aurit looked pointedly at Jason—"*beliefs* to a person's membership in—"

"Greer Cohen," Jason finished.

"—a racial group." Aurit's words were orphans. She grimaced when she heard Greer's name. Even Hannah, who had indeed struck Nate this evening as nice as well as smart, raised her eyebrows.

"Good for Greer," Elisa said, like some kind of Stepford hostess whose good manners extend even to those who aren't present.

"Who's Greer Cohen?"

"A writer. Of sorts," Aurit said to Kevin/Devon and his lawyer girlfriend.

Nate's friends then began offering up various, mostly uncharitable assessments of Greer's talent and speculating about whom she'd slept with and whom she'd merely flirted with.

"I do think she's a good writer," Hannah conceded.

"It's not so much her writing I object to," Aurit said. "It's her willingness to trade on her sexuality and call it feminism."

Nate leaned back in his chair and stretched his legs under the table. He felt no inclination to join in. He, too, had recently received a sizable book advance (though nowhere near four hundred thousand dollars). He could afford to be magnanimous.

His glass was empty again. The open wine bottle was on the far side of a vast, primitive-looking wooden salad bowl. He pivoted to reach for it, and as he turned, his torso momentarily blocked out everyone but him and Elisa. She met his eye and gave him one of her sultry looks, tilting her face bashfully downward and smiling a little lopsided smile that was peculiarly suggestive, the shy but flirtatious look a woman might wear when she confessed to some slightly offbeat sexual fantasy.

Nate's body tensed. He became panicky and hyperalert. He felt, he imagined, like a soldier who had been having a rollicking time on guard duty until he heard the crackle of approaching gunfire. Previous reports of improving conditions had proved false. Situation on the front was actually bad, very bad.

The wine made glugging sounds as it hurried out of the bottle and splashed against the fishbowl contours of his glass.

"Careful, buddy," Jason said and laughed. Nate ignored him. He needed fortification for later, when, he was now certain, Elisa would keep him back after the others left, insisting they needed to "talk." Ill-conceived advances would lead to a reprise of old accusations. The night would end as their nights so often had, in tears.

He exhaled loudly. An ex-girlfriend—not Elisa—once told him he was a histrionic breather.

When he looked toward the cabinet near the door to make sure there was another bottle of wine on reserve, he thought he felt something brush his leg, near his kneecap. He made the mistake of turning to investigate.

Elisa coyly withdrew her fingertips.

Nate bolted out of his chair and, as if overcome by a sudden and maniacal desire to study its contents more minutely, made for the bookcase. Borges, Boswell, Bulgakov. He ran a finger along their spines, most marked with yellow "used" stickers from the Brown bookstore.

When he dared to look up, careful to avoid the part of the room containing Elisa, he saw Hannah silhouetted in the kitchen doorway. She was wearing a blue top and narrow skirt. She really did have a nice, slim figure. She was carrying a stack of dishes and had turned partly back to respond to something someone said. She laughed, a real laugh, hearty and open-mouthed.

As it subsided, Hannah's eyes met his. She smiled. It was a friendly smile, a sane smile, perhaps the last he'd see tonight. He wondered if she was dating anyone.

2

Nate had not always been the kind of guy women call an asshole. Only recently had he been popular enough to inspire such ill will.

Growing up, he had been considered "nice." He was also a wunderkind of Advanced Placement classes, star debater, and fledgling songwriter whose extracredit homage to Madonna for Math Appreciation Week—"Like a Cosine (Solved for the Very First Time)"—had, unfortunately, been broadcast to the entire upper school. Despite playing on the varsity soccer and baseball teams since tenth grade (granted, his was a Jewish day school), he never quite achieved the reputation of an athlete. He didn't repel girls, exactly. They sought him out for help with bio or calculus, even for advice about their personal problems. They flirted with him when they wanted an ego boost and then they told him about their crushes on Todd or Mike or Scott.

He wasn't much to look at back then. Dark-haired and skinny, he had a pale, sunken chest that he felt made him look cowardly, as if he were perpetually shrinking back. Though he wasn't painfully short, he wasn't tall either. His hands, eyebrows, nose, and Adam's apple appeared to have been intended for a much larger person. This caused him to hold out hope, even as high school progressed, that he might spring up another couple inches, into the five-foot double digits. In the meantime these attributes didn't add much to his existing stock of personal charms.

Todd and Mike and Scott were his soccer and baseball team-mates. Scott was the most popular guy in their class. He was tall and broad-shouldered and had that combination of crudeness and confidence that rendered intelligence not only irrelevant but slightly ridiculous, a peculiar if not entirely unamusing talent, like the ability to ride a unicycle. Todd and Mike and Scott were not exactly Nate's friends—at least not on terms of equality—but they thought he was funny. They also relied on him for help with calculus. (Todd and Mike did anyway; Scott never made it past trigonometry.) Nate went to their parties. Nate got drunk. Jokes were made about how funny it was that Nate, bard of the math department, with the 4.0 GPA, was drunk.

Nate pined for girls like Amy Perelman, the stacked blonde siren of their class, whose bashfully averted eyes and modest smile were nicely offset by her clingy sweaters and ass-hugging jeans. Naturally, Amy went out with Scott, although one day she confided to Nate that she was worried about their future: "I mean, what will become of him? Like, if his dad's stores"—liquidated designer goods—"don't keep doing well? My dad says that they are, like, overleveraged. But Scott can barely read—I mean, he can read. Just not, like, whole books. But I can't see him doing well in college and getting a regular job. It just wouldn't be him, you know?"

In retrospect, it wasn't surprising that Amy Perelman, who was not actually stupid but only affected stupidity in her speech because that was the fashion, eventually ditched Scott and got an MBA from Wharton. At the time, however, Nate had, somewhat to his surprise, come to Scott's defense.

"He's a good guy, though. And he really likes you."

Amy looked thoughtful but not quite convinced. "I guess."

In those years, nice-guy Nate, friend to girls in need, devoted copious intellectual resources to such questions as the verisimilitude of various household items to female genitalia. After school, while his parents were still at work, he roamed the eerily quiet ranch house in search of erotic inspiration, leaving the lights off as darkness began to swirl through its corridors. Slinking like a burglar from room to room, he sized up fleece-lined mittens, condiments, even his mother's pantyhose for possible requisition. One day, in his parents' bedroom, he discovered a surprisingly racy book by a woman named Nancy Friday, and for a time, his equipage also included a "scrunchy" that Amy Perelman had used for her ponytail and which she had left behind in physics lab one day. During lonely afternoons of television and self-ministration, Nate, buoyed by Friday's assurances that women too have dirty thoughts, sniffed the yellow-and-white cloth until the smell of Amy's blonde waves had finally been depleted. Whether he'd literally inhaled it all or whether overexposure had desensitized him, he didn't know. Hoping a hiatus from daily use would restore the hair band to its former glory, he hid it in the back of his bottom desk drawer, behind an old graphing calculator and some tins of colorful, animal-shaped erasers he'd collected in elementary school. Before the experiment could be concluded, he'd forgotten about it— baseball practice had begun, cutting into his autoerotic afternoons. Still, he must have reeked of self-love because around that time Scott branded him "Learned Hand" (a surprising indication that Scott had paid attention in social studies class at least once).

Years later, when Nate and his college girlfriend Kristen had come to Maryland to pack up his old bedroom before his parents sold the house, she'd come across Amy Perelman's scrunchy.

She held it up. "Why do you have this?"

A few blonde hairs, which Nate had once been ever so careful not to displace, still clung to the fabric.

As soon as he realized what it was, Nate snatched the scrunchy from her hand, horrified, afraid that she'd catch something from it, a debilitating skin disease or a whiff of his former self.

"It must be my mom's," he mumbled.

Nate did have one admirer during high school: frizzy-haired

Michelle Goldstein. It wasn't that Michelle wasn't pretty—he'd been interested in girls who looked worse—but there was something painfully self-conscious about her. While it should have been refreshing to see *someone* at their school engrossed in Mary Wollstonecraft's *A Vindication of the Rights of Woman,* Michelle's embrace of culture seemed affected. She had an inexplicable fondness for the phrase *pas de deux,* which Nate had once, frighteningly enough, overheard her use in reference to her "relationship" with him.

Still, at moments, he felt real affection for Michelle. One spring night—it must have been after a school play or concert—they sat together for hours on a bench outside the upper school, gazing down a grassy hill toward the dark expanse of the athletic fields. Michelle spoke, intelligently, touchingly, about the music she liked (moody female singer-songwriters with socially progressive lyrics) and of her intention to live in New York one day, to go often to the Strand—"a huge used bookstore downtown."

Nate wasn't sure if he'd even been to a used bookstore. There weren't any in their suburb, he didn't think.

"You should go to New York sometime," Michelle said.

"I've been. We didn't go anyplace like that."

From his family's weekend in New York, Nate had photos, taken by his dad, of him and his mother huddled together on the Observation Deck of the Empire State Building. They wore newly purchased ponchos and smiled wanly while a cold drizzle fell on their heads.

Michelle smiled sympathetically.

In the light that spilled over from the parking lot, Nate thought Michelle's freckles and straw-colored hair were cute. He nearly reached out across the bench and touched her—her hand or her thigh.

It wasn't even about sex. Nate's life had been somewhat short on friendship, real friendship, distinct from the sort of conditional alliance he had with Scott and company. There had been Howard from summer camp and Jenny, a tomboyish girl on his street who moved to Michigan when he was in sixth grade and from whom Nate had received the occasional letter for several years after, and Ali, also from his neighborhood, who went to public school. He and Nate had drifted apart after junior high. Sitting on the bench with Michelle, Nate felt as if the two of them shared something, some nebulous, slightly melancholic sensitivity that made them different from their classmates.

But at school on Monday, Michelle seemed to have reverted back to her other self.

"I can't believe you got an A on that test," she said after calculus. "What a coup d'état." She gave a little wave as she walked away. "Ciao, chéri."

"Coup," he wanted to shout. "You mean just plain coup."

Yet he and Michelle were constantly lumped together and treated as a couple. Scott repeatedly asked him if her cooter smelled like mothballs because of all the vintage clothes she wore. Michelle's ambiguous social status, neither cool nor uncool, apparently made her his female equivalent. They even went to senior prom together. Nate had been working up the nerve to ask a pretty sophomore, and he felt both resentment and relief when Michelle's asking him foreclosed that possibility. On prom night, he thought Michelle might have been willing to have sex, but he didn't really try, although they made out—more than made out, actually: he had a brief opportunity to assess Scott's hypothesis vis-à-vis the bouquet of her female parts (the word he'd use was *musky*). Nate didn't push because at that particular moment in his life, he didn't want to get entangled with a girl who was slightly repulsive to him. Nor could he imagine sleeping with Michelle and then blowing her off, the way that Todd or Mike might have (although not Scott, who for all his crudity was sensitive and unwavering in his devotion to Amy). There was something that rubbed Nate wrong about Todd and Mike's attitude toward girls— their implicit belief that whatever befell a foolish or unattractive one was her just deserts. Empathy, they reserved for the best-looking girls. (Amy's most minor setbacks, a B-plus or mild cold, elicited coos of grave concern.)

Besides, by prom, Nate had largely begun to pin his erotic hopes on college, where, he imagined, even girls who looked like Amy Perelman would be smart and, more important, *mature*, a word he had lately begun to interpret as "willing to have sex with him." If he were to list the biggest disappointments of his life, freshman year of college would be near the top, right behind the realization, much later, that even something as seemingly sublime as a blow job—his penis in a woman's mouth! *his penis in a woman's mouth!*—could be boring, even slightly unpleasant, under the wrong circumstances or performed inexpertly.

Had he been an urchin rescued from the back alley where he'd foraged for food in dumpsters and solved millennia-old math problems on the inside of torn cereal boxes, he couldn't have been more naive, more uneducated in the social mores of a place like Harvard. And if he'd been a homeless autodidact, he would at least have reaped the social benefit of being exotic. What had seemed normal back home screamed Mall of America, middle management, and mediocrity on a campus where the tone had been set long ago by Puritans with names like Lowell, Dunster, and Cabot. Todd and Mike and Scott, with their gelled hair fanning up from their foreheads and with their polo shirts and BMWs, shrank in size. The kids who seemed to belong at Harvard—the ones who seemed at ease, chatting breezily in the Yard, greeting old friends and throwing their heads back in laughter—drove beat-up Volvos, ordered clothing from catalogs (an activity Nate had previously associated with isolated prairie farms and early Montgomery Ward circulars), and, in a flat English shorn of all regional accent, reeled off the names of places he had never heard of: "Yeah, I've been to Islesboro!" "My uncle has a house there!" "We go to Blue Hill every summer."

Before arriving in Cambridge, Nate had mentally prepared for

Park Avenue, for country clubs, yachts, caviar, for the heedless extravagance of Tom and Daisy Buchanan, but Maine, *Maine* caught him by surprise. Nate was used to summer locales that advertised themselves as such in their names: *Long Beach Island, Ocean City.* His new classmates were not playboys or debutantes. They didn't wear blazers; the girls weren't named Muffy or Binky. A fair number had gone to public schools (albeit largely a specific breed of elite public school). They were thin, ponytailed girls who wore no makeup and slouching guys in T-shirts and khaki shorts. They spoke of kayaking and hiking as the ne plus ultra amusements of their young lives. Nate, who had done those things at summer camp, hadn't accorded them any special significance beyond that of the other required activities, such as singing around the campfire and making finger puppets from strips of felt.

When Amy Perelman's family had gone to Vail for spring break, everyone at school knew they stayed at a ski lodge that sounded like some kind of alpine palace staffed by a regiment of liveried bellhops. People at Harvard, on the other hand, referred to their family's "places" in Vermont or New Hampshire as if these were cabins that their parents or grandparents had personally built, log by log, and they seemed almost to compete about whose had the fewest amenities. ("We never have enough hot water because we rely on our own solar generator, totally off the grid.") Amy spoke of the five-star steakhouse her family ate at after a long day on the trails; Harvard people talked of standing out in zero-degree weather waiting for their charcoal grills to heat up, as if their families had never bought into the whole indoor-stove fad. Nate, too, had been skiing. With a group of kids from his synagogue, he spent a weekend on a barren mountain in Pennsylvania that was also home to an abandoned mine. The trip was called a *Shabbaton*. They stayed at a Holiday Inn and ate at the Denny's across the parking lot.

Nate had never thought of himself as disadvantaged. His parents were immigrants, but the kind with good jobs. They worked for defense contractors. He grew up in a detached house with a lawn

and a metal swing-set in the back. He attended a private, albeit
religious school, where he got an excellent education. His parents
had graduate degrees (masters in engineering from Polytechnic
University of Bucharest, rather than, say, PhDs in art history from
Yale). Growing up, Nate discussed current events at the dinner
table; as a family, they watched *60 Minutes* and *Jeopardy!* Apparently, though, some parents read the *New York Review of Books*
and drank martinis. In time, Nate would learn to make finer distinctions between the homes of his most sophisticated
classmates—the old-school WASPs versus the academic intellectuals (Jew or gentile)—but in the first weeks of college it seemed
to him that all of them, from the children of well-known leftist
firebrands to the spawn of union-busting industrial titans, spoke
the same language. It seemed that way because they did. (Many
of them had gone to the same prep schools.) When it came right
down to it, these groups were like the Capulets and the Montagues.
Whatever their differences, they were both wealthy Veronese families. Nate's family was from Romania.

Before he arrived at Harvard, Nate had read *War and Peace* and
Ulysses for his own edification, but more important he had shown
up without ever having heard of J. Press—so he couldn't mock it.
(Eventually, he gleaned that it was a clothing store.) He had only a
distant familiarity with the *New Yorker* and no idea how easily an
apple could be converted into a device for smoking pot. Nate had
been captain of his high school trivia team. He knew many things—
for example, the capital of every African country as well as each
nation's colonial name, which he could reel off alphabetically—but
he did not know the kinds of things that made a person knowing at
Harvard in the fall of 1995.

He was, as a result, more than happy to be led about by his
suitemate Will McDormand. Will's great-grandfather had been a
railroad executive prominent enough to have been personally
despised by Eugene Debs. After long days straining to make conversation at orientation activities, Nate gaped at the parade of

"dudes" who came to drink with Will. Even chugging cans of
Miller Lite and ribbing one another about the pimply girl who had
been free with her favors at boarding school, they were clearly the
kind of young men who shook hands firmly, made old ladies blush
and giggle, and uttered the appropriate condolences at funerals
(before escaping to the deserted part of the cemetery to smoke a
little weed). They wore expressions of light irony, and their conversation dexterously dodged all serious, intellectual, or sentimental subject matter. When Nate brought up a course he was looking
forward to, an embarrassed silence fell over the room.

Nate believed passionately in the equality of man, disdained
inherited privilege, and bemoaned on ideological grounds the failures of the French and Russian Revolutions; just the same, during
those first few days at Harvard, every time there was a knock at the
door, he popped up from the sofa with eager anticipation. He was
trying to make out which new arrival was a nephew of a cabinet
member and which was a grandson of the Nobel Prize–winning
economist, details Will tossed off with a nonchalance that Nate
tried to mimic in his replies. (The ransom a kidnapper could have
collected if he'd snagged the roomful of guys watching the Red Sox
with the sound turned off while the Smashing Pumpkins played
on Will's stereo!) Will singled Nate out from their other two
suitemates—Sanjay ("Jay") Bannerjee, an affable but slightly stiff
kid from Kansas City, who tried and failed to conceal nervousness
about the beer drinking, and Justin Castlemeyer, a Young Republi-
can from a small town in North Carolina—both of whom Will
treated with a noblesse oblige that, as the semester progressed, grew
increasingly smirking. But Will thought Nate was "hysterical."
He liked when Nate said "smart things" while pounding shots
of vodka, tequila, Jägermeister, peach schnapps, or whatever happened to be on hand. Will particularly liked hearing Nate recite
the African countries' colonial names. "You're like a wind-up toy!"
he cried. "Again! Again!"

It took Nate a long time to realize that "thank you" was not the only possible response to Will's offer of friendship. For most of his freshman year, he found himself among Will's friends, lusting after surprisingly vacuous girls, who, though they had energy sufficient for sailing expeditions and weekends in the country and though they *got into Harvard*, shrank not only from abstract conversation but from any form of culture unrelated to drinking or the outdoors (including movies with subtitles and anything that fell under the umbrella of "performance"). Every once in a while, in private, to Nate only, one of these tanned, healthy girls made whispery reference to a middlebrow novel that she had once read at her summer house after a wayward guest left it behind. So clearly they *could* read. Nate was aware that there were other kinds of girls on campus, but these girls, the ones Will hung around with, many of them boarding school classmates or daughters of family friends or girls whose families had summered near his for so long that they were "like cousins"—these girls seemed like "the best," the ones who really belonged here.

Other classmates were ruined for Nate after Will made fun of them. Girls who liked theater were "thesbos," activists were "lacktits," and would-be campus journalists were "muffrakers." When Nate spent time with other people, Will seemed threatened. At least that's how pop psychology taught Nate to interpret it. (Years later, Nate would conclude that Will was simply a dick.) "Doing the ugly people thing tonight?" he would ask. "If that's what floats your boat, fine, but if you get tired of limpydick and the barking dogs, come to Molly's suite. We'll be playing quarters— or else tackling the mind-body problem." As if Nate had come to Harvard to play quarters! Yet, inevitably, he'd wind up slinking out of the dorm room where a group would be watching *Mystery Science Theatre 3,000* or a Godard film and head over to Molly's. Where he would play quarters with drunk girls who called him "cute" and asked, in giggly, slurring voices, whether Will was seeing anyone and if he was really as big a player as they'd heard. (Nate couldn't tell if the answer they hoped to hear was yes or no.)

It wasn't until midway through his sophomore year that Nate grew thoroughly tired of Will's world. It was too late. He didn't have much in the way of other friends. He sometimes hung out with his former roommate Jay, but for the most part he'd alienated all the nice, thoughtful people he'd tentatively, kind of, maybe liked freshman year by constantly dropping them for Will. When, through one or another extracurricular activity, he did hang out with other people, other types of people, he couldn't stop thinking in Will's terms. Every time he saw a girl in colored tights, no matter how cute or how into poetry, he thought "thesbo" and heard a howling sound in the background. And the nice kids' outings, to the movies or a lecture on campus and then to a coffee-house or diner, were depressingly tame, alcohol-free affairs. Many of these fiery debaters and ardent newspaper editors drank a lot of coffee and, in voices that grew squeaky at moments of high tension, discussed the allegorical implications of *Seinfeld*.

It was then that Nate began, really, to read. It seemed to him as if all the reading he had done back in high school had been tainted. Some part of him had been aiming to impress, reaching for a sophistication he had thought would serve him—socially—in college. (Ha.) The spring of his sophomore year, he began to read from feverish loneliness, a loneliness he began to fear would be permanent. After all, if he, if someone like *him*, wasn't happy in college, where and when would he be happy? His disappointment and isolation made him bitter, and he judged the world around him harshly, with the too-broad strokes of a crank. Except for people like Will, who already had enough privilege that they could afford to take it for granted, his classmates were blindly striving to climb up the meritocratic ladder, as if their lives were nothing more than preparation for business or law school—or, if they were "creative," Hollywood writing jobs. Only when Nate read, and occasionally in class discussions or during professors' office hours, did he feel any fluttering of hope. Perhaps his personality wasn't so ill formed if at least he found kinship somewhere, even if it was among the words of men who were long dead. Or in class, which everyone knew was the least important part of college.

In the middle of junior year, he met Kristen. They were in a political science seminar together. From her comments in class, Nate could tell that she was very smart. She was good-looking, too, with the healthy, athletic look common to Will's gal pals. She had the kind of quiet confidence that comes from faith in her own sturdy self-discipline and quick good sense. She and Nate often found themselves on the same side in discussions. Soon they exchanged smiles whenever a particularly fatuous classmate spoke. They began to walk from class together and discovered that their upbringings were similarly modest. New England–bred Kristen seemed intrigued by his immigrant parents. She laughed at his jokes. Still, when he finally mustered the courage to ask her out, Nate fully expected that she'd turn him down—whip out the boy-friend in Hanover or Williamstown or her latent lesbianism or a chastity vow effective until the implementation of universal health care. But . . . Kristen said yes. She'd recently broken up with her boyfriend (Providence).

Kristen was premed, bighearted, the kind of girl who spent winter break doing Habitat for Humanity projects in the Hondu-ran jungle, but she was also hardheaded and acerbic, prone to a withering disdain for foolishness or absurdity that was both win-ning and slightly intimidating. People instinctively wanted her approval. Between this authoritative air and her sunny good looks, Kristen was, in the world's crude judgment, a catch for Nate, several notches above him in the college social hierarchy. Nate wholeheart-edly concurred with the world: he felt himself to be extremely lucky. If Kristen didn't share his love for literature—well, that seemed beside the point, like insisting your girlfriend share your preference for Pepsi over Coke. It wasn't as if she were willing to date only biology majors.

Around the same time that he met Kristen, Nate met Jason, in a literary theory class, and through Jason, he met Peter. In some ways it was sensitive, thoughtful Peter with whom Nate felt a strong connection. But three worked better than two. There was something too breathily eager about two guys drinking whiskey and talking endlessly into the night about books and the corporate-financed rightward shift of the nation and whether it was fair to say that Marxism had been tested or not because Soviet-style communism was such a perversion. Jason as a third leavened the dynamic. His cheerful bluster dispelled Nate's and Peter's bashfulness and gave their outings the social imprimatur of a guys' night out.

Senior year of college, alternating his time between Jason-and-Peter and Kristen, Nate was happy. For many years afterward, he wondered if he was happier then than he'd ever be again. It was so new—the girl and the friends. And he'd waited so long for both. After graduation, he followed Kristen to Philadelphia, where she started med school and he wrote freelance pieces for a left-of-center magazine in D.C. He missed Jason, who worked at a glossy magazine in New York, and Peter, who was getting a PhD in American Studies at Yale. Home by himself—freelancing—Nate felt isolated. Perhaps he expected too much of Kristen. She had a different type of mind, and besides she was busy and tired. Medical school fulfilled her, mentally and socially.

Over time, Nate began to grow frustrated by her lack of literary sensibility, the sheer practicality of her intelligence, as well as a certain rectitude or squareness on her part—in other words, by her essential Kristen-ness, which he had once revered. He visited Jason in New York more and more frequently. He started to notice there were women who dressed differently, who wore neat-looking glasses and sexy high-heeled boots and had cool hair that made Kristen's ponytail seem uninspired. Many of these women seemed to be reading Svevo or Bernhard on the subway. At home, he'd read Kristen bits from Proust, and she'd get this pinched look on her face, as if the sheer extravagance of Proust's prose was morally objectionable, as if there were children in Africa who could have better used those excess words. Kristen also seemed to disapprove of Nate's homebound lifestyle on a visceral, almost Calvinistic level that she couldn't justify according to any of her core principles. (In theory she was devoted to the poor and idle.)

But the animosity accumulated so slowly that for a long time Nate hardly noticed it. He was genuinely shocked when Jason floated the notion that the relationship might be less than perfectly happy: "I don't know," he said, "it's just the way you sound when you talk about her—it's like 'Kristen, sigh, this' 'Kristen, sigh, that.'" Nate had gotten so angry that it was all he could do not to walk out of the bar. Never mind that in the past twenty-four hours he'd silently accused Kristen of being prudish and narrow-minded a dozen times. Never mind that only seconds before Jason had spoken, he had been imagining their Goth-looking waitress going down on him.

That spring, Kristen signed the two of them up to serve as guides for the blind in a 5K at Fairmount Park. The morning of the race Nate wanted to stay in bed and read, and then maybe, *maybe*, have a Bloody Mary or two a little later, as he read some more at a sports bar with a game on.

"Why does everything always have to be so goddamn wholesome and sunny and do-gooder-y?" he said.

He wasn't shouting, but he was close.

Kristen was sitting on their desk chair, bent at the waist as she pulled on her sneakers. She glanced at Nate, not with concern but with surprise that curdled quickly into annoyance. Then she returned to the business of her shoes. This angered him even more.

"I'm not fucking Jimmy Stewart," he said, mixing up *Pollyanna* and *It's a Wonderful Life*.

A spasm of irritation—out-and-out contempt, really—flickered across Kristen's face.

"If you want to sit around in your underwear all day, go right ahead," she said. "I'll go get you a beer from the fridge if that's what you want."

Nate had brought his laptop into bed. Now he closed it and looked at the wall beyond Kristen's head. "That's not what I meant."

Kristen began pulling her hair into a ponytail. "I'm going to go to the race now," she said in the doctor's voice she'd been cultivating: neutral and distancing and only dispassionately empathetic. "I think you should, too, because you said you would, and they're counting on you, but it's your decision."

Of course Nate apologized. Of course he began getting ready. But the truth was he still wished he didn't have to go. He felt he was right somehow, even though he was clearly wrong because he had promised and because it would suck to be blind and he was fortunate to be blessed with the gift of sight.

After that, their squabbles began to feel more like sublimated judgments of the other's entire person. For a while, each fight was followed—on Nate's end, anyway—by a strong internal counter-reaction. He felt uneasy about the precipice to which his resentful thoughts seemed to lead. He wanted to take back, retract, even in his mind, his criticisms of Kristen and restore the mental status quo (Kristen was the greatest, he adored her) that had served him so well, for so long. But as the fights persisted, his subsequent urge to backtrack began to diminish. Meanwhile, Kristen became increasingly interested in spending time with her classmates. Nate found he was relieved to be left to himself. Soon, they acknowledged that they'd "drifted apart."

Their breakup was very amicable—it was as if simply by agreeing to part, their frustrations with each other shrank to manageable dimensions—and although Nate was a little surprised by how quickly afterward she got together with one of her medical school classmates, there was, to this day, nobody he respected more than Kristen in that good, sturdy, upright citizen way.

Nate moved to New York. He had high expectations, both professionally and romantically. The growth spurt he'd longed for had never come to pass, but he had filled out. His proportions had harmonized. He also felt as if he'd been vetted and Kristen's seal of approval would, through some new air of self-confidence, be transmitted to all other pretty girls. After all, when he had still been going out with Kristen and he had, say, exchanged a look with a girl across a subway car, it had felt as if, surely, were it not for the existence of Kristen, he and the attractive stranger would have gotten off the train together and headed to a dive bar for a drink and smart, fizzy conversation. Once single, however, Nate quickly became aware of the vastly complicated chain of events that had to take place before a look translated into a conversation and a phone number, let alone drinks. It turned out that many of these good-looking girls who gleamed so promiscuously on the subway had boyfriends waiting for them aboveground. Or so they claimed.

When he did manage to get a date with a girl he picked up in public, he was usually in for a series of surprises. Yes, those girls with the boxy glasses reading Svevo or Bernhard or, more commonly, Dave Eggers (Nate had to admit that Svevo and Bernhard had always been much rarer sights, even on the F train), were, as a general category, very attractive. And when the sum total of Nate's knowledge of such a woman had been what he gleaned from her clothing, posture, reading material, and facial expression, he had effortlessly filled in the blanks. She would be nonvegan, catless (or at least only one-catted), left-leaning, sane, and critical of the inadequacies of the American educational system without embodying them personally. He had been extremely naive.

It was around this time that he began to understand what was meant by the phrase *low self-esteem*, something he used to think he identified with intuitively. But what he had himself experienced was nothing like the total habituation to being treated badly that he encountered in some of the girls he met his first year in New York. He went out with a girl named Justine, a Pratt student who lived in a tiny studio in Bed-Stuy with a poodle named Pierre and a cat called Debbie Gibson. Several nights after Nate had gently suggested they might not have a future, she called him on his cell.

"I thought maybe you'd want to come over," she said.

It was 2:00 a.m. Nate said he probably shouldn't. "I think—well, I'm not sure I'm over my ex."

Although Kristen had just told him that her new boyfriend was moving into the apartment they had shared, and although he had been, uhm, *surprised* by the dispatch with which this had transpired, what he told Justine was not, strictly speaking, true—he wasn't pining for Kristen. But it was the best he could come up with on the spot.

Justine started to cry. "I guess Noah was right."

Noah was *her* ex. Apparently, he had told her she needed to get breast implants if any guy was going to want her. Obliged to disprove this prince, Nate said he'd be there in twenty minutes.

The next day he felt ashamed. What did boxy glasses and edgy tattoos matter if you were talking about a girl who suggested, in a heartbreakingly resigned monotone, that he might like to do her with porn on "because that's how Noah liked it"? (Nate wondered how Noah felt about Pierre-the-poodle's wiry-haired silhouette flitting across scenes of spanking and anal penetration as the ill-natured canine chased Debbie Gibson around the room.) Nate felt bad for Justine—because she'd grown up in an infinitely bleaker suburbia than the one he had known; because her mother had repeatedly chosen "the asshole" (her stepfather) over her; because, art school notwithstanding, she grimly expected to be a waitress or secretary all her life ("I don't know the right people"); and because guys like Noah and Nate himself took advantage of her. But pity couldn't be transmuted into romantic feeling, and Nate knew the best thing he could do for Justine was to stop seeing her.

Besides, he had problems of his own. Unhappy with the way one of his articles had been edited, he had—in a moment of pique or high principle, depending on how you looked at it—vowed never again to write for the left-wing magazine that had been his main source of income as well as credibility. This decision had disastrous consequences for his career and his finances.

When he first moved to New York, he'd had some notion that he'd paid his dues during his years in Philly. This turned out to be false, risibly so. Even with Jason's connections at up-market men's magazines, Nate had trouble getting assignments in New York. He took a temp job that became a full-time, indefinitely termed job in the library of a private equity firm, with the intention of writing at night. The job was so demoralizing that he wound up mostly drinking during his off-hours. It was a bad year (closer to two, actually). His industrious parents, who for his sake had emigrated to an unfamiliar land and whose uncreative and not particularly fulfilling labors had funded his lavish education, were, understandably, displeased. They wanted him to get a real job or go to graduate school. Nate was, however, determined to make a living writing.

Looking back, he was proud that he'd "persevered," by which he meant that he hadn't gone to law school. He'd moved to a cheaper apartment, which allowed him to quit the private equity job in favor of shorter bouts of temp work and freelance proofreading for a law firm. He worked on fiction and pitched articles and book reviews, getting assignments here and there. His critical voice improved. He began to get more assignments. Toward the end of his twenties, it became evident that he'd managed to cobble together an actual career as a freelance writer. The achievement was capped off when a major online magazine offered him a position as its regular book reviewer.

By then, he'd mostly stopped picking up girls at bars (let alone on the subway), having learned that he had a better chance of meeting someone he could have a conversation with if he dated women he met at publishing parties—editorial assistants and assistant editors, publicists, even interns. They weren't all brilliant, but chances were slim that they had an ex-boyfriend named Noah who told them to get breast implants. They'd never met anyone like Noah, not in a romantic context anyway, not at Wesleyan or Oberlin or Barnard. And if they hadn't read Svevo or Bernhard—and let's face it, most hadn't—at least they knew who they were. ("*Zeno's Conscience*, right? Doesn't James Wood, like, love that book?")

Conveniently, such women tended increasingly to like him. The well-groomed, stylishly clad, expensively educated women of publishing found him appealing. The more his byline appeared, the more appealing they found him. It wasn't that they were outright social climbers so much as they began to see him in a flattering light, the light in which he was beginning to see himself. He was not underemployed and chronically low on cash—he wasn't only those things, anyway. He was also a young, up-and-coming literary intellectual.

Nate felt not only glad but vindicated, as if a long-running argument had finally been settled in his favor. His unpopularity, though persistent, had never seemed quite right. He was not and had never been a nervous, nebbishy sort; his interest in science fiction, never very intense, had peaked at age thirteen. He had always been a rather well-disposed and agreeable sort of person, if he said so himself.

He knew he'd truly arrived when he began dating Elisa the Beautiful. Not long after, he began making rapid progress on the book that had gone on to win him a six-figure advance from a major publishing house, further enhancing both his professional reputation and personal popularity. Water, as they say, eventually finds its level.

3

The block of text that appeared on his computer screen was oppressively dense. Nate reached for his coffee mug before he began to read.

The e-mail was from Hannah, from Elisa's dinner party. "I was wondering something," she had written. "The other night you said that the indifference to suffering that was normal in Dickens's times still exists. We've just gotten better at keeping it at a remove. But back then things like child labor were tolerated in a way that they aren't tolerated now. They have, literally, been outlawed. Doesn't that matter?" She continued in this vein for another couple paragraphs before ending on a friendly note: "I had a lot of fun the other night. It was nice talking to you."

Nate's coffee mug contained flat Coke. This was not his top-choice beverage first thing in the morning, but he didn't have the wherewithal to make coffee, in part because he hadn't had the wherewithal to make coffee for so many mornings in a row that he was afraid to face the live cultures colonizing his coffee-maker.

After reading Hannah's e-mail, he set down the mug. Its impact on the desk caused a stack of books to wobble. As he reached out to steady it, the stapler that was perched atop an adjacent stack fell forward, landing on the back of his outstretched hand. He yelped.

Several minutes passed before he clicked back on Hannah's message. He frowned as he reread it. Sober, in the daylight, he felt strangely hesitant to pursue the connection. The reason for this was unclear.

On the other hand, he wasn't awake enough to start writing his commodification-of-conscience essay. And he didn't have anything else in particular to do. When he'd been working on his book, he'd always had something to work on. Even when he wasn't up to writing new material, he could always go back and tweak sentences he'd already written. Now that the book was in the hands of his publisher, he missed that.

He hit REPLY. "Isn't it true, though"—his fingers tap-tap-tapped across his keyboard in a pleasing clatter of productivity—"that we are as acquisitive, if not more, than people were back then? We want comfortable lives, and if we don't have servants, we have laborsaving devices made in China. Only now we want to feel good about it, too. So we make sure the exploitation happens out of sight. China is ideal."

After he pressed SEND, Nate checked for new mail. He was expecting something from Peter, who had recently moved from New Haven to Maine for an academic job. But, no, nothing.

He got up and looked out the window. His street was barren, the trees that lined its sidewalks short and spindly, their leaves sparse even at the height of spring. They had been planted a few years ago as part of an urban revitalization scheme, and they had about them a sad, failed look, as if no one but civil servants had ever cared for them. Maybe they were also the wrong species or simply poor examples of their type. The wealthy residents of, say, Park Slope, one neighborhood over, would have known better than to let the city plant such gnarled, runtish saplings on their streets. The people of Park Slope probably imported their own lush, verdant, perhaps even fruit-bearing trees.

The smell of bacon wafted through the window. Nate wondered if he'd missed anything the last time he'd scrounged around his cupboards for food.

As he walked to the kitchen, his socks stuck on the hardwood floor. Coffee droplets, dating from the days before he'd sworn off the coffeemaker, had congealed, turning his hallway into a strip of flypaper for dust and balled-up receipts and the tiny paper disks spewed by his hole puncher.

He gazed into his refrigerator, looking for he didn't know what. A ready-made breakfast of eggs Benedict with a strong cup of coffee would have been nice. Alas. Not even a stray carton of rice from his favorite Chinese delivery place, whose motto was *Always YOU Will Find Deliciousness*. He poured the last of the Coke into his mug and threw out the bottle. A rancid odor rose from the trash can. He pressed the lid shut.

From the other room, his computer pinged. Nate hurried back to his desk. "Even so," Hannah had written, "doesn't it matter that forms of exploitation that were openly tolerated in the past have been forced under the table? Doesn't that say something about how our conception of what's acceptable has changed?"

She had a point. Nate leaned back in his chair. It was not a deal-breaking point, but something he'd have to address in his essay. Perhaps as we become more ethically ambitious, we have more incentive to hide our failings from ourselves? He scrawled "Rawls" on a Post-It note and stuck it to the screen of his laptop.

Then he began to consider more closely the personal implications of these e-mails. Why did he feel so wary?

There was Elisa. He didn't think getting mixed up with a good friend of hers would go over well, and Hannah had been at her dinner party. Still, it wasn't clear that they were good friends. He'd never heard Elisa mention her. And Hannah was older than Elisa, at least thirty, closer to his age than Elisa's. And she seemed, just, different from Elisa, more mature or something. They didn't seem likely to be bosom buddies.

No, something other than Elisa was holding him back. Nate closed his eyes and pictured Hannah turning around in Elisa's kitchen doorway. She was nice-looking, sort of striking and appealing at certain moments, when her expression was animated, but there was something about the stark line of her eyebrows and the pointiness of her features that wasn't exactly pretty. And while she had a nice body, she was on the tall side and had something of the loose-limbed quality of a comic actor, goofy and self-conscious, good-humored but perhaps also a bit asexual.

If Hannah had been more obviously hot, he was pretty sure that he would have given her more thought before the other night, when she had been the only woman present who was at all a viable candidate for his interest. That had to mean something, although Nate wasn't sure what exactly. When he was younger, he had imagined that as he grew up, he would become progressively less shallow and women's looks wouldn't matter as much. Now that he was, more or less, grown up, he realized it wasn't going to happen. He wasn't even particularly shallow. Many of his friends were far colder and more connoisseur-like in their attitudes toward women's appearances, as if the tenderer feelings that had animated the crushes of their younger years had been spent. What emerged in their place was the cool eye of the seasoned appraiser, who above all knows how to calculate the market rate.

Physical attraction had driven him straight into the beds of Elisa and Juliet. This was not exactly a proof of its wisdom. With Kristen, on the other hand, there had been a brief window, before they'd spoken, when he thought she was a bit plain, slightly rabbity and prudish-looking. Later, when Kristen was achingly beautiful to him, his harsh initial assessment became hard for him to believe.

The problem, he realized now, wasn't Hannah's looks.

Nate wandered back to the window, pulling up blinds all the way and squinting at the milky white sky. The problem was that

he was not particularly interested in the kind of relationship he'd
had with Kristen.

He thought of Juliet, the look on her face the other day right
before she turned away from him. Then, later, Elisa. *Jesus.* When
the others had left, she'd tried to kiss him. "I don't think it's a
good idea, for either of us," he'd said, disentangling himself. She
was upset, whether embarrassed or angry, he didn't know. He was
both. He couldn't believe she was going to put them through this
again. While she cried and dredged up old grievances Nate thought
had been put to rest, he downed the rest of the wine and then
started in on a bottle of vodka he'd bought her ages ago and found
still lying on its side in the back of her freezer. An hour later, she
was still going. He was by then so angry he was tempted to fuck
her—just to shut her up. But he didn't. He had done his share to
create this situation, and he knew it. After a while, they both
calmed down, and he coaxed her into her bed. "Just so you know,
it wasn't about sex," she said from under the covers. He was leaning on her bedroom door, about to slip out. "I just wanted to be
held," she said. "I wanted, for a little while, not to feel alone. You
know?" "I know," he said. As he picked up his messenger bag and
closed the door to her apartment, he too wanted to cry.

Contrary to what these women seemed to think, he was not
indifferent to their unhappiness. And yet he seemed, in spite of
himself, to provoke it.

When he was twenty-five, everywhere he turned he saw a
woman who already had, or else didn't want, a boyfriend. Some
were taking breaks from men to give women or celibacy a try.
Others were busy applying to grad school, or planning yearlong
trips to Indian ashrams, or touring the country with their all-girl
rock bands. The ones who had boyfriends were careless about the
relationships and seemed to cheat frequently (which occasionally
worked in his favor). But in his thirties everything was different.
The world seemed populated, to an alarming degree, by women
whose careers, whether soaring or sputtering along, no longer pre-

occupied them. No matter what they claimed, they seemed, in practice, to care about little except relationships.

The sun had come out from behind the clouds. A bead of sweat rolled down Nate's neck and was absorbed into the limp fabric of his undershirt. As he pulled off the T-shirt and tossed it to the ground, it occurred to him that maybe Hannah just wanted to be friends. Maybe he was being presumptuous?

He returned to his computer and tapped on the spacebar. When the screen came to life, he skimmed Hannah's e-mails again. Dickens this, child labor that. Even if she weren't offering outright to suck his cock, she was, in a sense, doing just that. It was in her careful, deliberate friendliness even as she disagreed, in the sheer length of her initial note. These e-mails were invitations for him to ask her out. If he went along, sooner or later his dick would wind up in her mouth.

To Nate's surprise, the thought of Hannah going down on him caused a slight flutter in his crotch. Interesting. Wearing only gray boxer briefs, he swiveled his chair away from his desk so he could stretch his legs and contemplate a blow job from her—for research purposes, to ascertain his level of interest.

He was distracted by an ominous crack in his wall, inching downward from the molding above his bed. Arrow-shaped, it seemed to point accusingly at the squalor below. Parts of his black futon mattress were exposed because the ugly black-and-white sheets, purchased at one of those "department stores" that sell irregular goods in not-quite-gentrified urban neighborhoods, were too small for the mattress and nightly slipped from its corners, tangling themselves like nooses around his ankles. His green comforter spilled over onto the floor, a corner dangling into an abandoned mug.

Because his apartment had no living room, his bedroom was his main living space. Someone had once told him that not having a couch was an effective way to get girls into bed, though that presumed bringing a girl here wouldn't immediately repel her. At the moment, his apartment was like an ungroomed human body, with fetid odors seeping out from dark crevices and unruly patches of overgrowth sprouting up here and there. Nate wasn't big on cleaning or on having someone else in to do it. It wasn't even that he didn't want to shell out the sixty or seventy dollars every couple months. It tormented his conscience to see a stooped Hispanic lady scrubbing his toilet; he held out until the level of filth was unbearable. When finally she came, Consuela or Imelda or Pilar looked at him with big frightened eyes, as if a person who lived this way was most probably dangerous. He didn't blame her. Casting about in his own detritus, Nate often felt ashamed. When there was an unexpected knock at his door, he felt as panicky as if he had to hurriedly pull up his pants, untie the pantyhose from around his neck, and hide the inflatable woman doll in his closet.

After a moment, Nate gave up on his "investigation." He climbed back into bed—to gather strength.

Jason would say to fuck Hannah if he wanted. But Jason—with his finger, Nate made a circle the size of a dinner plate in the air above his pillow—wasn't the right person to consult about this sort of thing. Although he was technically good-looking (and three—three and a half—inches taller than Nate), Jason lacked the good-with-women gene, the thing that Nate had come to realize he had, even back in the days when they mainly wanted to be his friend. For all his gonzo talk, Jason was prissy, almost squeamish when it came to physical contact. He would break off making out with a girl to tell her she should use higher-powered lip balm. "What?" he'd say, genuinely baffled, if you called him on this kind of thing. The belief that he was entitled to only what was most desirable was so deeply ingrained that Jason not only felt disgust at women's minor flaws but took for granted that his disgust was reasonable. "How could I make out with a girl whose lips were like sandpaper?" he would ask. Okay, Jason, fine. Alienate every single fucking woman who gives you half a chance. Go home by yourself and watch porn. *Again.*

Yet Jason gave Nate advice: "Stop overthinking, dude. You're acting like a girl." Nate hated, really hated, being told he thought too much. Jason wasn't the only one who said it: hippie-dippie types who romanticize the natural and the "intuitive" also prefer feeling to thought. But not thinking was a way of giving oneself license to be a dick. If Nate consulted only his "feelings," he'd fuck Hannah without regard for anything else.

Nate sniffed the air several times rapidly. Something was rank. It wasn't the apartment. It was his sweat, musty and animal. He leaped out of bed. For a while now, his stomach had been hissing and yowling like a pair of mating cats. He'd need to go get something to eat soon. Showering was a good idea, forward-thinking.

Afterward, he stood in front of his bathroom sink with a towel wrapped around his waist. In the steamy mirror, his body appeared to be in a state of panic. His nipples were pink Os that the wiry hairs on his chest, pointing every which way, appeared to be riotously fleeing. He had developed a small paunch that protruded sullenly above the white towel. His eyebrows, thick and bushy like the hair on his head, were in need of a trim. Elisa had introduced him to the concept of eyebrow grooming, just as she'd introduced him to many other aesthetic innovations, such as socks that didn't climb halfway up his calves. "Like tomatoes on a vine," she'd said, frowning at the ring where his socks ended and his leg hair came bounding out, wild with gesticulative fervor.

In the mirror, Nate tightened his jaw and pressed his lips together. The expression was suggestive of a cable news pundit taking a moment to consider his response to a thorny question: When will Al Qaeda strike next? Does Iran have sufficient quantities of plutonium for a nuclear weapon? Although Nate had never ceased to consider his nose problematic (bulbous and peasantlike, like that of the dissipated monk in a farce), his literary agent, a brash, jolly doyenne of the industry, had told him he had a telegenic face: intelligent without being priggish, attractive but not, she told him cheerfully, so attractive as to undercut his credibility. This last point Nate heard with slightly less good humor than she had delivered it with.

While getting dressed, he glanced at his laptop. He still hadn't decided how to respond to Hannah. As he pulled on a pair of brown socks, he noticed that one had a dime-sized hole near the seam. He rotated the fabric so the hole wouldn't catch his toe as he walked. Then it occurred to him: he was a man with a book deal. Recently, on the strength of that book deal, he'd even hired an accountant, a singular development in the life of a person who had for years come close to qualifying for the earned income tax credit. Other people, people like Jason and Peter, took for granted a much more exalted sense of what they deserved. Jason prized his well-being too highly to consign his foot to a hole-ridden sock. And Peter, struggling academic though he was, probably wore hand-sewn silk socks he special ordered from an aged Italian sock maker. Weren't Nate's feet entitled to the same consideration? Nate cast off the brown socks. He found another pair in his drawer.

Before leaving, he checked his e-mail one more time. Just mass mailings from various news outlets. Annoyed, he hid the mail program. In its place appeared the last Web site he had visited. A naked woman stood with her breasts pressed against a brick wall, her ass jutting out behind her as she tottered on tiptoes.

It had been a long time—nearly two months—since he'd slept with anyone. At a party the weekend before, he probably could have slept with, or at least fooled around with, a young editorial assistant, yet he'd decided at the last minute to cut out of there, to go home, by himself. Recently he had been undone by the mere dread of tears, female tears, theoretical future female tears that might never even come to pass. (Not every woman he hooked up with liked him!) In the midst of hooking up, all he needed was a moment's fleeting sobriety for his mind to conjure up the fraught, awkward scene that might ensue after one night or two or three, when he tried to skip out of her apartment without committing himself to seeing her again, not meeting her eyes because he knew she knew what he was doing. And then the call a few days later, when, in a studiously cheerful voice, willing herself to be optimistic, she'd casually suggest that they make plans to do something. Holding the phone next to his ear, Nate would feel not only bad but culpable. Had he led her on, acted just a tad more interested than he was out of some perverse combination of tact and strategy and unwillingness, for both their sakes, to ruin the moment? Once this happened—once his mind stepped out of the drunken, groping present to contemplate this bathetic, déjà vu–inducing future— the whole thing might just become . . . undoable. *Unbelievable.* This was Nate, whose unflagging hard-ons had formerly caused him to worry that he was a latent sex addict, liable to wind up arrested for masturbating in a Florida porn theater. But, instead of setting his mind at ease, his new sexual temperance filled him with another kind of anxiety. It made him feel like a wuss.

Fuck it, he thought as he grabbed his wallet and keys off the dresser. Maybe he should go ahead and fuck Hannah, as well as every other willing girl from Red Hook to Williamsburg. Maybe he'd start at the coffee shop, with Beth, the cute girl who worked behind the counter.

4

The light was dim and reddish at the bar Hannah chose on Myrtle (once known as Murder) Avenue. The music, an early 1990s alternative album distantly familiar to Nate, wasn't too loud. A large exposed pipe ran along the ceiling. Tables were topped with old-fashioned desk lamps, an upscale touch in a place that was on the whole studiously dingy, a dark, heavily curtained wannabe dive. As Jason said, you can tell a real dive by its bathrooms. If they don't reek, it's no dive, no matter how much graffiti is on the walls.

Hannah arrived a few minutes after eight, apologizing for being late. "I have no excuse," she said as she slid onto the bar stool. "I live just down the street."

Nate caught a whiff of coconut shampoo.

While Hannah deliberated between a Chianti and a Malbec, with her head tilted away from his and her lips slightly puckered, Nate noticed that she looked a lot like a girl he knew in high school. Emily Kovans had been in the tenth grade when he was a senior. He could still picture Emily sitting outside on the strip of grass between the upper school building and the cafeteria. Her long, dirty blonde hair, shiny like Hannah's, but lighter and less auburn, had a bit of string braided into it, and she wore bunches of silver bracelets and rings with colorful stones. Her sandals sat beside her; her small feet poked out from under a long, flowery skirt. Nate hadn't generally been drawn to hippie chicks, but for months he nursed a tender longing for little Emily Kovans.

Hannah murmured thanks as the bartender set down her glass. Nate asked her about the neighborhood.

"I love it," she said. "Of course, the last time my parents visited they saw a drug deal go down in front of my building." She smiled as she combed a hand through a smooth curtain of hair. "They're not so keen on it."

Nate continued to study her face for hints of Emily. The resemblance came and went, depending on the angle. After a moment, Hannah's smile began to falter. Nate realized it was his turn to say something.

"Mine dislike all of Brooklyn," he said.

Hannah cocked her head. "How come?"

With his thumb and forefinger, Nate rotated his glass on the bar. "Even the son of my mother's chiropractor lives in Manhattan," he said. He lifted his gaze to meet Hannah's. "And he, as my mother likes to point out, didn't go to Harvard."

Hannah tittered. "Nice."

"They get that I moved here when I was broke," Nate continued. "They can't figure out why I stay. I told them I like it. That all my friends live here. I told them that the whole publishing industry lives in Brooklyn."

Hannah was still smiling. "And?"

"And I fell into a trap. My dad says, 'See? It's just like I always told you—no one makes money writing. Except for Stephen King. And as far as I know he doesn't live in Brooklyn.'"

Hannah smiled and then with a jaunty little toss of her chin, flipped the hair off her face.

Nate was back in high school. History class, Mrs. Davidoff's gravelly voice describing FDR's battles with the judiciary (Scott, covering his mouth with his hands and forming the words *Learned*

Hand every time she mentioned the courts) as Nate gazed out the window at Emily.

He couldn't remember when he'd last thought of Emily Kovans. In this dark bar, where the smell of cigarettes wafted from people's clothes and a pink neon martini glass glowed sullenly on the wall, he remembered not only Emily but what the world had felt like to him then. He could see what he hadn't seen at the time: how much his thrilling and uniquely angst-free crush had been bound up with youth, with the particular headiness of a Harvard-bound senior in the months of April and May—college and adulthood glimmering before him like rewards for good behavior. (How naively he had believed what his teachers and school counselors told him about the joys of college.) He didn't know then that the ability to feel the kind of sincere and unqualified longing he felt for Emily would pass from him, fall away like outgrown skin. His current self was considerably more louche—buffeted by short-lived, largely prurient desires, whose gratification he no longer believed would make him happy, at least not for long.

"I used to love this song."

Hannah's voice brought him back to the present. Nate listened. *Those sheets are dirty and so are you,* a vocalist intoned to cheerful, California-surfer pop accompaniment. It was from a different album than the one that had been playing before. He didn't recognize it.

"I listened to it all the time when I was in high school," Hannah said. "Freshman year of college, too."

She told him that she'd grown up in Ohio and had gone to a big public school, the kind where cheerleading was taken seriously.

She took a sip of wine. "You can imagine why punk seemed really cool."

"Ohio, huh?"

"Yup."

She ran a finger along the seam of a cocktail napkin she'd folded into a triangle. "Most of my friends from home are still in Cleveland. Maybe Chicago, if they were ambitious."

She said she'd gone to Barnard on a whim and wound up staying in the city for journalism school. "Nobody I know from home writes or does anything close," she said. "They have regular jobs, at banks and insurance companies. Things like that."

She rested her chin on her palm. A thin silver bracelet slid down her arm and disappeared into the sleeve of her sweater. "What about you?" she asked. "Did you feel remote from this world before you got here? Or is your family . . . ?"

Nate knew what she meant. "Did I tell you what my dad thinks of writing as a profession?"

Hannah had a warm, throaty laugh.

Nate was charmed by something he couldn't quite identify, a tone perhaps, a sort of pervading archness. Now that he was alone with her, he found Hannah to be a little different than he'd expected. He'd formed an impression of her as the kind of cheerful, competent person one likes to have on hand at dinner parties or on camping trips, but she struck him as more interesting than that.

"I definitely didn't grow up in a fancy intellectual environment," he told her. "But I was determined not to stay in Baltimore. I interned in D.C. one year, and I met kids whose parents were politicians and *Washington Post* columnists. I knew I wanted that, what their parents had. I felt like if they had it, there was no reason I couldn't."

Hannah leaned in, poised to be amused. "What was it you wanted exactly?"

Nate caught a glimpse of cleavage beneath the neckline of her loose-fitting V-neck T-shirt.

He didn't have a game plan for the evening. He hadn't even made a conscious decision to ask her out. The day after he'd gotten her e-mail, he'd simply been restless. In the same spirit that he flipped through stacks of takeout menus, he scrolled through the names on his phone, reaching the end—Eugene Wu—without seeing one that appealed to him. Everyone's shtick felt tired, overly familiar. Hannah offered, if nothing else, novelty. He wrote back to her suggesting they continue the conversation in person.

"What did I want?" he repeated. "You really want to know?"

"I really want to know."

He toyed with a whiskey-coated ice cube inside his mouth, pressing it against his cheek. He recalled old daydreams: a generically handsome, professorial man with a strong jaw sitting in a wood-paneled office, a line of students waiting out front and a beautiful wife on the phone. Sometimes, the office wasn't wood-paneled but chrome and glass, with a secretary who patched his calls through and a wall of windows opening onto the skyscrapers of New York. There was also a little hut in Africa where he'd dispense antibiotics and teach the villagers to love Shakespeare.

"On the one hand, to do something interesting," he said. "And on the other, to be admired for it."

Nate remembered something else: the belief that success was something that just happened to you, that you just did your thing, and if you were deserving, it was bestowed by the same invisible hand that ensured that the deli would have milk to drink and sandwiches to buy. Wouldn't that be nice? Nate sometimes envied people less clear-sighted, people so seduced by success itself that their enthusiasm for successful people was wholly genuine. Nate knew perfectly well when he was currying favor—or trying to—and he was more than capable of feeling dirty about it.

"I used to think—" he started to say. But he didn't know how to finish. He began fiddling with one of the buttons on his shirt. "It's more complicated than I thought, the whole thing—ambition and writing," he said finally. "More sordid."

Hannah laughed. "Sold your soul lately?"

"Only in bits and pieces."

"Lucky you," she said. "I've tried. No takers."

Like him, Hannah was a freelance writer, but Nate was pretty sure she wasn't as far along yet. He remembered that she was trying to get a book contract. "They'll come," he assured her.

When Hannah got up to use the bathroom, she walked with her shoulders hunched and her head tilted slightly down, as if she were accustomed to rooms designed for shorter people. She was wearing a cardigan sweater over her T-shirt and jeans tucked into boots, a style that had reminded Nate of Wonder Woman when girls started adopting it en masse a year or two earlier. Her outfit seemed almost deliberately unsexy. But she had what seemed like a nervous habit of pulling the two sides of her sweater more tightly closed, which had the effect of making her (not insubstantial) breasts more prominent. As she walked away, the long sweater prevented him from getting a fresh read on her ass.

"Want another?"

Nate swiveled his head. The bartender, a young woman, was staring at him. She wasn't so much pretty as stylish, with a slightly beakish nose and pouty lips. Her dark hair was separated into two long ponytails that hung on either side of her face.

"Yeah, thanks," he said. He nodded at Hannah's empty glass. "And another Chianti for her."

"She was drinking Malbec."

"Malbec then."

She leaned over the bar to scoop up Hannah's crumpled cocktail napkin. *Her* cleavage was frank and undisguised. The top few buttons of her plaid shirt were undone, and even though she had on a tank top underneath, it too was low cut.

She glided off to the other end of the bar. While he and Hannah had been talking, more people had filtered in; the room swam with their long, swaying shadows. A disco ball cast roving splotches of red and blue on the walls of the long, narrow space.

When Hannah returned, she glanced at her wine glass. "Thanks. Next round is on me."

Jason had a theory that girls who offer to pay on dates suffer from low self-esteem. They don't feel they deserve to be paid for; it's a sign there's something wrong with them. Nate wasn't sure he agreed. Sometimes, it was just nice, only fair—especially if you weren't Jason, who had never been short on cash because he was, Nate was sure, on the receiving end of significant income supplements from his parents or grandparents. Not that he and Jason discussed such things openly. No one in their circle did.

Jason would never go out with Hannah anyway. He was only interested in women who were very conventionally attractive, a preference he had once defended on the grounds of social justice: "If smart people only mated with smart people, class structures would ossify. There'd be a permanent underclass of stupid people. But when smart men mate with beautiful women, smart or not, you undermine that kind of rigid caste system. Dumb rich kids do everyone a favor by eroding any justification for birth-based privilege." Jason was a jackass. Still, the thought of his friend's appraisal—Jason would probably call Hannah a seven ("coworker material")—bothered Nate. He didn't like the idea of dating girls Jason wouldn't. That seemed wrong, since Nate was clearly the better person—more successful as well as more deserving.

This was not a helpful line of thinking. "What's your book proposal about?" he asked Hannah.

"What? Oh . . . *that*." She began to adjust the folds of her cardigan. "Class and college in America," she said. "It's kind of a history and analysis of a national obsession. The Ivy League as our own version of aristocracy." She nodded at him. "Nice shirt, by the way."

Nate looked down. He'd unbuttoned the top buttons of his Oxford. Underneath, he was wearing an old T-shirt. Just visible were the crimson-colored letters *A-R-V*. He laughed.

Fuck Jason. Nate was having a good time.

"When does your proposal go out?" he asked.

Hannah touched a hand to one of her earrings, a silver dangling thing. "I'm not finished yet," she said. "It's taking longer than I hoped."

Nate nodded. "It's a lot of work. You want to make it as strong as possible."

A moment later, he made a throwaway comment about how it's sad that so few people read these days. "It's hard not to feel irrelevant in a world where a book that does really well sells maybe a hundred thousand copies. Even the lamest television show about time travel or killer pets would be canceled instantly if it did that badly."

"Oh, I don't know," Hannah said, turning to face him on the bar stool. "I think it's vanity to want it both ways. You know, to want to write books because that's your thing but also to want to be treated like a rock star."

She held her wine glass rather elegantly if precariously by its stem, at nearly chin level. There was about her manner now a certain devil-may-care majesty not quite of a piece with her earlier timidity.

"Are you really so indifferent to the fate of books?" Nate asked. "You said the other night you love Nabokov. Wouldn't it be a bad thing if people stopped reading *Lolita*?"

"I think people who are likely to appreciate *Lolita* will read *Lolita*," she said, her expression challenging—flirtatious. "I don't care about the rest. I mean, I don't care what they do for fun."

It flashed through Nate's mind that Hannah's position wasn't very feminine. She sounded more like an aesthete than an educator, and women, in his experience, tended by disposition to be educators. He felt intuitively that she was paraphrasing someone else (a professor? Nabokov's *Lectures on Literature*?) and that the someone was a man.

"You're saying most people are philistines and no amount of education or cultural outreach will change that?" he asked.

She raised an eyebrow. "Not exactly. I mean, who even says 'philistine' anymore?"

"You know what I mean."

"I don't think they are worse people because they don't like novels, if that's what you mean."

"You don't?"

"They could be, I don't know, scientific geniuses or Christians who devote their lives to charity. I don't see why being a person who reads novels makes me or anyone else superior."

"Do you really mean that? Or are you just paying lip service to the idea because it's politically correct?"

Hannah laughed and her cardigan fell open, revealing the contours of her breasts through her T-shirt.

"I mostly mean it," she said. "I try to mean it."

Nate realized he was having a conversation with Hannah—that is, he wasn't going through the motions of having a conversation with her while privately articulating her tics and mental limitations. When it came to dating, his intelligence often seemed like an awkward appendage that failed for the most part to provide him with whatever precisely was wanted—dry, cynical humor; gallantry; an appreciation for certain trendy novelists—but nonetheless made a nuisance of itself by reminding him when he was bored. He wasn't bored now.

"Is it snobbery to think that *Lolita* is better than a television show about pets?" he persisted.

"It's snobbery to think you're a better person than someone else just because they don't happen to get off on the world's most elegant account of child molestation."

Her eyes flashed in the light cast by the disco ball.

Nate suggested they order another round.

As the bartender brought their drinks, he remembered something. "I didn't know you and Elisa were friends," he said.

Hannah looked at the black Formica bar. With her fingertips, she pushed her wine glass along its surface, guiding the glass like a hockey puck on ice.

"We're not really," she said. "To be honest, I was surprised when she invited me to her dinner party." She looked up. "Pleasantly surprised, I should say."

This made perfect sense. Elisa wasn't great at maintaining friendships with women. She often pursued new female friends eagerly, but from year to year there was high turnover. Nate didn't think it a coincidence that half the guests at her dinner party had been his friends rather than her own.

"What about you?" Hannah asked. "You and Elisa . . . ?"

"We used to date," Nate said quickly.

Hannah nodded. Nate nodded back. He suspected that Hannah already knew about him and Elisa. For a moment, they continued to nod at each other.

"It's great you're still friends," she said, finally.

She suggested they go outside for a cigarette. Nate was glad for the chance to stand up.

It had been a chilly June; the outside air was cool. He and Hannah stood with their backs to the bar. Across the street, in a brightly lit new bodega, a table was piled high with pineapples and bananas. Its back wall was lined with stacks of Nature's Harvest toilet paper wrapped in bucolic green cellophane. Next to the bodega stood a shabby, glass-fronted insurance office.

Hannah sifted through her purse and passed Nate a pack of cigarettes. He held the yellow box at a distance from his body, like a teetotaler forced to handle a martini glass.

"I didn't know you smoked," he said.

She continued to dig through her bag. "Only when I'm drinking," she said. Her voice had become a bit singsong. She'd kept up with him drink for drink. That had surprised him.

The traffic light turned green. Two yellow cabs with their empty lights on shot past, hightailing it back to Manhattan. Hannah retrieved a plastic lighter. Nate watched as she put a cigarette in her mouth, cupping it with one hand and lighting it with the other. When she inhaled, her mouth formed a small O. Her eyelids drooped languidly. Pleasure seemed to ripple through her.

"You're like a junkie."

Without meeting his eye, she gave him the finger. The gesture surprised Nate into laughter.

"I just get so sick of the antismoking thing," she said. "It's so totalitarian."

Before he knew what he was doing, Nate leaned in and kissed her. He descended upon her so swiftly that she made some sort of girlish, giggling noise of surprise-cum-accommodation before she began kissing him back. He felt the cigarette fall to the ground.

Her mouth tasted mildly of ashtray. It didn't bother him. He liked that she found the antismoking thing "totalitarian."

He began walking her backward until her upper back touched the brick front of an adjacent building. He leaned into her, one hand on the wall above her head for support, as his other moved down to the curve of her hip. Then, abruptly, he felt a tightening in his chest, as his body reacted to a thought before it had fully formed in his mind. Without at all wanting to, he had begun to wonder whether this was a good idea, if the spontaneous affection he felt for Hannah weren't a signal that this was the last thing he ought to be doing.

No. The hand on the wall balled into a fist, scratching against the brick; his other hand found its way to where the small of Hannah's back dimpled and flared into her ass, which was indeed nice, *very nice*. Through his shirt, he felt her hand climbing up his back. He told himself to shut the fuck up and enjoy the moment.

5

Nate held his coffeepot up to the light. Its bottom half was a mash-up of pale brown stains with dark outlines, a fossil record of every pot of coffee he'd made since the last time he cleaned the thing. He began scrubbing the inside with a warm sponge.

After a little while, his thoughts turned to Hannah. He'd had fun with her the other night. That wasn't so unusual. He generally liked first dates. What was unusual was the impression of her he had taken away, one of both reasonableness and intellectual depth. Although it wasn't something he'd admit aloud, he often thought women were either deep or reasonable, but rarely both. Aurit, for example, was deep but not reasonable. Kristen was reasonable but not deep.

Sometimes he wondered whether he was a bit misogynistic. Over the years, various women had complained that almost all the writers he admired were not only dead and white but male. Although this was pointed out to him with prosecutorial glee, Nate didn't think it meant all that much. Women had faced systemic barriers to education and opportunity for most of history. They hadn't written as much.

What he didn't say—why aid the prosecution's case?—was that the kind of writing he preferred seemed inherently masculine.

The writers who impressed him most weren't animated by a sense of personal grievance. (They were unlikely to, say, write poems called "Mommy.") Of course that wasn't an accurate characterization of all, or most, writing by women. Still, the fact was that when he read something he admired, something written today—fiction, nonfiction, didn't matter—there was about an 80 percent chance that a guy wrote it.

He thought women were every bit as intelligent as men, every bit as capable of figuring out how long it would take for train A to crash into train B if the two were moving toward each other at an average speed of C. They were as capable of rational thought; they just didn't appear to be as interested in it. They were happy to apply rational argument to defend what they already believed but unlikely to be swayed by it, not if it conflicted with inclination or, worse, intuition, not if it undercut a cherished opinion or nettled their self-esteem. So many times, when Nate had been arguing with a woman, a point was reached when it became clear that no argument would alter her thinking. Her position was one she "felt" to be true; it was, as a result, impermeable.

Even self-consciously intellectual women seemed to be primarily interested in advocacy, using intellect to serve a cause like feminism or the environment or the welfare of children, or in the interpretation of their own experience. Take Aurit. She was one of the smartest women—people—Nate knew. She was clear-sighted and original, and not, like a certain type of woman, intellectually timorous; she was comfortable challenging conventional wisdom. But her subjects—Zionism, Judaism, patriarchy—stemmed from her life. When she tried to do more abstract writing, the result was comparatively thin. She wasn't interested in international relations or Middle Eastern politics; she was interested in growing up in a crazy, conflicted Israeli family that functioned like a two-headed monster, liberal socialism and primitive tribalism everywhere bumping up against each other. In other words, she was interested in being Aurit. And that was fine. But it was a difference.

Of course, if you pointed this out to Aurit, she'd be furious. And for Aurit, the fact that something made her feel bad was reason enough to reject it. She didn't even like it when Nate mentioned things outside her ken. If he got to talking about philosophers she hadn't read—which is to say, most of them—her face would grow taut, tight-lipped, with a pulsing around the temples, as if Nate, in talking about Nietzsche, were in actuality whipping out his cock and beating her with it. Even Jason—and Aurit was surely a better person than *Jason*—was far more fair, intellectually.

And that was Aurit, who was brilliant. If Nate were honest, he also thought that women as a general category seemed less capable of (or interested in) the disinterested aesthetic appraisal of literature or art: they were more likely to base judgments on a thing's message, whether or not it was one they approved of, whether it was something that "needed saying."

By now, the coffeepot was reasonably transparent.

Nate set it aside and inspected the coffeemaker itself, examining the caked-up grounds that clung to it. When he turned the lightweight plastic apparatus upside down, compartments came flapping open, swinging wildly on plastic hinges. The machine began to slide from his hands. Crouching quickly, he caught it, hugging it against his stomach. He set it in the sink and began jabbing at it with the limp sponge.

When he finished, he left the coffeemaker to dry on the counter next to the carafe. As he walked to his bedroom, he took off his damp T-shirt. The air in the bedroom was thick with a restless gloom as wan late afternoon sunlight mostly failed to pierce a thick blanket of clouds. A light layer of condensation dotted the windowpane and gave the room a sealed, hermetic feel.

He felt a wave of affection for his little garret. Its particular brand of squalor appealed to him on a basic level. Real squalor was not this but the barren utilitarianism of his parents' suburban condo, where various unseen appliances hummed monotonously like hospital monitors. Or it was the plasticky faux-elegance of the ranch house they'd lived in when he was growing up, an immigrant's version of the American home, culled from TV shows of a generation earlier, with artificial flowers and a living room that was rarely used. Even the tasteful, high-end prewar co-ops that some of his friends had purchased in recent years, with their baby gates and wine refrigerators (wine refrigerators!), were to Nate more squalid than his little apartment, which was, in contrast, the home of a person who lived for things other than the sort of domestic and domesticating coziness that almost everybody seemed to go in for.

He'd done some cleaning. That helped. Nate's day-to-day life was characterized by bursts of productivity punctuated by downward slides into lethargy, loneliness, filth, and gloom. His bad moods had a self-perpetuating quality. He hadn't a job or consistent routine to stop the slough, and his general recourse—drink—tended to be helpful only in the short-term. Still, Nate had never really been incapacitated by his moods, not for more than a day or two, and ever since his book had sold, his low bouts had been both less frequent and less severe. If his relative success hadn't exactly made him happy, it had, on average, made him less unhappy. Today the approach of a deadline had spurred him out of inactivity. He had a book review to write, and write fast. In preparation, he'd launched into hyperproductive mode. In the past several hours, he had gone for a run (five miles in forty-one minutes and thirty-eight seconds), mailed an overdue RSVP card to a friend's wedding, dropped off his laundry, and ventured to the grocery store, where he'd bought beer, milk, three Celeste Pizzas for One (on special), and an ample supply of Total Raisin Bran and Lucky Charms (his breakfast of choice was a bowl of the former followed by a "dessert" of Lucky Charms).

Feeling entitled to a moment of repose, Nate pulled his bedroom window open and leaned outside, breathing in mouthfuls of moist air. His apartment's two windows—one in the bedroom and one in the kitchen—were the only features that a yuppie might covet. South-facing, they let in lots of sunlight, and from the sixth floor, the view was decent—if you looked above the roofs of the neighboring buildings and into the skyline rather than at the street below. But his block was more dear to him for its ugliness. Its proximity to fashion—appealing bars and restaurants, coffee shops, his friends—was convenient, but its unfashionableness was what he loved. At the corner, a tire repair shop's yellow awning read, "Open 7 a.m. to - -" On Sunday mornings, the storefront church across the street drew a crowd of black women whose calf-length skirts clung to their legs in the breeze.

Such vestiges of the neighborhood that this had once been were especially touching now. In his own building, people who had lived for many years in dark, mildewy apartments with cracked linoleum tiles watched from their doorways as surrounding units were gutted, then redone with gleaming new windows, hardwood floors, and stainless steel appliances—and a different type of tenant, the kind who paid several times the unrenovated rent. Nate had moved in a few years before the current wave of ubergentrification; that his own apartment had hardly been improved was a source of pride.

Still, like the newer arrivals, he only superficially lived among the poor. They walked the same streets and rode the same subways (the buses, however, were largely ceded to the underclass), but the two groups might have existed on different layers of the earth's atmosphere that only from a distance appear to be on the same plane. A store called National Wines & Liquors, Inc., where both liquor and cashier were enclosed behind bulletproof glass, was not actually a competitor to the much newer Tangled Vine, which specialized in organic and local wines and exhibited the work of area artists at its Thursday-evening tastings. Even at the bodegas, where all paths in fact converged, the different strata of residents rarely handled the same merchandise. Nate reached for the *New York Times* (which they had only begun to stock relatively recently— when he first moved to the neighborhood, he had to walk to Park Slope to get it), while the cabbies and construction workers grabbed the *Post*. He bought six-packs of beer to take home rather than single-serving twenty-four ounce cans. Only the cash that passed back and forth across the counter touched all hands.

From the street, Nate heard the guttural throb of an unmuffled engine, followed by the screech of brakes. Nate could hear shouting but not the words as a pair of young women crossed the street in front of a stopped car.

He thought again of Hannah. After they'd kissed the other night, they'd gone back inside the bar and finished their drinks. He walked her home, and they made out a little more in front of her building. Even in retrospect, he found her—her easy willingness to contradict him, her unfeminine but not at all unflattering outfit—strongly sexy.

But he knew he should be careful. He had a bad habit of initially zeroing in on one or two things he liked about every new girl he found himself interested in, as if to justify his attraction. This one (Emily Chiu) was not just beautiful in a petite and delicate way he found particularly compelling, but he and she had also had, on first meeting, an intense and bonding conversation about being children of immigrants. That one (Emily Berg) was funny. A third was dazzlingly impressive in a certain sane and competent and businesslike way. (Yes, early on, he'd thought maybe he would fall for Juliet.) But early impressions were unreliable. Juliet, for example. She prided herself on being a person who had the courage to speak her mind, who called things as she saw them, but after a few dates, Nate had felt *aggressive* was perhaps a more fitting description. She was a repository of truths both obvious and rude: a friend should go on a diet, a struggling coworker should accept his limitations and stop trying to be "some hotshot reporter he's not cut out to be." She rarely asked Nate questions about himself except to wonder if he'd been to such-and-such restaurant and to marvel when the answer was no. They couldn't seem to hit on many topics of mutual interest; Nate spent much of their time together affecting interest in subjects that held only moderate appeal for him: personnel issues at the *Wall Street Journal*, the vast number of business reporters who lacked a solid understanding of business, the relative merits of whole grains versus refined ones. Also, the high percentage of New York men who were, according to Juliet, intimidated by successful women.

There was nothing *wrong* with Juliet—Nate had no doubt that many other men found her desirable—but it had been obvious that he and she weren't right for each other. Still, when he realized that he had been mistaken in his initial impression—of Juliet or of any of the women he dated—he invariably felt like a jerk for having seemed, initially, more enthusiastic than he would turn out to be.

Of course, these women ought to have listened when he told them he wasn't looking for anything serious. But on a certain level, it didn't really matter if it was stupid of them. Ethical people don't take advantage of other people's weakness; that's like being a slumlord or a price gouger. And treading on weakness is exactly what dating felt like, with so many of these women—with their wide-open hopefulness, their hunger for connection and blithe assumption that men wanted it just as badly.

Based on what? On whom?

The outside air began to chill his bare chest. Nate edged back inside, ready now to begin. The book he was reviewing was written by a left-leaning Israeli novelist. In the past few weeks, he had read all of the author's earlier works and other related books but not, until today, the book he was actually reviewing. He quickly grew absorbed in the text, rarely looking up as the sun sank behind a jagged gray horizon of six- and seven-story buildings. He was already growing disenchanted with the text—it was rife with sentimentality, its politics were pat and self-congratulatory— when he realized he was squinting to read in near darkness; he switched on his desk lamp. He finished the book around midnight and began making notes. Several hours later, he turned out the lamp to take a short nap. He was back at his desk, bent over his laptop, when the first hint of salmony orange began tingeing the darkness outside. He walked to the window. Even the storefront church looked austere and dignified in the dawn mist. *The city doth now, like a garment, wear / the beauty of the morning, silent, bare* . . . He vowed to pay attention to the sunrise more often, when he hadn't been up all night. Which is what he always said when he'd been up all night.

By midmorning, the sun was brilliant, hard and glinting. What clouds remained were reduced to stringy tendrils kicked around by the breeze. Nate shut his blinds to block out the glare. By then, he was laying out the heart of his argument. While he shared the author's outrage at certain developments in contemporary Israel, there is, he wrote, an inevitability about the country's rightward shift. When a nation claiming allegiance to liberal-democratic principles is founded on explicitly nationalistic grounds, the contradiction is bound to come back to haunt it, even if nationalism is dressed up as Zionism. Because Israel was from its birth riddled with evasion—like the United States, in terms of slavery—there isn't firm ground on which to argue with the growing number of Israelis, particularly Orthodox Jews and Russian immigrants, who dismiss liberal principle as mere weakness. Eventually, a true reckoning, not a mere hand-wringing, will be necessary. (Aurit, Nate realized, was going to hate the piece.)

Every once in a while, as he considered a phrase or conceived a counterargument, he stood up to pace, clasping his hands together behind his head as he roamed his apartment's small perimeter. In the late afternoon, he opened his blinds and looked outside. Cloud shadows passed so quickly over the tops of buildings that he had the sensation of being himself in motion.

It was early evening when he sent off the completed review. He felt like he'd emerged from some dark, intimate chamber. He showered and then left a trail of wet footprints as he walked back to the bedroom with his towel around his waist, his cheeks tender and pink from the razor. He resisted the urge to e-mail his editor with a few minor corrections that had come to him as he shaved.

Instead, he picked up three cereal bowls, two mugs, an empty can of Bud Light, an orange ceramic plate full of pizza crusts, and several greasy paper towels. It didn't seem like much detritus for twenty-four hours of pretty much straight work.

Sitting at a nearby sports bar an hour or so later—his hunger sated, and his interest in the Yankees game on the flat-screen TV waning as their lead over the Orioles grew larger—he felt a yearning to see Hannah. He wanted to talk to her about his review, which he was largely happy with. He'd made a glancing reference to Nabokov that he thought she would appreciate.

He toyed with the idea of calling her to see if she wanted to join him. But that was ridiculous. He was practically falling asleep on the bar stool and felt drunk after a single beer. There was also the fact that he was wary of starting something.

He left a few dollars under his glass and nodded good-bye to the bartender, a gruff, muscular guy about Nate's age. As he emerged onto the street, a deliveryman on a bicycle whizzed by, causing him to step back. It occurred to him how ridiculous he was being, how *neurotic*. He was making way too big a deal out of this. He made up his mind to call her the next day.

The restaurant they met at was one of those bistro-style places, with red leather banquettes and a black-and-white tile floor, a decor inspired by *Casablanca* and French colonialism. When Nate arrived, Hannah was leaning on the bar with a drink in her hand. A ray of sunlight from the window cut a stripe on her slender back and then, as she turned to face him, across her chest and shoulders.

She was dressed in a fitted blouse and a narrow skirt that wasn't exactly a miniskirt but didn't quite reach her knees. She looked nice. "You look nice," he said.

"Thanks."

Nate tugged at his T-shirt, only to notice that his gut jutted out a bit in the front. He sucked it in and saw that his jeans, fashionable ones that Elisa had picked out for him, sagged from too much time between washings. His pockets, full with wallet and cell phone and keys, bulged unattractively.

"Expecting rain?" Hannah asked.

She nodded at the umbrella he was carrying and tilted her head toward the window. Bright blue sky was visible above the rooftops.

"Maybe I got bad information," he said.

He told her he'd been given the umbrella that afternoon by the girl who worked at his regular coffee shop. Someone had left it weeks before.

"Can't beat free, right?" he said. Then he squinted at the umbrella. It was oversized, with a purple-and-white canopy. "Well, it is maybe a little conspicuous."

When Hannah smiled, the Emily Kovans resemblance struck him again.

"I hope I'm not turning into my dad," he said after they'd been seated at a table in the back of the restaurant. "He likes to brag about how he never has to buy dishtowels or washcloths because he just takes the ones they give you to use at the gym."

Hannah asked what his parents were like—"when they aren't stealing household items, I mean."

Nate immediately wanted to take back what he'd said. He didn't like the derision that habitually crept into his voice when he talked about his parents, as it had the last time he'd seen Hannah, when he'd mocked their attitude about Brooklyn. Seeking to entertain, he too often found himself making fun of their middle-class immigrant ways: their un-PC remarks about minorities, their defensive, almost childlike assertions of superiority over Americans and the American culture that they so often misread, their too-naked concern with money and frequent suspicion that people intended to take advantage of them. All of those stories were true, but when Nate trotted them out something didn't translate. He felt more empathy for his parents than his tone implied, and he suspected that what he was really trying to say was "I'm different—I'm of Harvard, of New York, not of these rubes." This had been especially bad with Elisa. Perhaps he never forgave her for the remorseless quality of her laughter when he'd told her about how, long ago, they had oohed and aahed at the furniture in the window of a rent-to-own store. They had said the cream-and-gold lacquered coffee table and the bed with the swan-shaped headboard reminded them of Versailles.

"They're not so bad," he said to Hannah as a waiter dropped down menus. "They're nice people."

She was more forthcoming. Both her parents had grown up on the west side of Cleveland ("the wrong side"). Her father was the brainy son of an autoworker who'd wooed and won a popular girl, Hannah's mother, when they were students at Kent State. "She literally was homecoming queen," Hannah said. Her father was a corporate lawyer. She had two older sisters, both well-adjusted and successful, "more midwestern" than she was. They were married; one lived in Chicago and the other in Cleveland. East side.

When they finished their cocktails, Nate ordered a bottle of wine.

"What a proper meal this is turning into," Hannah said. "Very WASPy."

She told him that she'd visited a friend's Cape Cod beach house a couple weekends before. She described the house's wine cellar and the bedroom she'd stayed in, which opened to a screened-in porch that led to the beach. She said she couldn't quite believe she was there. Nate remarked that the rich enjoy being hospitable to smart, artsy types. They need an audience of people discerning enough to truly appreciate all they have. It helps them to enjoy it more. Hannah suggested that he was being overcynical. Her friend's family had money. Why should that make her hospitality more suspect than other people's? Nate said that he didn't mean to insult her friend. He was talking on a macro level.

"Oh, a *macro* level," Hannah said. "I see then."

Nate was immediately embarrassed. Why had he used that word? He had a bad habit of getting carried away, unwittingly revealing his pedantic precision, the academic cast of his mind. In writing, he could cover this up with deceptively casual language, a hard-won conversational tone that often eluded him—in conversation. In contrast, Hannah had about her, in spite of her slight shyness, an air of cool; it was in her amused, ironic, slouching posture, her default arch tone, even in the careless way she held her drink.

"I mean—" he began.

"I know what you mean," she said. "I just think any overarching theory based on a misconception, or an exaggeration, is bound to be off."

She smiled innocently.

Nate laughed. Why did women say men were threatened by women who challenged them?

The waiter poured the last of the wine into their glasses. When they left the restaurant, the buildings and sidewalks were slick and shiny. Nate wiped a large drop of water from his forehead. Hannah looked indignantly skyward.

Nate waved the umbrella victoriously. "I knew it!"

Hannah rolled her eyes, with the sort of mock exasperation women like to affect when they're flirting. As she got under the umbrella with him, her hip brushed his. She was so close Nate could almost feel her hair on his face.

"Let's go to your place," he said.

Hannah's expression became searching. She pushed her hair back behind her ear and pulled back from him as much as she could while remaining under the umbrella. She seemed to be considering the question very seriously. Nate was tempted to touch her, but something, perhaps the fact that she was busy "considering," held him back, as if to do so would constitute an illegitimate interference, like jury tampering.

"I want to see your book collection," he said instead.

"Gag me."

"I'm taking that as a yes."

The cab he hailed seemed to move like a bumper car on the shimmering street, spewing water as it slid to a halt about twenty feet in front of them. They ran toward it, laughing drunkenly as they scrambled into the backseat. The small, balding driver grumbled when they told him they were going to Brooklyn and, muttering into his cell phone in a South Asian language, banged a fist against his doily-covered steering wheel. This also struck them as extremely funny.

Crossing the bridge, Nate turned to take in the Manhattan skyline behind them. The chains of white lights lining the cables of the other East River bridges were like dangling necklaces beneath the brightly lit towers, a fireworks display frozen at its most expansive moment. The view, familiar and yet still—always— thrilling, in combination with the plastic smell of the taxi, made him feel almost giddy. He had sort of a Pavlovian reaction to cabs. He rarely took them except on his way to bed with a new girl.

Hannah's apartment was right off Myrtle, on the second floor of a walk-up building. Nate waited near the door as she circled the living room, switching on a succession of small lamps. The space lit up only gradually, as she got to the third or fourth one. Its wood floors were scuffed, but the walls were a very clean, stark white with original moldings at the top and very few pictures on them. One wall was lined with bookshelves. On the other side, a half-wall separated the kitchen from the living area. The room seemed unusually spacious for New York, in part because it had relatively little furniture. There was, Nate noticed, no couch. No television, either.

Hannah gestured for Nate to sit near the window where two mismatched upholstered chairs sat on either side of a small, triangular table. On the windowsill sat an ashtray.

A breeze blew through the window screen. The air, heavy with moisture, smelled clean and fresh. Hannah put some music on a record player, a stoned-sounding guy on a guitar, his voice ethereal and sad.

"I thought you were into punk," Nate called as Hannah walked toward the kitchen.

"What?"

She turned around. "Oh, right . . . the Descendents. Different epoch."

Epoch. Nate liked that. The music wasn't bad, either, though it reminded him of Starbucks.

The breeze rustled up the air again. Nate leaned back in his chair, experiencing the pleasant sensation of being outside time and normal life. It was officially the first day of summer, and for a change his mood was in sync with the calendar. He felt free and heady, the way he had when he was young, when summer was a long possibility, a state of mind, not a period when work was slow because editors were on vacation.

Hannah moved around the apartment with dizzy cheer, pivoting shakily on the balls of her feet every time she changed direction. On her tiptoes, she retrieved a bottle of bourbon and two thin, blue-rimmed glasses from a kitchen cabinet. She placed the glasses on the little table next to Nate and began to pour the bourbon, holding the bottle high above, like a bartender, the long, amber stream glimmering in the lamplight. As she moved from one to the other, she spilled a little so that a dotted trail of liquid linked their drinks.

Nate picked up the one closer to him. "Cheers."

He noticed some blue-and-white china crockery on Hannah's countertop. "That reminds me of stuff my mother brought with her from Romania," he said. Though he'd brushed her off when she asked, he'd wanted to tell Hannah about his family ever since she told him about hers. She wasn't at all like Elisa.

He told her about the redbrick ranch house they'd lived in

when he was growing up. After school, Nate and his mother would sit at the table, a Formica thing, in their sunny 1960s kitchen and drink tea—this was before his mother worked full-time. He remembered stirring in sugar cubes from a porcelain bowl with delicate fluting around the rim and gold-plating inside. Because the little bowl was one of the few things she'd been able to take with her when she and his father emigrated, it was regarded in their household as a treasure of inestimable value. In retrospect, he told Hannah, it was striking how his mother conveyed something aristocratic about her life in Romania, something very Old World and romantic, in spite of the poverty, the anti-Semitism, the dreariness. "She still has some of that European snobbery," he said. Over tea, she had told him that children there don't read "this, this"—and she'd scrunched up her nose—"*Encyclopedia Brown*." She gave Nate a copy of *Twenty-Thousand Leagues Under the Sea*. It was also over tea that she first spoke to him about the novels she loved. She'd tossed her long, honey-colored hair over her shoulders as she explained how Anna Karenina simply couldn't take it anymore. Mr. Karenin was a good man, but his kind of goodness—and Nate could remember the way his mother grasped his arm with a bony hand as she said this—his kind of goodness could be stultifying. The rim of her teacup had been stained with red lipstick.

"I guess she didn't have many friends back then," Nate said quickly, feeling suddenly that he'd said too much. "She and my dad are really different."

Hannah nodded.

Nate was relieved that she didn't question him about his parents' marriage, and what, as an adult, he had come to think of as his mother's somewhat self-serving interpretation of it.

He got up to peruse her bookshelves. "You've got a lot of Greene."

She had mostly old paperback editions, their titles printed in modish 1960s fonts above Graham Greene's name.

"I did grow up Catholic," she said.

She had padded to his side, bringing with her the sweet scent of bourbon. Nate turned and kissed her.

A moment later, she pulled away. She looked at the ground. Lamplight glinted on her long eyelashes, giving her face a languorous, abandoned aspect. The next words out of her mouth spoiled the effect. She told him that he was welcome to stay over if he wanted, but she'd rather not . . . well, you know. She bit her lip. "I probably should have told you before you came over."

Nate stepped back as if he'd been reproached. He wished she wouldn't look so nervous. He wasn't some brute who was going to fly into a rage because she wouldn't fuck him. He looked toward the kitchen.

"That's fine," he said. "Whatever makes you comfortable."

"It's just . . ." Hannah's eyes shot from the ground to his face. "Just that we don't know each other that well. That's the main thing."

Nate began to crack the knuckles of his right hand with his left one. He'd live without sex, but he really didn't want to get drawn into a long and uncomfortable conversation about it.

"Hannah," he said. "I get it. It's not a problem. Really."

He must have sounded impatient because she seemed to bristle. She flashed a quick smile. "Great," she said.

Nate put his hands in his pockets. He began looking at the bookshelf again.

"Just tell me one thing," he said after a moment. "Does this have to do with your being Catholic?"

For an instant, Hannah looked taken aback. Then she raised an eyebrow. "No. It has to do with your being Jewish."

Nate laughed, a real and hearty laugh. When he stopped, the awkwardness he'd felt the minute before was gone. Hannah, too, seemed to have gotten past her irritation. She leaned against the bookshelf, looking amused. Nate touched her cheek.

"If it really is all right, I'd like to stay."

She nodded. "It's all right."

6

Nate and Aurit had a go-to restaurant. Located halfway between their apartments, the place was moderate enough in price to suit him but not so devoid of culinary pretension as to be unacceptable to her. It was also, somewhat mysteriously, as far as Nate was concerned, hip. Certain medieval touches—dark walls, tall wooden benches, torchlike lighting from iron ceiling fixtures—had a themey-ness that could easily have gone the other way.

Nate arrived first and was seated at a table near the kitchen.

Aurit showed up ten minutes later. She scanned the room. "I don't know why you'd want to sit here when there are booths free," she said.

Nate glanced at the time on his phone.

After they changed tables, Aurit began telling him about a party she'd gone to the weekend before. "I overheard these two ugly, completely lame guys talking, at full volume, about which woman there they most wanted to go home with. I wanted to be like, 'Do you not understand that people can hear you? Do you imagine that you are speaking in some exotic tongue?'" She shook her head. "Did I mention they were ugly?" Another night, she'd had dinner with a friend, who "is otherwise nice but has this habit that drives me up the wall. You remark on anything, and she starts *explaining* it to you, as if you are totally clueless. You say, 'So many people are moving to the South Slope these days,' and she says, 'Well, it's more affordable than other neighborhoods,' and you're like, 'Thanks, and by the way, I'm not an *idiot*.'" Nate laughed. "It's actually amazingly annoying," Aurit continued. "But it's also kind of tragic. She must alienate people all the time without having any idea why."

Their waitress had white-blonde hair with dark roots and elaborately tattooed forearms. After she took their orders, Aurit asked Nate what had been going on with him. He told her about his book review, leaving out aspects that he thought she'd find objectionable.

"Hmm . . . uh huh, uh huh . . . That's interesting."

She seemed far more interested when he mentioned that he'd gone out with Hannah again. "Do tell."

Nate described their date, surprising himself by how effusive he sounded. Aside from that one tense moment, it had been a really nice night.

"That was, when, Wednesday? Thursday?" Aurit asked. "What about since?"

She was buttering a slice of bread. When Nate didn't immediately answer, she put the bread down. "Nate. Have you not called her?"

Sometimes Aurit reminded him of the Lorax, the glowering little Dr. Seuss character who climbs out of tree stumps to hector the greedy capitalist. Like the rook in chess, she was short and big on top, with large maternal breasts and broad shoulders that were like the top of a triangle, tapering to petite hips that she liked to show off in close-fitting jeans. She had dark skin and attractive, small, almost gaunt features. Her black hair was short, but it had a baffling quality of not seeming short, or at least not striking Nate as androgynous the way short hair sometimes did. It had lots of wispy layers so that there was always plenty of it around her face, longish pieces that fell almost to her chin and were always tumbling forward and being pushed back behind her pixieish ears.

Aurit had long ago explained to Nate that the two of them had never gotten romantically involved because when they started spending time together, he was going out with Elisa. By the time he and Elisa broke up, it was too late: he and Aurit were already in the "friend zone." For a long time Nate had believed this because Aurit said it so authoritatively and it sounded plausible and he was in the habit of thinking that Aurit had more insight than he did into such things. Until it occurred to him that he'd never been attracted to her. He had been perfectly capable of finding women other than Elisa attractive. She just wasn't one of them. This realization had scared him a little. He'd nearly been convinced of a false account of his own feelings merely because Aurit was so emphatic. He was also relieved. Aurit had a way about her. If she had wanted him for her boyfriend, there was a good chance that, attraction or not, he would at this very moment be carrying her shopping bags.

The waitress arrived with Nate's burger. She brought Aurit a large plate of shootlike leaves and then retreated quickly, as if to forestall any additional requests.

"What is that?" Nate asked Aurit.

"You haven't answered my question," she said. "How many days has it been?"

Nate leaned forward for a better look. "Is it arugula? Bamboo shoots?"

"Four? Five?"

"Clovers of some sort? Do you get anything else with it?"

"Do you get off on making her wait? I'd just like to know what men are thinking when they pull this sort of thing."

"Are you on some kind of extreme diet? Should I be worried?"

Aurit was too proud of her slim figure to let that go. "It's a *pizza*."

"Maybe where you come from, they call that pizza. Here in the United States, we call it a grassy knoll."

"For your information, it's a prosciutto and arugula pizza." Aurit used her fork to rake off a section of shrubbery. Nate saw that underneath there did appear to be a fairly standard pizza with cheese and prosciutto. She set down her fork, and the arugula layer fell back in place.

"So . . . *Hannah?*"

Nate began pouring ketchup on his burger. "Why are you bent on giving me the third degree? I only went out with her twice. I haven't even slept with her."

In Hannah's bed that night—*four* nights ago, as a matter of fact—they had alternately talked and engaged in what felt like a prolonged and fairly innocent bout of adolescent groping. It had been pretty nice, though. Perhaps he was getting old, but there had been surprising consolation in the knowledge that he was not going to wake up with the chalky feeling of embarrassment that often followed drunken hookups. In the morning, he'd hung around for a while. He walked home along a street he particularly liked, with mansions set back from the sidewalk. Built by nineteenth-century industrialists, the mansions had degenerated, in the mid-twentieth century, into single-room-occupancy boardinghouses. Recently, the neighborhood had turned again, the SROs converted to upscale apartment buildings. On that summer morning, the shady street was lush and fragrant. Nate had felt unusually cheerful as he made his way home.

"So, what?" Aurit said. "It doesn't matter? You can just do whatever you want because you didn't slip your thing in?"

For god's sake.

Nate put the bun on his burger, picked it up with both hands, and took a bite. He winced as some ketchup squirted out from under the bun and onto his hand. He could feel Aurit's eyes on him. She had a very particular way of staring. She was still except for a slight widening of her pupils, which managed to suggest that her mind was hard at work, trying to accommodate some new and terribly damning truth she'd just discovered. Nate looked intently at the bun of his burger, imagining he was on a gently rocking sailboat. The only thing on the boat with him was a big, juicy cheeseburger. The idyll was short-lived.

"It's just great, Nate," Aurit said. "While writing the book review of the year and whatever the hell else you've been doing, you happen to go out with a girl a couple times, spend the night with her—who cares if you actually slept together?—but for you, it's out of sight, out of mind. As soon as she's not in the room, you're back in Nateland. What about her?"

Nate wished he'd called Jason instead. You could eat a fucking cheeseburger with Jason.

He eyed the opposite wall, where some kind of menacing lancelike weapon was on display.

"I think it would be a little strange if Hannah were all that invested after two dates," he said finally. He felt that responding at all was giving in to Aurit, but he didn't see an alternative that wouldn't set her off even more. "I don't think you're giving her much credit."

"Two dates that you said yourself went really well," Aurit said. "So she's thinking about you and wondering if maybe she imagined it, maybe she was crazy for thinking you guys had a lot of fun, because otherwise why haven't you called?"

"Maybe she's thinking I haven't called because I've been busy. Which happens to be true. Or maybe she hasn't thought anything because *she's* busy. She's a smart girl and has stuff going on. I really don't think you're being fair to her, turning her into this sad creature who is sitting around waiting for my call. Maybe she doesn't even like me much." Nate arranged his features into a smile he hoped was charming. "Shocking as it may seem, not every woman finds me irresistible."

Aurit plucked a single sprig of arugula from her pizza. "No offense, Nate, but you sound really defensive."

He dropped his burger to his plate.

Aurit began making dainty little strokes with her fork, clearing away tufts of salad greens from the surface of her pizza. She cut a tiny triangular bite. She was about to put it in her mouth when she spoke instead.

"The thing is, Hannah seems cool, like someone you might actually like." Aurit spoke in a deliberately soothing tone, wagging the fork with the pizza across the air above her plate. "You usually pick the wrong women. You see someone pretty, and you come up with a reason to find her interesting. Then, when it doesn't work, you act like the problem is 'women' or 'relationships,' instead of the women you choose . . . Like that ditzy Emily, who might as well have been sixteen years old."

"Which Em—?" Nate started to ask. But she obviously meant Emily Berg. He closed his eyes for a moment. "I really don't want to talk about this," he said when he opened them. "Can we please drop it?"

He knew that Aurit would interpret his reaction as "defensive." He was not defensive. He was frustrated by her (unjust) dig at Emily and her facile analysis of his personal life—delivered, naturally, with unwavering certainty of tone.

"Fine," Aurit said.

"Thank you."

Nate took a bite of his burger.

"It's just that I don't understand," Aurit said. "It seems to me that when you do meet someone suitable and you have a nice time with her, you should tread carefully, take it seriously . . ."

Nate felt like he was the subject of a highly sophisticated type of torture in which the torturer listens to your objections, even seems sympathetic, and then continues to administer electric shocks.

Aurit had once espoused a system of categorizing people that he found useful. She said some people were horizontally oriented, while others were vertical. Horizontally oriented people were concerned exclusively with what others think, with fitting in or impressing their peers. Vertically oriented people were obsessed only with some higher "truth," which they believed in wholeheartedly and wanted to trumpet no matter who was interested. People who are horizontally oriented are phonies and sycophants, while those who are entirely vertically oriented lack all social skill—they're the ones on the street shouting about the apocalypse. Normal people are in the middle, but veer one way or the other. Nate was tempted to tell Aurit that she had been sliding into tone-deaf vertical territory.

"Can we please talk about something other than dating?" he said instead. "I mean, there is a lot more in the world than who wants to date whom and 'Oh my god, have you called her yet?' We might as well be on fucking *Sex and the City*."

Aurit raised her eyebrows and tossed her head back, chin up in the air, so that, diminutive as she was, she seemed to be looking down at him from some kind of perch. "Oh, I'm sorry, Nate. I forgot how deep you are. Silly me, I can't believe I bored you with my girlish prattle. Maybe we should talk about nuclear disarmament."

How did he come to be in the wrong? Nate didn't know what happened, but now there was no help for it.

"I'm sorry," he said. "I'm just tired."

"Whatever." Aurit shrugged. "It's fine. I just hate the way so many men treat 'dating' as if it's a frivolous subject. It's boneheaded." She smiled frostily and tilted her head in his direction, lest there be any uncertainty about who exactly she was calling boneheaded. "Dating is probably the most fraught human interaction there is. You're sizing people up to see if they're worth your time and attention, and they're doing the same to you. It's meritocracy applied to personal life, but there's no accountability. We submit ourselves to these intimate inspections and simultaneously inflict them on others and try to keep our psyches intact—to keep from becoming cold and callous—and we hope that at the end of it we wind up happier than our grandparents, who didn't spend this vast period of their lives, these prime years, so thoroughly alone, coldly and explicitly anatomized again and again. But who cares, right? It's just girl stuff."

Classic Aurit. Take whatever she was personally interested in and apply all her ingenuity to turning it into Something Important. It never occurred to her that there was anything more worth caring about or thinking about than upper-middle-class women's search for happiness, in the cozily coupled, fatally bourgeois sense of the word. She thought if she could just convey *how much this meant* to women—articulate it once and for all—the world would come around. Never did she realize how limited her perspective was, how insensible she was to all that fell outside the sphere of her own preoccupations.

"I don't know," Nate said in a tone intended to be placating even though he was about to disagree. "It's easy to overstate the importance of whatever you're personally affected by. It's like mothers whose kids don't test well think standardized tests are the worst thing in the world. I just don't think dating is quite the scourge of modern life you're making it out to be. I don't think it's that big of a deal. It's just one aspect of life and certainly not the most important one."

"No, you wouldn't think it was that big a deal, would you?" Aurit mused. Her voice was no longer pissy but thoughtful, as if she were a naturalist classifying a homely new species. "Next time you feel lonely, my guess is that you'll think it's a pretty big deal. But as long as you're feeling calm and collected and you're able to focus on your book and your highly intellectual, oh-so-important book reviews and whatever else, I can see why it reinforces your sense of self to act as if you're too deep to care much."

Nate was amused. "I'm boneheaded is what you're saying."

Before Aurit could respond, the waitress approached. "You done?"

"Uh, *no*," said Aurit, who was poised to bite into a forkful of pizza.

The waitress scowled and walked away. Aurit's nostrils flared. Bad service was a source of great frustration for her, an irritant that might at any moment set her off, like science was for the medieval church.

"When she comes back, I'm going to tell her there was too much arugula on my pizza."

"Hi guys."

Both Nate and Aurit looked up. Standing beside their booth was Greer Cohen—Greer Cohen whose book advance had aroused such animosity at Elisa's dinner party. Greer was smiling gaily, as if running into them was the best thing that had happened to her in weeks.

Seeing Greer wasn't such a surprise, really. In Brooklyn, everyone turned up everywhere. Though the parts of Brooklyn congenial to people in their demographic had expanded dramatically in a widening web of faux-dives and mysteriously hip restaurants, to Nate the place seemed never to have been smaller, so dense was it with people he knew.

"I thought it was you guys," Greer said, in her girlish, vowel-elongating lilt.

Greer's manner of speaking was not merely flirty but flirty like a teenage girl with bubblegum in her mouth and a tennis skirt and tanned thighs.

"We heard about your book," Aurit said. "Congratulations. That's a great opportunity."

Greer smiled and shrugged a little bit, as if to say "Who me?" As though the book deal had simply fallen into her path, and she'd barely taken the time to notice it. Now, *Greer* was a horizontally oriented person. Even her sexiness had something artificial in it. Some people reeked of sex; Greer, in spite of a tomboyish style of dress, reeked of a manufactured sexiness more tartish than slutty, like a pinup girl from the 1940s.

The last time Nate had seen her, at a party, they had gotten into a long and tiresome argument. Nate had said that in a certain sense, and only in a certain sense, it's harder for men to say no to sex than it is for women. When a woman says no, nobody's feelings are hurt. Men expect to be shot down. But when a man says no, the woman feels as if he's just said she's fat and undesirable. That makes him feel like a jerk. Greer thought he was being a sexist asshole who didn't think women should hit on men and refused to grasp the seriousness of sexual harassment and rape. Nate thought she was strident and unsubtle, either deliberately misunderstanding him for effect or simply unable to grasp the distinction he was making.

Now, however, as Greer described her book to Aurit ("it's partly a memoir about my teenaged misadventures but also sort of an art book with photos and drawings and song lyrics"), he was entranced by her cleavage. She began nodding vigorously at something Aurit said. Greer's breasts, snug in an olive-green tank top, were his favorite size, just big enough to fill a wine glass (a red one). When he tried to meet her eye, they were squarely in his line of vision.

"It was good to see you guys," she said finally. "I'll see you later."

Nate watched her heart-shaped ass bounce in tandem with her jaunty little stride as she turned the corner into the bar area.

"Did I tell you Hans is coming to town in a couple weeks?" Aurit asked.

Aurit's boyfriend Hans was an affable German journalist who wore circle-rim glasses and sometimes struck Nate as more of a prop of Aurit's than a figure in his own right. His existence in her life, however semimaterial given the long-distance nature of their relationship, gave her authority to lecture others about their romantic lives.

Nate was still contemplating Greer's ass. "That's nice."

Sunlight sloped through the windows of "Recess, open 7 a.m. to 9 p.m." (no ungrammatical dashes there), and collected in glittering eddies of dust underneath chairs and behind display counters laden with coffee beans.

Whatever his feelings about gentrification, Nate appreciated the abundance of coffee shops that had lately appeared in his neighborhood. It was hard to believe that, once upon a time, the pale, bleary-eyed freelancers and grad students who gathered daily at places like Recess would have typed away all by themselves, grimly holed up in rooms of their own. "Sometimes you just want to see another human being, you know?" Nate had tried to explain to his

dad, who clucked about the waste of money and extolled the virtues of the home espresso machine. Nate didn't tell his father that
working at Recess prevented him from looking at porn, easily boost-
ing his productivity enough to earn back what he spent on coffee.

Nate had chosen Recess on the dual bases of proximity (a block
and a half from his apartment) and Beth, who worked behind the
counter. He met Beth's eye now. She smiled and looked questioningly at his computer. He shrugged and made a face, as if he were
trying to work without success. In fact, he'd been scanning an
e-mail from a national office supply retailer. It seemed there had
never been a better time to buy a home copy machine.

In truth, he was having a hard time focusing. His mind kept
drifting. Personal stuff. Hannah.

He had not called her the day after his dinner with Aurit. He
had waited until the day after. The extra day was sort of a fuck you
to Aurit. She had been a real pain in the ass that night. But . . .
calling Hannah seemed like a good idea. It was the right thing. He
had spent the night with her. She'd made him breakfast. On the
phone, Hannah's voice, contra Aurit's dire prognostications, had
not been full of tearful reproach, even though he had taken—
gasp—six days to get in touch with her. She sounded a bit sleepy
at first, her consonants not quite distinct. After a pause just long
enough to alarm him, she said, "Sure, let's do something."

Since then, Nate had been busy making revisions to his review
of the Israel book and filling out a long, detailed questionnaire from
his publisher's marketing department. The fact that in February
his book was going to be in stores across America was beginning
to feel more real. When he thought about seeing Hannah, he felt
a mild sense of anticipation. Not only did he like her, but they'd
be on good behavior with each other, not touchy and peevish the
way he and Aurit had been the other night, but the new-person
versions of themselves: attentive, polite, and good-humored. This
iteration felt to Nate like not just his better self but his real self,
except that, like a skittish housecat, this magnanimous and

engaged person materialized only occasionally, under very particular circumstances. New people brought him out. So did the receipt of good news. Nate had never been more tolerant of other people than in the weeks following the sale of his book.

But he and Hannah were soon going to move past new-person territory. That whole bit about not wanting to sleep with him, about not knowing him well enough, made clear that she wasn't looking for something casual. He had tacitly agreed to her terms when he asked her out again. (This was the real reason he'd hesitated about calling her, which he would have told Aurit if she hadn't immediately begun haranguing him.) After the other night, it would be harder, more awkward, for him to tell Hannah he wasn't looking for anything serious. Also something had stopped him from delivering such a line either time they'd gone out. He had sensed it would be, for Hannah, a deal breaker—that she wouldn't bat her eyelashes and say, "I'm not looking for anything serious either" the way a lot of girls did, as if this were part of the challenge of dating. Each time he'd been out with Hannah, he had found himself reluctant to say anything that would throw water on their fun, flirty dynamic. No doubt he'd feel the same hesitation tonight.

Outside, the brakes of a bus squealed. Nate set his elbows on the table and rubbed his temples with the heels of his palms. Aurit wouldn't have been any help anyway. She didn't understand (she willfully refused to understand) that in the little mental space where she stored fond images of cuddling, Nate saw himself struggling to read in bed while some alien presence breathed moistly at his side and asked if he would be ready to turn off the light soon. He imagined gazing in farewell at his apartment as he closed the door and left for some girlfriend's place "because it *is* more comfortable, isn't it?" He saw touchy-feely sex and dutifully concealed porn and movie nights—well-reviewed indie comedies on Netflix, or maybe, if they were feeling especially ambitious, a documentary.

Nate was devoted to humanity in the abstract—to human rights, equal opportunity, the eradication of poverty. He was, in theory, sympathetic to the limitations of others: you had to take into account root causes, the punishing handicaps posed by stupidity, an infantilizing consumer culture, et cetera. But when he trained the microscope more closely, human beings took on, in his view, an increasingly unattractive cast. They appeared greedy, grubby, hypocritical, self-deceiving. Sex, the sexual impulse, was a lure—an illusion engineered by an animal organism that sought only to perpetuate itself. The makeup, the hairstyling, the waxed limbs and gym-toned musculature, the urbane posturing and protective veneers of youth and achievement and even kindliness—weren't they all merely cover for the pathetic, grasping "I" underneath? It wasn't misogyny. Men laid similarly bare, stripped of pretensions, would be equally unappealing. But Nate wasn't both attracted to and repelled by men. Men didn't force him into contact with their least attractive aspects. The cesspools of need, the pockets of self-pity, the most vain and ugly of the thoughts that roiled Nate's male friends as they lay awake in the middle of the night remained largely hidden from him, like foul odors sucked into the exhaust fans of modern bathrooms.

But maybe he was kidding himself. Certainly abstract ideas hadn't prevented him from enjoying many other things he found philosophically objectionable, such as consumer goods from China, jet travel, Tori Amos. If he wanted to be in a relationship, no argument would change his mind. Perhaps the salient issue was not *why* but simply *that* he didn't want to be in a relationship. His work fulfilled him, and his friends provided all the conversation and companionship he needed.

Was this so wrong? Why do women get away with pathologizing men for not wanting girlfriends? There are entire Web sites written by supposedly smart, "independent" women who make no bones about calling such men immature at best, assholes at worst. Nate wanted to argue, if only he had someone to argue with, that women want to be in relationships because on a gut level they don't like being alone. They aren't noble, high-minded individuals, concerned about the well-being of the nation or the continuity of the species. They simply swoon at images of cooking dinner together, of some loving boyfriend playfully swatting their ass with a dishtowel while the two of them chop vegetables and sip wine and listen to NPR (preferably in a jointly owned prewar apartment with an updated kitchen). And that's their prerogative. But what right do they have to demonize a counterpreference? If Nate's idea of a nice dinner involved hunching over his kitchen table with a Celeste Pizza for One and a copy of Lermontov's *A Hero of Our Time*, who is to say that his ideal is worse?

Nate knew what the response would be: maturity, it's what adults do, et cetera, et cetera. But the same women who are so quick to call men immature when they don't order their lives around snug domestic relationships would never call a woman immature because she doesn't want to pop out babies. They resent the hell out of anyone who implies there's anything wrong with *her* choice. No, women only pull out that talk about mature adulthood when it's convenient, when they want grounds to resent some poor guy who doesn't want what they want. It isn't merely inconsistent: it suggests an unwillingness to take seriously other people's preferences. As such, it's a tyrannical impulse. And somebody really needs to say so.

Out the window, sunlight reflected off the windshields of parked cars. Nate finished the last of his coffee and set his mug down.

The problem was that no matter how unfair they are, no matter how insanely bent on domestication, Nate was unable to entirely discount the claims of women—those he slept with or might sleep with. If only, like those cock-swinging writers of the last century— Mailer, Roth, et al.—he could see the satisfaction of his sexual desire as a triumph of spirit, the vital and needful assertion of a giant, powerful virility whose essence was intellectual as well as erotic. Either Nate was less poetic, unable to rise to such dazzling heights of imaginative fancy, altogether more pedestrian and earthbound—and no doubt he was—or he was less self-dramatizing. He didn't, couldn't, adorn his basic desire to get off, *to squirt his stuff*, with such baroque justification; so it was harder to see why his desire ought to trump everything else, trump women's post-coital unhappiness. The dreary voice of Kant, insisting on impartiality, the egalitarianism of the age—every person equal as a claimant to empathy—were, for him, lodged too deep.

"You okay, Nate?"

Nate turned to look at Beth's broad, friendly face, the kind of face that retained a whiff of the well-loved girl who hung pictures of horses on her bedroom wall. "You've got this big scowl going on," she said.

"Just focusing, I guess. How're you?"

She waved the rag she was holding. "Oh, you know, another day in paradise."

On his table, Nate's cell phone began to vibrate, flailing like an overturned cockroach struggling to right itself. When he reached for it, Elisa's face stared back at him. In the screen shot, her pouting lips were painted a deep red, and her blonde hair was messily pulled back from her face, with just a few stray clusters falling forward. The flash had flushed her skin, and the angle was askew because she had taken the picture herself with an outstretched arm. She still looked beautiful. But if she had been trying to endear herself to him by setting this picture to appear when she called, she'd miscalculated. The implicitly accusing expression on her face always filled him with dread. He hit DECLINE.

Then he opened a new message window on his computer. "I'm sorry," he wrote to Hannah. "I got swamped with edits on the Israel book review. I'm not going to be able to get together tonight."

He added a few pleasantries, signed his name, deleted his name, replaced it with the letter *N*, deleted the letter *N*, and finally settled on the lowercase *np* as signifying just the right amount of intimacy.

As soon as he pressed SEND, relief washed over him.

7

The next night an acquaintance of Nate's was reading from his new book at a bookstore in Lower Manhattan. Nate arrived early, in part because his friend Mark had called and asked Nate to hold a seat for him.

Jason showed up soon after and took one of the seats next to Nate's. "Hey, man, you're coming out after, right?" Jason's voice dropped to a stage whisper. "I've got gossip. I can't tell you here."

Nate had once suggested to Jason that there was something prurient in the intensity of his interest in other people's lives. In response, Jason had paraphrased Bellow paraphrasing Allan Bloom: "When I do it, it's not gossip. It's social history."

Nate's friend Eugene Wu arrived and started to sit on Nate's other side. Nate was about to tell Eugene that the seat was saved for Mark. He stopped himself. Eugene was a suspicious, bilious sort of person. He was apt to take even this as a personal affront. There was something fey about seat saving anyway.

Mark walked in just as the author was being introduced. Nate waved his arms and made a sad clown face, trying to suggest that he had done his best. The author began to read. Nate tried to focus, but Mark distracted him. Forced to stand beside a rack of foreign periodicals, he visibly shifted his weight from one leg to the other while glowering in Nate's direction. Nate tried to avoid looking at that part of the room.

Afterward, a large group walked to a nearby bar. On the way, Nate wove in and out of various conversations. The thrashing of car horns and the whoosh of traffic lent a pleasant urban ambience as the group ambled along Houston Street in the humid dusk. Nate felt a wave of contentment. Sometimes he remembered how lonely he had been in high school and the early part of college, even in his early years in New York, after he and Kristen had broken up. Surrounded by friends and reasonably established, he felt lucky. He knew he'd been lucky.

The inside of the bar was scarcely populated, with only a few diehards watching baseball on a flat-screen TV and another group gathered around a pool table. But its large, gravelly backyard was packed. Standing under a scraggly tree, Nate got into a conversation about payday loans with a girl named Jean. She was writing an article about urban poverty.

"I had to take out a couple over the years," Nate told her.

"Really?" she said. "You're not exactly the target demographic."

Jean wore cute faux-librarian glasses and had a cheerful abundance of curly hair that bounced energetically when she nodded, which she did frequently, as if to offer encouragement to the person she was speaking with.

"I had some bad years," Nate said. "I couldn't always afford to wait two months for some magazine to get around to cutting me a check."

As Jean groaned in sympathy, Nate started to roll up his sleeves. He wished he'd worn a T-shirt. The warm air was thick, a physical presence.

"Can I ask why you didn't just get a cash advance on your credit card?" Jean asked.

"I forgot my PIN," Nate said.

Beyond Jean's shoulder, he noticed a very cute brunette. She was talking to a girl he knew slightly, and she seemed to be looking in his direction. The gravel beneath Nate's feet crunched as he shifted position to get a better view.

"Seriously?" Jean asked.

Nate turned back to her. "I figured if it was one I knew by heart, it would be too tempting," he said. "I made up a random one, wrote it down, and lost the paper."

Jean pushed her glasses up on her nose. "Did you think about retrieving it from the credit card company?"

"I kept answering the security questions wrong."

"You're kidding," Jean said.

"My mother's Romanian. Her maiden name has a lot of vowels. I may also have been drunk. They didn't ask so many questions at the payday loan place."

Jean had a guffawing laugh, which, while not particularly feminine, seemed uninhibited and heartfelt at least.

She was someone Nate liked, someone he was always happy to see at a party. Yet he inevitably ran out of things to talk about with her. She knew a lot about obscure bands and indie actors, but she almost never spoke personally or volunteered an opinion not in accord with right principles and liberal piety. After a while, this unwavering good nature left Nate tongue-tied.

The brunette went inside the bar.

Nate patted Jean on the shoulder. "I'll be just a minute."

The girl—and she was indeed young enough that Nate didn't think calling her a girl was politically incorrect—was leaning over the bar, the soles of her feet rising out of her ballet slippers as she stood on her tiptoes.

Nate took the place next to her. "I think we're with the same group. You were at the reading, right?"

She sank back into her shoes. She came up to, maybe, his chin. "Yeah," she said warily.

"So you'll help?"

"With what?"

Nate pointed with his thumb at the bartender. "You stand a better chance of getting his attention than I do."

Her name, Nate soon learned, was Cara. She had graduated from Stanford a couple of years before. She had since gotten a master's degree in writing from Johns Hopkins. She was interning at an august literary magazine and looking for a full-time job. She was open to something in publishing or magazines, but it was hard, in spite of her degrees.

"It's really awful that there aren't more full-time jobs for people in our field," she said. "I'd even take an assistant-level job."

To Nate, this sounded more than a little entitled. But she was young, and it was no easy task—getting started professionally— and she seemed sweet. It helped also that she was model pretty.

They returned to the backyard with their drinks. It had grown appreciably darker. One by one, windows in the surrounding tenements switched from black to yellow as inside lights were turned on.

Nate and Cara leaned against a brick wall. She let on that she knew who he was, that someone had pointed him out to her and she'd read something of his, or at least heard it spoken of. Naturally Nate was flattered. She told him she lived in the South Slope with roommates. She liked it. She had never felt like a true Californian. And Baltimore? No, she couldn't say she much liked it, even if it was Nate's hometown.

After a couple of minutes, Nate found himself eyeing Jason and Eugene, who were huddled together on the other side of the patio. He still hadn't heard Jason's gossip. He was growing a little bored, but he wasn't ready to extricate himself. Cara was petite. Her dark hair fell in long, loose waves around her face, which was delicate and appealing, with well-shaped lips and thick but shapely eyebrows. Olive-skinned, almost Persian-looking, she wasn't just goodlooking; she appeared intelligent, soulful. And clearly she was smart. She would have to be. It was impossible—*wasn't it?*—that she could actually be as boring as she seemed.

What began, after a few more minutes, to irritate him was that she didn't even attempt to be engaging—made no effort toward wit or color in her replies. Only an attractive young woman would take for granted a stranger's interest in the minutiae of her life.

Perhaps she was shy.

He asked how she liked the internship. Her answer was not unintelligent, yet it struck Nate as academic and passionless. At another point in his life, he would have felt a challenge in her stiffness—that air of complacent acquiescence rather than enthusiasm. He would have tried to get her to say something inflected with feeling, if only gossip or a complaint about her coworkers. He would have done so in part because he wouldn't have wanted her to come away thinking *he* was boring. But he didn't feel motivated to make that kind of effort. He thought of Hannah and felt a pang—of something, he didn't know what. He didn't choose to examine it.

He was getting ready to slip away when he found himself telling Cara that he pretty much had no choice but to live in New York because he was a terrible driver. "I couldn't live in a place where you need a car to get around."

"Did I hear you mention driving, Nate?"

Mark approached, holding out his hand to Cara. "Hi, I'm Mark," he said, his tone self-effacing, as though he doubted whether someone of Cara's importance would want to meet him. That was part of his shtick.

"Did Nate tell you his theory about driving?" Mark asked.

He sounded bored, lugubriously so, as if he'd told this story a hundred times and was sure she wouldn't be much interested.

Cara shook her head no.

"Well, let me tell you. He's a *terrible* driver."

She smiled. "So he said."

She already looked more animated than she had when Nate had been alone with her.

A magazine editor, Mark was thin, slight, with tidily cut dark hair; he was always neatly dressed in business casual. He looked at first to be almost trifling, but he had cultivated a dry, everyman persona that he played to great advantage.

"He says—" Mark began, his voice thick with disapproval. He broke off, as if overcome, and started again. "He told me and our friend Jason a couple years ago, when we were on a road trip, that his brain is like a Mack Truck."

Cara's smile was now a little confused. Nate was shaking his head, but he began to laugh, partly in embarrassment, partly in amusement. He'd nearly forgotten this story. He had to give Mark credit as far as Cara went. Mark was bringing far more panache to the job than he himself had.

"Nate says that good drivers are people who can put their brains on cruise control. Their brains are like small Japanese cars. He, on the other hand—well, his brain is this huge roaring engine that needs to be constantly monitored. It's too powerful to be put on a default setting where it can seamlessly change gears or pick up on a stoplight ahead."

Mark shook his head reproachfully. Cara, hands on her hips, pivoted toward Nate, for some sort of defense.

Nate tried to look endearing. "What he's not telling you is that those two—he and Jason—were on my case all weekend about my driving. I had to say something."

Mark frowned at Nate before turning back to Cara. "Personally, I thought it was extremely elitist. I was very offended."

"Also," Cara said with sudden energy. "I think trucks *do* have cruise control. I mean, airplanes do, right? Autopilot? Why not trucks?"

"Smart!" Mark turned to him. "What do you have to say to *that*, Nate?"

Nate held his hands up. "Whether they do or not, I concede. It was a stupid theory."

He had finally started having fun.

When Cara left to use the bathroom, Mark turned to him. His face was submerged in shadows cast by the tabletop umbrellas. "I think she kind of dug me, but if you're—I mean, you got there first."

"Go for it," Nate said. He meant it. He still felt a little bad about the seat-saving incident. That wasn't the main thing, though. "We didn't have much to say to each other."

Even in the semidarkness, Nate could see that Mark looked surprised. "I'd do her no matter what she has to say."

"Best of luck."

[illegible]or another drink. While he waited at the b[illegible]ghter rang through the beery air. Nate felt s[illegible]n. It was hard to say why. The night simply seemed empty, almost pointless.

When the bartender handed him his drink, he finished it too quickly. It was his third or fourth, and consumed so fast, it was enough to nudge him from buzzed to drunk. He ordered another immediately.

He awoke the next morning to embarrassing recollections— going up to Jean and putting his arm around her, for one. "So, what is your deal?" he'd asked. "Who are you, really?" She'd laughed, but he had felt her edging back from him. He wasn't, he had realized even through the haze of his drunkenness, coming off as bold and daring, only buffoonish. And sweaty. He also had a distinct memory of passing Cara on his way out. There was something pitying in the way she looked at him.

After four Advils, a large iced coffee, and the passage of several hours, he felt significantly better. In the early afternoon, he called Hannah.

"Well . . . ," she said slowly, when he asked her to reschedule the date he'd canceled. "It's not really a great week for me." Nate played dumb, cheerily suggesting the following week. Hannah said she was busy then too. But there was a slight laugh in her voice that gave him confidence. "What about coffee at ten a.m. on Tuesday?" he asked. "You can't be booked for ten a.m. on a Tuesday, can you? It's not like you have a job or anything—by which I mean no offense. I don't have one either."

She conceded that she might have a free evening that she'd forgotten about.

When he arrived in midtown, at Bryant Park, Hannah was already sitting with a book at a small green café table, lightly thumbing the edge of the page as she read. Her hair, lighter than usual in the sunlight, fell forward, on either side of her face. She glanced up from her book as he approached. When she stood up, the spindly metal chair she had been sitting on rocked on the cobblestones.

"Hi."

Nate felt uncharacteristically nervous as they smiled at each other.

"I brought you something," he said, reaching into his back pocket. He pushed a copy of Graham Greene's *Travels with My Aunt* across the table. "I noticed you didn't have it," he said, looking not at Hannah but at the book.

"Oh! That was nice of you. Thank you."

The concert they had come to hear wouldn't begin for another few minutes, but the park was full of activity. Across the wide swath of grass was the carousel, and to their left, in an old-timey booth, a "sandwich artisan." A few kids, maybe six or seven years old, were playing on the grass nearby. "Look!" cried a little Asian girl in pigtails and a white dress. She was speaking to two blond boys, twins. The little girl leaped from a chair, her skirt billowing up from her split legs. The boys didn't even pretend to care. They ran off, and she followed, pigtails flying behind her. "Wait!"

Back in the 1980s, the sociologist William Whyte said that you couldn't have found a more villainous-looking crew of dope dealers than the ones who hung out at this park if you hired them. Nate told Hannah that, and she laughed.

"Did you write something about him?" she asked. "I seem to remember reading something. It was . . . good."

Nate was pleased she'd read it. The piece was one he liked, about the materialism of the age.

The musicians began to play. Hannah turned to face them. She had suggested the free evening concert. "They're going to play some late Beethoven quartets that are really wonderful," she'd said. Nate was less keen on these kinds of performances. He thought there was something grating about upper-middle-class New Yorkers' love of high culture in city parks. It was so full of self-congratulation, as if a few lousy performances made up for systemic economic inequality. "Uh huh," Hannah had said. "You know you sound like one of those, uhm, *philistines* who doesn't see the use in art, right?" That had shut him up.

Now, Nate began to wonder what Hannah had really thought of his essay. There had been something coy, something withholding, in the way she'd said it was good.

The music stopped. Nate nearly started clapping before he realized it was only the end of the movement. Hannah whispered that the next one would be slower. Nate nodded meaningfully. When the musicians resumed playing, he closed his eyes to filter out distractions. Hannah had told him that these quartets were bridges between the classical and romantic periods. That was interesting. But the crisscross slats of the metal chair were gnawing the flesh on the back of his legs. It seemed as if the chair had been designed back in the 1980s to keep the dope dealers from getting too comfortable.

He was contemplating some of the wording his editor had suggested for his book's catalog copy when people abruptly started clapping. As soon as he realized, he began banging his hands together with great zeal.

He failed to convince. "I take it you aren't a classical music lover?" Hannah asked.

Nate let his hands drop. "I took piano lessons as a kid. I guess they didn't take."

When they left the park, he and Hannah were swept into a mass of people exiting an office tower. All around them briefcases bumped against thighs; cell phones clicked shut. They passed a subway entrance, and the crowd began to thin. They walked west, toward the setting sun.

Hannah told him that she played the cello through college. She asked what kind of music he liked.

"Honestly, I'm kind of an idiot about music," Nate said. "I usually wind up liking what people tell me is good." He glanced at her, a little shyly. "I liked the music you played at your apartment the last time."

Shielding her eyes from the sun with her hand, Hannah turned to him. "Elliott Smith? I wouldn't have guessed."

"What can I say, I like sad music."

She tossed her hair over her shoulder. In the sharp light, it glinted red-gold. "Interesting."

It was one of those cheerful dusks. Puddles that pedestrians would have had to make long arcs around the day before had dried up and disappeared. Convivial laughter rose from sidewalk cafés and echoed through the streets, which, in the fading heat, seemed to unfurl at the edges and relax into evening. People moved jauntily as if choreographed. As he and Hannah stepped from the sidewalk into a street, Nate touched a hand to her lower back. He felt glad to be exactly where he was.

8

The following week he brought Hannah to his apartment. The bulbs were out on his stairwell's third and fourth floors; he and Hannah climbed in near darkness. His door, when he pushed it open, emitted a piteous, multisyllabic whine.

"I hope you're not expecting much."

Hannah peered into the kitchen. Then she walked down the narrow hallway toward his bedroom. Nate trailed behind her. He had tidied in preparation for her visit, but his apartment cleaned up was unconvincing, like a career hoodlum dolled up for court by his lawyer. The rag he had used to wipe his desk and dresser sat in a heap on the windowsill. One of his dresser drawers, too crammed to shut all the way, had fallen wide open. He had hastily made the bed, but a triangle of garish black-and-white sheet poked out from beneath the comforter.

"It's nice," Hannah said slowly. She pointed to the wall above his desk. "I like that picture."

Nate had found the print, El Greco's *View of Toledo*, on the street. The angry blue sky and hilly green cityscape had appealed to him. He'd fixed the frame with duct tape.

"Thanks."

He came up behind her and placed his hands on her jeaned

hips. Leaning his head against hers, he closed his eyes and breathed in the scent of her hair.

After the concert the Friday before, they had gotten dinner and gone back to her place. Nate had stayed the rest of the weekend. On Saturday, they went out for breakfast and then walked around her neighborhood. They drank Bloody Marys at a well-air-conditioned Moroccan restaurant that was nearly empty between the brunch and dinner shifts. Afterward, he tagged along on her evening plans with a couple of her girlfriends from journalism school, skipping a party that he didn't much want to go to anyway (half the people who would be there he'd seen at the reading the week before). Sunday afternoon, Hannah practically pushed him out of her apartment. "I totally intended to work on my book proposal this weekend. If I don't get on it, I'm going to be writing health news my whole life." She had a regular freelance gig writing a weekly roundup of health news for the *Times*'s Web site.

Now, she relaxed against him, her hips pressing into his. Nate began to get hard. In the course of the weekend he'd spent at her apartment, she had rescinded the ban on sex.

He hadn't exactly changed his mind about wanting to be in a relationship. But now that he'd met Hannah, now that he found that he liked her, he couldn't see any other way to be. It was with the pleasure of cynicism defied that he had come to believe that she was in fact different from other women he'd recently dated. Though she came from the same sort of upper-middle-class background as most people he encountered socially, she seemed to him to be sort of savvy, not as blinkered as many of the women he knew—there was nothing precious or sheltered-seeming about her. Smart rather than "smart," she was neither timid nor humorless in her thinking. She didn't venture opinions with a question mark at the end. He'd looked up her work online and was surprised he hadn't noticed her stuff more before. Her reviews and essays were lucid, well-informed, and often wonderfully acerbic. She had a voice of her own, an energetic moral outrage tempered

by irony and warm, self-aware humor. And she was nearly as well read as Jason and Peter and even Nate himself. (To be honest, that had surprised him.) She was fun, too—quick to smile and to laugh.

She also had a way of insinuating that she hadn't entirely made up her mind about him that he enjoyed. He felt as if she was taking his measure, according to some exacting standard of her own devising. He respected her for it. He felt instinctively that her standard was a good one, that she was, in some essential way, *good*. Not just in the sense of being kind to orphans and kittens, nor in the do-gooder sense in which Kristen had been good, but good in some other way. Honest, fair-minded, unsnobbish.

A gunshotlike crackle cut through the room. Fireworks, no doubt left over from the Fourth of July holiday several days before. The rumbling soon gave way to the shriek of car alarms and shouts from the street below.

"Sorry about that," Nate said, letting go of Hannah and pushing the window partly shut. "My neighbors take America's independence very seriously."

Hannah walked to the milk crate next to his bed and began examining the books stacked on it.

"Do you want some wine?" Nate asked.

"Sure."

As he walked to the kitchen, Nate yawned. It was late. They'd already been out to dinner.

The wine he'd purchased earlier from the Tangled Vine was in a plastic bag on the table. He uncorked the bottle and retrieved a pair of wine glasses, holding them in one hand with the stems crisscrossed.

Hannah was standing expectantly, even docilely, in the middle of the bedroom. Nate set the wine and the glasses on the crate before he went to her.

The first time they'd slept together, as well as the second, the following morning, had been urgent, feverish, as if there had been

a tremendous amount of buildup, rather than just a few weeks' worth. He wanted to take it slower this time.

She was nearly his height. He barely had to bend down to kiss her. He slid his hands around her waist and beneath her shirt. Her back was taut and sinewy. He found the clasp of her bra: he felt her hands on his back, gently kneading the flesh under the elastic of his boxer briefs and moving along his belt line. The area was tender, and he enjoyed her touch, but he grew conscious of being a little thicker there than he would like, a little paunchier on the sides and in front, and he tried to pull in his abdominal muscles.

He nudged her toward the bed. His desk lamp lent the room an institutional cast, so he switched it off. He began unbuttoning his shirt. His eyes adjusted to the dark, and he saw Hannah watching him from the bed. Holding his gaze, she slipped her shirt over her head.

Nate poured wine into one of the glasses and handed it to her. While she sipped it, he sat down beside her and touched her breasts. She gave the glass back to him, and as he drank, she began to unfasten his jeans. He set the glass down. Then he took hold of her, pushing her onto her back and tugging at her jeans as he pressed himself against her.

As he had been the previous times, he was quickly swept up in a current of feeling, the intensity of which surprised him. His most recent encounters before Hannah—months ago now, and with women he'd scarcely known and had had little desire to see again—had been strangely tensionless, almost masturbatory.

He and Hannah had plain missionary-style sex, no theatrics, and it was—for him—really good. He thought it was for her, too. Her body seemed keenly responsive to his touch. That was part of what made it so good for him—that, and its lack of artificiality: he wasn't conscious of playing a part, conforming to expectation. The intensity, mysterious as it was, and the temporary forgetting of self, was real. After he came, he buried his face in her neck as waves of tenderness, embarrassingly strong, washed over him.

For a few minutes, they remained quietly curled in each other's arms. Then Nate began to recover himself. Quotidian thoughts pressed upon him. He became aware of feeling clammy and got up to throw out the condom.

Returning to the bed, he took in the sight of her, sprawled out before him. "You have such a nice body," he said. "People must tell you that all the time."

He could see the taut muscles of her stomach tense up as she laughed.

"I'm, like, totally tired of hearing about it," she said. She turned on her side. "If there's one thing women get sick of, it's being complimented. We're just so secure about our bodies."

Nate poured more wine. They began to talk, for some reason, about her ex-boyfriend Steve, whom she'd been with for four years. Nate pressed her for details. She had an intelligent, novelistic way of describing people that he enjoyed. "He had this culturally conservative streak," she said. "He read a lot. He was a lawyer, but he read philosophy, fiction—even poetry. I respected that, but after a while the gentleman-scholar thing got on my nerves. It seemed like he was trying to recreate something, like he had a little too much nostalgia for the past, for aristocracy and class privilege, really."

She said Steve was practical and organized and critical of her for being too careless, making her out to be some kind of hapless wild-child. Over time, their relationship devolved into a series of proxy battles. "In the last year we were together, I could feel him constantly inspecting me from top to bottom. A missing button or tiny stain was an *aha* moment in which my fundamental failure as a person was exposed." She began toying with a lock of her hair. "But I'm not being fair. The truth is I was doing the same to him at the end—building a case as to how rigid and unsubtle and bullying he was. He was always accusing me of rolling my eyes or smirking at him. I guess I was."

An hour had gone by. They had lost interest in the wine. Nate brought glasses of water from the kitchen.

He found himself telling her about Kelly Krebs, the girl he'd lost his virginity to between freshman and sophomore years of college.

"We met at the beach. Ocean City. She was a type I'd never really known before—middle-class, all-American, gentile. Not all that smart and not at all concerned about it. She thought it was weird I went to Harvard. I think she was embarrassed for me."

Because of her ski-slope nose and because she attended a second-tier state college, his friends from high school called Kelly a *grit*, which he explained to Hannah was a Baltimore term for a hick. ("They called her that to her face?" Hannah asked, aghast. "No, no," he assured her. "Of course not. Just to me.") He told her that it said more about his friends' provincial, suburban Jewishness—to say nothing of their dickishness—than it did about Kelly. They lumped all gentiles together (except for the very rich ones, from whose ranks senators and presidents were culled). Kelly was no hick. Her dad was an accountant. Her mom worked part-time in a boutique. To Nate, who had none, she had what seemed a superabundance of siblings. Their house in Towson, a suburb adjacent to Nate's, was a crowded jumble of sports equipment—hockey sticks tilting out of umbrella stands, kneepads abandoned on the coffee tables—and unmissable signs of female habitation. Jars of nail polish were left open, their contents spilling onto the pages of fashion magazines. There always seemed to be a hair dryer on upstairs. His own house seemed funereal in comparison. The Krebses were warm; as a family, they seemed happy. Nate liked them. He was especially taken with Mr. Krebs, a plump bearded man with a booming voice who coached Little League and soccer and was constantly shepherding one or another Krebs child to a sporting event or to the mall. Nate had rarely encountered a father as cheerful as he was.

Nate could see that as a family the Krebses were proud of their salt-of-the-earth-ness, their friendly, unpretentious American-ness. Nice as they were, they exuded their own brand of self-satisfaction. He compared them to his own parents, with their pride in their bookish intelligence, their sobriety and self-restraint. He had wondered if everybody took the quality they had and treated it as the most important thing—used it as a basis for feeling superior to others.

Nate had been on his back, looking at the ceiling. He turned to Hannah. "The answer, I decided, was yes."

She was leaning on her elbow, with her chin in her palm. "It sounds like the germ of relativism."

He began fondling her breasts. While he'd been talking about the Krebs family, Hannah had reached for her shirt. He'd swatted her hand away. "Please don't," he'd said. "I can't tell you how happy it makes me to look at your breasts."

She asked what happened with Kelly.

"She broke up with me for a guy from her college. I was a little relieved, to tell you the truth."

It must have been close to three o'clock by then. At some point, Hannah went off on a writer she thought was overrated. He happened to be the son of a very prominent journalist.

"Couldn't it possibly be," Nate said, "that you just don't like his stuff as much as some people do? Or is every article you dislike proof of an industry-wide conspiracy—a plot on behalf of nepotistic overlords to keep down good, hardworking, talented writers, such as, ahem, Hannah Leary?"

She laughed. It pleased him that her laughter was not a prelude to hurt feelings or sulkiness.

"Maybe you have a point," Hannah said. "Maybe it's a defense mechanism on my part."

Nate reached for a clump of her hair and gently pulled her close to him. They started to fool around again.

Nate wanted to freeze and preserve an image of her, from afterward. She was standing naked at his window with her back to him. Her hair fell in clumps against her flushed skin as the orange tip of a cigarette glowed pensively in the dark.

It was after four when they finally fell asleep. Nate's nose was buried in her hair, an arm draped over her side. His hand rested on her breast, and her ass brushed against his now limp dick.

The weeks that followed ran together in what seemed like a near-continuous stream of conversation and sex, punctuated by bouts of sleep and work. Nate was productive, workwise, perhaps even more productive than usual (he finished the commodification-of-conscience essay). But the hours at his computer, the occasional evening he spent by himself, resting with a pizza and a book, even his weekly soccer games at the park, felt almost like extensions of sleep. The time he spent with Hannah—narrating his life, listening to her do the same, exchanging opinions, fucking—seemed like the real awake time.

He told her about his book, the way it had evolved in the years he'd spent working on it. He'd first intended to write a scathing critique of the suburbs, featuring an immigrant family with one child. A son. This son was intended to be the book's central character, from whose lips precocious wit and wisdom would flow and whose struggles—girls and popularity—would arouse readers' sympathy. He told her how the novel had started to come together only when this "insufferable" character had been shunted to the sidelines, in favor of the parents, with their quietly troubled marriage and off-kilter but also in certain ways sharp-sighted responses to American life. Hannah told him that growing up she'd felt underestimated. "People expect girls from good middle-class families to be smart—but what they mean by smart for a girl is to have nice handwriting and a neat locker and to do her homework on time. They don't expect ideas or much in the way of real thought." She said, for her, writing had been a way to be heard.

One night they went to a party hosted by a girl Nate was friendly with and Hannah knew slightly.

When they arrived at Francesca's apartment on the Lower East

Side, Francesca ran up to Nate and hugged him. "I want to introduce you to my friend Nicholas," she told him. He reminded her of Hannah's name. "Hannah, that's right. It's *so* nice to see you," she said. She turned back to Nate. "Nicholas is a huge fan of yours. He's looking forward to your book."

Francesca pulled him to the other side of the room. He lost sight of Hannah.

"Nicholas is very big in Canada," Francesca whispered.

Nicholas was a burly, mustachioed guy with an unlit cigarette hanging out of his mouth. After he and Nate exchanged a few words, Francesca laid a hand on Nate's arm. "What would you like to drink?"

Something in her smile made Nate suspect she wasn't personally pouring out gin and tonics for all her guests.

Several years older than Nate, Francesca was a prettyish, stylish writer who'd been extremely successful with her first book at a young age. After that, she'd been less successful, but she was well known. And she made a point of knowing everyone. It was only recently that "everyone" had come to include Nate. When he'd been a struggling freelance writer who did some legal proofreading on the side, she'd been merely polite.

In those years, Nate had often been dismayed not by Francesca in particular but by the vast number of women whose legs, like the doors to an exclusive club, parted only at the proof of a man's success. Now that he was—barely—on the other side of it, the tendency depressed him for other reasons. There was something in the almost wolfish way that Francesca was looking at him that nullified whatever attractiveness was there.

"Don't worry about it," he told her. "I know where the kitchen is. Nice to meet you, Nicholas."

He didn't find Hannah in the kitchen, but Francesca's apartment had a back window that opened to a fire escape and a flight of stairs.

The roof was strung with white Christmas lights that ran from an extension cord inside the apartment. Francesca's building was flanked on one side by a tall fortresslike structure with few windows. On the other sides, jagged rows of shorter buildings spread out around them.

Nate saw Hannah standing near the edge of the roof. She was talking to Eugene Wu. Nate walked up to them and looped his arm around her waist. "Hey," he said. Hannah flushed slightly and pulled back. Nate realized that this was probably the first public gesture of couplehood he'd made. They'd largely spent time together one-on-one. Amused by her reticence, he kissed her temple lightly.

Hannah ignored this. "Eugene was just telling me that yoga is the new Orientalism," she said. "It's a good thing I do Pilates."

Nate had to strain to hear her over the roar of an air-conditioning unit atop one of the neighboring buildings. "Same difference, isn't it?" he said loudly.

"Pilates was invented by an American," Eugene said. "In the 1920s."

Nate gaped at him. "How do you know that?"

Eugene held out one of his arms for their perusal. "How do you think I stay so lean?"

When Hannah broke away to talk to a friend she hadn't seen in a while, Eugene turned to Nate with his arms crossed in front of his chest. "I didn't know you were dating her."

From his tone Nate suspected that Eugene had asked Hannah out before and had been shot down. Eugene had long been eager to date a bookish girl, a member of the literary set; for him, Hannah, pretty (if not a knockout by Jason's standard), pleasant, and smart, would have been a natural object of desire.

"It's recent," Nate said.

"Hmm . . . ," Eugene said. "Well, she has a nice rack."

Nate didn't know if Eugene was trying to indicate that he wasn't envious or if he was simply pissing on Nate's fire hydrant. Eugene existed in a state of permanent aggrievedness. He felt it his duty to nip at the happiness of those more fortunate. He resented that Nate had gone to Harvard and had a book deal; he acted as if money and girls and writing gigs had been handed to Nate with his diploma. In fact, their professional lives had been similarly scrappy until several years ago when Nate got the regular reviewing gig and then sold his book. Still, Eugene was smart—and more serious, less exclusively careerist than many people he knew.

"What about you, Eugene?" he asked. "You dating anyone?"

"I'm thinking about going online," Eugene admitted.

Surprised, Nate tried to remove from his expression anything that Eugene, in his prickliness, might perceive as mocking. "Go for it," he said. "Can't hurt, right?"

Soon after Hannah returned, Nate saw Jason's large silhouette emerge from the fire escape stairs. Jason looked around for a moment before he came lumbering toward the corner they'd staked out.

When he had told Jason he was dating Hannah, Jason's response—"she seems like a nice girl"—had been so bland that Nate had silently seethed, hating himself because the number seven flitted across his mind. He hated himself even more as he heard himself extol Hannah's virtues: *she's really cool! fun! smart!* An undertone of desperation had found its way into his voice. Jason had nodded, doing nothing that Nate could call him out on, and yet something in his smile had reminded Nate of a WASPy hostess "overlooking" a breach of etiquette.

"Hannah," Jason said as he approached. With mock formality, he held out a hand for her to shake.

Hannah scrunched her eyebrows quizzically, but she smiled and matched his tone. "Jason," she said, giving him her hand. "It's nice to see you."

"You look lovely. As always."

"Thank you."

Nate began rubbing the stubble on his chin. There wasn't anything he could do. Either Jason would be a dick—he'd call it "shaking things up"—or he wouldn't. As a distraction, Nate let himself get drawn into a hair-splitting and incredibly geekish argument with Eugene about libertarianism. After a few minutes, he turned to Jason.

"Can I use your phone to look up something?"

"Dude," Jason said. "Get your own. You're like the last person in New York to not have a smartphone."

"Jesus."

Hannah reached into her purse. "You can use mine."

Nate took the phone from her and turned to Jason. "Do you see how it's possible to do someone a favor without commentary?"

Jason smiled exultantly. "Commentary is what I do," he said. "I'm a *social commentator*, remember?"

Jason had recently been interviewed on CNN about his essay on obesity.

Hannah let out a short, skeptical laugh. "Harassing Nate about his cell phone is social commentary how?"

Nate looked at her in surprise. The awkwardness he'd been dreading had materialized—from an unexpected corner. His "girl-friend" was stepping in to defend him. He wished she wouldn't.

"Hannah, Hannah, Hannah," Jason said. He was leaning on the roof's railing with his arms extended on either side of his body and his ankles daintily crossed. When he smiled, his wide jawline formed a gratuitously large canvas for his fleshy lips. In his head's narrower, more delicately constructed upper half, his eyelashes fluttered in a show of affability as disingenuous as the upturn of his mouth.

"There comes a point"—Jason unclasped his hands from the metal rail and lurched toward them like a cuckoo emerging from inside its clock—"when a technology becomes such a part of the mainstream that it is no longer, strictly speaking, optional. This is a social phenomenon; diagnosing it is like diagnosing narcissism in the 1970s. The moment of smartphone saturation, or you might say, of *cultural transubstantiation*, occurred at or around August of 2008, at least for people in our demographic—"

"That's ridi—" Nate tried to cut in.

"*After that*," Jason said, "not to have one is a statement. Especially when, like our friend Nate here"—Jason gestured grandly in Nate's direction—"you aren't exactly poverty-stricken. At least not anymore." He flashed Nate a quick, malicious grin before turning back to the others. "For Nate, today, not to have a smartphone is a high-pitched scream that he is a square peg who refuses to be wedged into a round hole. And that," Jason said, looking directly at Hannah, "is an invitation to the rest of the clan to shame him. That's how the social order is maintained."

"So in giving Nate a hard time, what you're really doing is embodying a repressive social order?" Hannah's eyebrows were raised and her voice was mocking, but her expression was amused, even a bit flirtatious. "You're like the guy who sewed the *A* onto Hester Prynne's dress?" She turned to Nate and Eugene. "And that's his defense?" she concluded with a shake of her head.

Nate felt his body relax. She'd been perfect.

Jason shrugged in defeat. "No one likes the enforcer," he said. "I guess that's just the way it is."

Nate pulled Hannah closer to him, feeling pleased both with her and in some more obscure way with himself.

"Incidentally, Hester sewed on the *A* herself," Eugene said.

"Thank you, Brainy Smurf," Nate said. He turned to Hannah. "Jason's very big on social order these days," he said, resting his hand on the place on her hip where her jeans ended and feeling really turned on. "He thinks it's gotten a bad rap—"

"—because of, you know," Eugene cut in, "Hitler. Mussolini."

"Social order, huh?" Hannah said to Jason.

Hannah's back was lightly touching Nate's shoulder. Her body language, tilting away from the group, suggested she was ready to shrink away from the spotlight, glad for its attention to refocus on Jason, who sighed loudly, though in fact he enjoyed nothing so much as pontificating, even if he had to play the buffoon to do it.

"As Aristotle said, man is a political animal—"

"I'm going to get a drink," Eugene said.

"Man alone is worthless," Jason continued. "Hairless, shivering, and physically puny, he's no match for animals or the elements. Only through our collective intelligence, through *society*, has man risen. The mistake people make is to consider human evolution from the perspective of the individual. The happiness of individuals is, evolutionarily speaking, irrelevant; what matters is the health of society."

Nate circled Hannah's waist with his arm and cocked his head so that his forehead was touching hers. Her hip grazed his upper thigh, and her hair brushed against his chin and neck. He wanted to get even closer, but as it was, he was already a bit too turned on. He took a few deep breaths.

Above, the strings of white Christmas lights cut diagonal stripes across the darkening sky; several stories below, city traffic streamed around them. Jason droned on.

When they returned to Hannah's apartment, Nate apologized for Jason. "He doesn't mean any harm. He's just kind of a blowhard. Some people have golf, some have girlfriends, Jason has his mouth."

"I like him, actually," Hannah said. "He's . . . *ebullient*."

"Ebullient?" Nate smiled. "I'll tell him you said so. He'll like it."

They were lying on top of Hannah's bed, staring up at her ceiling as if at the stars. Nate told her that in college he thought he had less in common with Jason than with his friend Peter, but that over the years, the balance had shifted.

"Jason's weird, especially about women, but he's not a bad guy," Nate said. "He's more, I don't know how to put it exactly— substantial, maybe?—than a lot of people. He doesn't look over his shoulder to see what other people think, the way someone like Mark does." Hannah knew Mark; he had edited her writing at the online magazine where he used to work. "Mark's great, of course," Nate continued. "Good at what he does and really funny—but his first allegiance will always be to his reputation."

Hannah asked what Peter was like.

"Smart. Lonely. He really wants a girlfriend. He lives in Water-town, Maine—he got a job teaching up there. There aren't very many single women in Watertown. And, well, he's kind of awk-ward with women."

Nate realized that in the past couple weeks he and Hannah had talked about many aspects of their lives, but they hadn't spent much time on their friends. "What about you?" he asked. "What are your friends like?"

Hannah told him that her close friends dated back to journalism school and her days as a newspaper reporter. They were reporters who covered politics and business. Although she and Nate had a number of common friends and acquaintances, she felt her foothold in Nate's literary circle was tenuous. For the past few years, since she and Steve had broken up, she had felt a little bit lonely, intel-lectually. Her choice to try and write a book while taking miscel-laneous freelance gigs was mysterious to many of her journalist friends in a way that it wasn't, couldn't possibly be, to Nate.

Nate stroked her cheek with his thumb. "I find that strangely touching," he said. "I mean, it makes me glad that I can do that for you. Understand that part of you. I promise you're doing the right thing. Your book will be terrific."

She kissed his chin. "Thank you. That's really nice."

The desire Nate had been holding back since the party started to well up again, and he began to touch her breasts through her tank top. But he could tell she was distracted.

"What are you thinking about?"

She turned on her side, so they faced each other. She didn't answer right away.

"Nothing really," she said finally. "Just that you've been kind of great. I mean, it's been really great, these past few weeks." She touched his chest lightly through his T-shirt. "I've been really . . . happy."

He curled a finger into her hair. "Me too," he said. "Me too."

9

Like Freud, Aurit had a coherent theory of the universe. From a single foundational myth, she had derived a large and growing labyrinth of substories, all internally logical and surprisingly convincing, as long as you accepted her initial premises. The most important of these was the belief that being part of a couple was *the* primary marker of psychological health. On such a basis, she came up with far-reaching analyses of everyone she encountered. This one, she would announce, was sexually dysfunctional due to a painful formative relationship. That one was stunted by a series of early professional successes that kept him committed to the same immature belief structure he'd possessed during his period of peak glory. (Single men were deemed particularly lacking in emotional well-being.) Aurit took her analyses very seriously, often liking, disliking, or feeling sorry for people based almost entirely on the narratives she constructed. In particular, the men who'd hurt her most had become objects of such a virulent strain of pity that one might suspect her motives for dating them had been philanthropic.

Nate was reminded of this the following Saturday afternoon. He and Aurit were walking to Prospect Park, where some friends were hosting a picnic to celebrate their recent City Hall marriage. Aurit wanted to hear all about Hannah.

"It's been, what? A month? A little longer?"

"Something like that." It had been six weeks since he and Hannah first went out, about four since they'd begun to see each other in earnest.

"I'm really glad for you, Nate."

Aurit was nodding and smiling at him like he'd made it through naptime without wetting his pants.

Suddenly, it was essential to Nate that he complicate Aurit's narrow viewpoint. "It's not *that* big a deal. Who knows what will happen?"

Aurit had just purchased an iced coffee. Through the plastic lid, she had been stabbing at the caramel-colored liquid with her straw.

"Oh?" She looked up at him. "Is something wrong?"

"No. I just don't want to blow it out of proportion, that's all."

Aurit frowned. "Uh huh."

What he wanted to get across was a general demurral from Aurit's romantic monomania. He didn't see his getting together with Hannah as quite the epic, life-defining event that Aurit's relationships were for her. His new relationship, though consuming when he was with Hannah, wasn't the only thing on his mind, especially as time wore on and he became more acclimated to her presence in his life. Particularly in the past few days he'd had new preoccupations. He had gotten a journalism assignment that he was pleased about, a big and well-paid piece for a glossy magazine. Jason had recommended him for it. He had also had the germ of an idea for another book. And it wasn't only writing. The relationship, nice as it was, shared space in his mind with other things— with his interest in thinking abstractly, about things other than his personal life, for one, even with his interest in sports. But he couldn't think of a way to explain this to Aurit that wouldn't seem to her to imply discontent with Hannah.

They walked in silence. The plastic bag with the bottle of wine Nate bought for the picnic bumped rhythmically against his knee and shin.

"Is she coming today?" Aurit asked finally.

"No. She wanted to do some work. She's working on a book proposal."

Aurit nodded. Then she took a big sip of her drink and glared into the plastic cup.

"Ugh. An iced mocha shouldn't taste like chocolate milk."

Nate had nothing to say to that.

For the last day of July, the afternoon was lovely—not too humid, the sky a non-washed-out shade of blue—and the scene, as they entered the park, was idyllic, almost too idyllic. Technically, Prospect Park's natural amenities (wooded hills, rolling meadows, crescent-shaped pond with requisite ducks and swans) probably didn't outshine those of other parks in other cities. But unlike the parks Nate had known growing up in the suburbs, frequented almost exclusively by delinquent teens, gay cruisers, and sundry procurers of crack, this one didn't feel rickety and abandoned. ("When people have their own backyards, they grill alone," Jason had said once.)

Prospect Park teemed with cheerful people doing cheerful things: walking, running, biking, playing Little League, watching Little League, eating drippy ice cream cones while watching Little League. Groups of young professionals toting canvas bags from local bookstores staked out places on the grass next to Caribbean families with plastic coolers full of elaborate foods that somehow all smelled of plantains. The park was a liberal integrationist's wet dream: multiracial, multiethnic, multiclass.

When he and Aurit arrived at the picnic, a rapid-fire exchange of effusions ensued. "Congrats!" "It's official!" "Thanks for coming!" "Have something to eat!"

On an adjacent picnic blanket, Jason was holding court. "I'm sorry to have to tell you, but no amount of quality day care or liberal education is going to produce a nation of self-critical adherents to the Golden Rule," he was saying. He was speaking to two bemused-looking women and paused only long enough to nod at Nate and Aurit. "It's just not in everybody's DNA. Virtue is its own reward for some—but not for everyone. And that's a good thing. There are a lot of things that moralists are incapable of doing."

"Like what, building pyramids?" Aurit muttered. "It's amazing what you can do if you're willing to use slave labor."

"Exactly!" Jason said. "Pyramids, the settling of the New World, industrialization. Think of the brutality!" He beamed. "Moral people wouldn't have pulled off any of it. And then where would we be? Not sitting here in lovely Prospect Park with our cushy jobs and preening social consciences."

The women he was talking to—or at—exchanged a glance. "What about the victims of these immoral people?" asked one, a friendly-looking redhead.

"Of course, there's a social tax we pay for having psychopaths running around," Jason conceded. "But society needs the cunning to make things happen, just like it needs the conscientious to enforce the rules, to keep the thing from turning into a game theorist's nightmare. Just like it needs *artists*"—he spoke the word with mocking emphasis—"by which I include writers, musicians, and the like, to attract would-be loners to the communal campfire and fold them into the clan."

"That's a moving theory," the redhead said.

The argument petered out. The redhead, whom Nate sat down next to, told him she was a grad student in art history. Before she went back to school she had been an editor at his publishing house. She and Nate began running through various common acquaintances.

Jason turned to him. "Where's *Hannah*?"

Nate's jaw tightened. He knew Jason thought he had the temperament of a sad, whipped schmuck, a conviction that certain women might have found hard to credit but was nonetheless unshakable as far as Jason went. (Jason had, in the past, attributed this to Nate's "squirrelly, smarmy" need for everyone to like him.)

"We're not attached at the hip," Nate said.

He turned back to the redhead. After a few minutes, their conversation began to run dry. He wished there were a way to politely exit, but she was so smiley and friendly that Nate didn't want to hurt her feelings. Finally, she nodded at the red wine he was drinking. "I think I'm going to look for some white," she said.

"Of course!" Nate said.

He remembered something he wanted to ask Mark. He flicked Jason's upper arm. "Is Mark coming today, do you know?"

Jason shook his head. "Dunno . . . I haven't seen him for a while. You know he started dating someone, right? The hot little ticket from that reading? Carrie? Cara?" He whistled. "*Cute girl.* Hey, wait. Didn't you talk to her first?"

"Maybe," Nate said, tugging a blade of grass from the ground. "Yeah. I guess I did."

"And you didn't . . . ? Oh, that's right." Jason smirked. "*Hannah.*"

Before Nate could respond, a woman he had dated briefly years ago came up and said hello. She was now married with a small child, which she had brought along with her. When they dated, Nate had thought that she was a little too maternal for his taste. The well-being she projected now, as she held up the little blond thing for him to admire, seemed to confirm his intuition. When she put the child down, it lurched toward a squirrel. Laughing, she tottered off after it. "Good to see you!" she called behind her.

Nate accepted some carrots and hummus from a plate being passed around.

"Did I tell you Maggie started dating someone?" Jason asked.

Maggie was a girl Jason worked with. He had made out with her once the year before and talked about it frequently.

"The guy sounds like a real douche," Jason continued. "Some kind of freelance Web site designer or something that basically anyone could do in their spare time."

The sun had emerged from behind a cloud. Nate lifted a hand to shield his eyes. "Not that you care, right?"

"I care about Maggie a lot," Jason said, swatting one hand against his arm. "*Fucking mosquito.* Maggie's happiness is extremely important to me."

"Right . . ."

Nate's cell phone rang from inside his jeans pocket.

"The girlfriend?" Jason asked as Nate fished for the phone.

Nate hit the DECLINE button to make Hannah's name disappear from the screen. "You know, Jase," he said. "I was trying to remember. When actually was the last time you got laid? Who was president? Did you have dial-up or broadband?"

Jason stared at him for a moment. Then he smiled broadly. His distended lips reminded Nate of the bellies of starving children. "I can't help it if I have high standards," he said.

The group was called to attention to toast the couple.

Afterward, Jason turned to him. "I get the feeling you think I don't like your new girlfriend."

"I didn't—" Instinctively, Nate started to deny that he'd given the subject any thought whatsoever, but Jason continued over him.

"That's not true. I might have thought she was a little mousy at first, but I was wrong. I think she's a cool girl."

Nate was surprised to hear this—also surprised, and a little embarrassed, by just how glad he was to hear it. He nodded with studied casualness. "She is cool."

"I was surprised, at first, only because I didn't think she was your type."

This was clearly a provocation. Nate knew he should ignore it. "What do you mean, not my type?" he asked.

"You know . . ." Jason said. "You usually go for—I don't know how to put this—sort of girly, high-maintenance women. You know, like Elisa."

"That's ridic—!" On the other side of the picnic blanket, Aurit, in conversation with someone Nate didn't know, glanced up at him. Nate lowered his voice. "—ulous. Don't you think I liked Elisa in spite of her being, as you put it—so generously, I might add—'girly and high-maintenance,' and not because of it?"

"Well, I'm sure you think so—"

"There were a lot of reasons I liked her. Not one of them had to do with her being high-maintenance. That did have something to do with why I broke up with her."

"Calm down," Jason said. "All I'm saying is that we're hard-wired to respond to certain things—I know I am—and not all of them are what I'd call good."

"Kristen wasn't girly or high-maintenance."

"No, she wasn't," Jason agreed. "Anyway, it doesn't matter. If you're happy, that's great. As I said, I think Hannah's a cool girl." Without giving Nate a chance to respond, Jason turned away. "Hey, Aurit, can you pass some of those vegetables?"

"Speaking of Elisa," Jason said a moment later, "what'd she say when you told her you were doing her friend?"

Nate started to react to that last bit but checked himself. "I haven't told her yet," he said. "I'm going to."

Jason was nibbling on a broccoli floret with a delicacy that was almost effete, especially in contrast with the leer that took shape on his lips. "Tell her if she needs a shoulder to cry on, she can call me," he said. "I've always got time for her tight little ass and big blue eyes."

"For fuck's sake."

Nate did meet up with Elisa several days later. He'd been putting it off, and indeed he should have done it sooner. She had already heard about Hannah from someone. To Nate's surprise, she was mad not at him but at Hannah.

"I thought she was my friend," Elisa said.

"She feels bad," Nate said. "She really likes you. She assumed it was cool since you and I are friends."

"I'm sure she feels *awful*. A person who dates her friend's ex, who she met at her friend's own house—at her friend's *dinner party* . . . I'm sure she feels terrible."

Nate studied the grain of the wood on the bar. They were at a steak place, in midtown, near Elisa's office. He was beginning to wonder whether this get-together was a good idea. Making such a big to-do about him and Hannah seemed to confer undue legitimacy to Elisa's anger.

Elisa was aggressively stirring her martini. "What a bitch."

"That's not fa—"

But as Elisa turned her eyes from the smoky mirror behind the bar to meet his, Nate let the words trail off. Sometimes, it hit him all over again, the rawness of Elisa's unhappiness. For all her beauty, she looked—around her eyes—haggard, stricken.

"I'm sorry, E," he said softly. "I really am. I didn't think you guys were close. I didn't mean to hurt you."

Elisa's lower lip protruded sulkily. She didn't so much shrug as raise a thin shoulder, causing her collarbone to jut out above the wide neckline of her blouse. Apart from her eyes, she looked as pretty and fashionable as ever, with her blonde hair swept up in a loose bun. She was wearing a long, loose white shirt and tight-fitting black pants.

"You'll meet someone," Nate said.

Elisa looked at him, her perfect features perfectly still. As one beat passed and then another, her expression seemed to deepen until her face projected a profound weariness.

"Maybe," she said finally.

Nate braced himself for her to start in on familiar accusations. He had poisoned her future relationships. She could no longer trust that a guy who claimed to love her wouldn't change his mind at any moment. He had made her feel that she wasn't smart enough or good enough. How was she supposed to recover from that?

But she must have sensed that for now she already had Nate's sympathy. There was nothing to gain by taking that tack.

"By the way," she said. "I'm sorry about last time. My dinner party, I mean. And afterward. I had too much to drink. I shouldn't have put you in that position. It's just . . . I don't know, things have kind of sucked lately. I've been feeling really down."

Nate shifted his weight on the well-padded bar stool. In his chest, various emotions—guilt and pity and simple sadness—swelled miserably. He almost preferred when she berated him.

"Don't worry about it," he said. "I'm sorry you haven't been happy."

Elisa shrugged again as she scrutinized one of her hands and began repositioning a ring that had slid off-center.

Nate sought something diverting to say. "What's the boss up to these days?"

Elisa very subtly shook her head as if in wry amusement, as if she knew he was changing the subject because he was a coward, but was by now resigned to his immaturity. With touching pliancy, she launched into an anecdote.

Elisa worked for a Very Important Magazine. Nate, as she well knew, liked hearing about the goings-on there. She told him about a well-known writer who'd pissed off her boss, the editor in chief, by withdrawing a piece rather than submitting to his editorial suggestions. The writer had then published the piece in a competing publication, incorporating many of those suggestions.

"He's never writing for us again," she said.

"No, I would think not."

Elisa looked deliberately at him. "What about you? It's only about, what, six months until your book comes out? You must"—her eyes twitched—"you must be really excited."

Nate stared at the row of single-malt scotches lined up on the shelf behind the bar. He had written much of his book while he had been with Elisa. In a way, she had been essential to his writing it. Although she had sometimes complained about the time he took away from her to work on it, she had always believed in the book and in his ability to pull it off. During periods when the writing wasn't going well, when he had seriously doubted it ever would, her faith had mattered a lot, had maybe been crucial. Then, before the book was finished and sold, he'd broken up with her.

"I try not to obsess about it," he said.

Elisa pushed her empty glass to the back of the bar. It was immediately whisked away by a bow-tied attendant. Nate began to call him back to ask for the check.

"Why are you in such a hurry?" Elisa asked.

Something familiar snapped back into place as her resigned tone gave way to one of complaint.

Nate held up his hands. "I'm not."

"Is *Hannah* expecting you?"

"No! I just—oh, never mind. Let's get another."

"Not if you don't want to."

"I want to!" he insisted. "I do."

It was after ten when he walked Elisa to her subway station. As she disappeared down the steps, Nate felt the kind of relief that has a physical component, like the release after a long run. On his way to his own subway station, several blocks west, he sent Hannah a text. *Is it weird that I miss you?* They'd seen each other only that morning.

Her reply came a moment later. *Yes, it's weird.* Seconds after, another arrived: *(but I kinda, sorta miss you too).*

After the evening with Elisa, Nate wanted nothing so much as to rebuild his mood in a different key. The light, easy banter he and Hannah tended toward—the implicit reassurance of her presence that he wasn't a heartless ingrate—was particularly appealing.

Before he got on the train, he wrote back. *I can be there in 45.*

{ 10 }

That night, Hannah asked what the deal was with him and Elisa. They were sitting in the chairs by her window. Nate paused before answering.

He had met Elisa three years ago at a publishing party. She had arrived with the editor in chief of the Very Important Magazine. Nate asked his friend Andrew about her. Andrew said she was the editor in chief's new assistant.

When her boss left, Elisa remained. Nate downed two or three thimble-sized glasses of wine. She was standing next to the food table, in front of a small mountain of fruit.

"Hi, I'm Nate."

She popped a red grape into her mouth. "Elisa," she said, almost drowsily.

For the next few minutes, she answered his questions, but she seemed slightly put out by the obligation he had imposed on her. Eventually, she asked what he did.

He said he was the book critic for an online magazine. She asked which one. He told her.

She eyed him. Nate tugged at the collar of his blue Oxford shirt. He noticed that one of his shoes was not merely untied but radically untied, as if he had only just now wrested his foot from a steel trap. Its gaping, brown tongue hung crookedly, crisscrossed with faint indentations where the laces should have been. He stepped on that foot with the other, swaying slightly, like a top-heavy kebab.

She told him that she'd recently finished a master's degree in comp lit from the Sorbonne. Before that she'd been at Brown. This was her first job in publishing. She wanted to write. She'd love to get coffee with Nate sometime. *She would?* Yeah, she'd love to talk about publishing.

Coffee turned into dinner and, a few days later, a sunset run over the Brooklyn Bridge and then a party at a Harvard friend/hedge fund guy's Upper West Side triplex and a Saturday night at the Brooklyn Museum. Nate was terrifically impressed by her. She dropped casual references to the work of aging intellectuals who contributed to the *New York Review of Books*. The polysyllabic names of avant-garde eastern European filmmakers rolled effortlessly from her tongue. Her father was a well-known professor whose books Nate knew by reputation. By that point in his life, Nate had dated any number of editorial types. Elisa seemed different, unusually serious and well informed, especially for someone so young. And so attractive.

Even Nate, who had had to be told by Jason not to wear pants with pleats, could tell somehow that among all the well-dressed young women of Brooklyn, Elisa looked especially nice. She knew where to buy anything, which stores were not so much expensive as tasteful, and also what was okay to buy at Target (from what Nate gleaned, things that started with the letter *T*: Tupperware, tights, toothpaste). In theory, Nate disdained "bourgeois status signifiers," but in practice he took pride in Elisa's whiff of smart chic. She radiated the effortless worldly ease of the popular girl. She was clearly first-rate, top-shelf, the publishing world equivalent of Amy Perelman in high school and Will McDormand's best-looking gal pals at Harvard: she was the thing that was clearly, indisputably desirable.

Her demeanor was smooth and preoccupied, even slightly sullen, and she spoke at times with an unnerving, almost anhedonic lack of affect. She often seemed bored. This edge of perpetual dissatisfaction made it all the more thrilling for Nate when he cajoled her into laughter and good humor: to impress her, one felt—he felt—was really something.

Back then he didn't have a book deal. His book-reviewing gig ensured a regular paycheck, but to call it modest, relative to the cost of living in New York, was an overstatement bordering on a lie. To get by, he needed to hustle for all the additional assignments he could get, both proofreading and writing. He worked alone, in his dirty apartment. Some days, he didn't bother to shower. He blew his nose with toilet paper. Cheap toilet paper. (Once when he was visiting from New Haven, Nate's college friend Peter had surreptitiously nabbed a few squares from the roll and folded them into the breast pocket of his shirt. He waited until their friends were assembled at a bar to pass them around. "Just feel it. Can you believe that *this*—the world's most diaphanous sandpaper—is what our Nate uses to wipe his ass? Talk about self-loathing.")

Nate had no health insurance, hadn't had it for years. After a while, he'd come to take for granted that he was the kind of scruffy, marginal person whose well-being was not deemed important by society. Elisa's well-being, on the other hand, was incontrovertibly important—to her, to her parents, to the magazine that lavished her with extensive dental, optical, and mental-health benefits. The universe itself seemed bent on accommodating her, with free drinks from bartenders, gentle treatment from otherwise gruff cab drivers, and kindly offers of advice from avuncular grandees of magazine publishing who never returned Nate's e-mails.

Nate was usually still sleeping each day when Elisa, lovely and carefully groomed, sailed past the guards in the lobby of that midtown Manhattan skyscraper, zoomed up to the zillionth floor in the express elevator, and took her seat at a desk with her nameplate above it. There, she answered phones, calmly assuring nervous writers that her boss would get back to them. She escorted various Important People into the big corner office. She sat in on certain editorial meetings and even, when asked, offered ideas about the magazine's content. For the most part, though, her work was administrative. It was, nonetheless, the start of a career. She was taking great care not to become someone fringy like Nate, at home in his underwear, sweating up his sheets, pondering such questions as whether he should take the earned income tax credit if he qualified, or if that would be wrong, since it was clearly intended for real poor people, not Harvard grads who eschewed regular jobs to pursue their idiosyncratic intellectual ambitions.

When he met up with Elisa at the end of a workday, he felt like he'd clawed his way out of a Morlockean underworld. With her, he was treated differently at restaurants. Other men sized him up with their eyes. Waiters and maître d's were more deferential. Even among his circle of friends and acquaintances, his stock rose subtly.

So it hardly seemed to matter that she was not a particularly nice girlfriend. Unless they coincided with hers, Elisa treated his desires as perverse whims, wholly negligible. An expensive restaurant she liked was a healthy indulgence; his craving for barbecue was "disgusting." A somewhat down-market local barbecue chain he especially liked? "Out of the question." After social engagements, she enjoyed regaling him with a list of criticisms of his behavior. She seemed to think that everything he did was first and foremost a reflection on her. When, at a dinner party, he made a bad joke, Elisa was mad at him for embarrassing her. "What made you think that would have been funny?" she demanded as soon as they'd rounded the corner from the Park Slope brownstone where they'd spent the evening. Nate was forced to admit he had absolutely no idea why he had thought that responding to someone's comment that we are living in an age of anxiety by saying that he thought it was the Age of Aquarius would be funny. As soon as the words had escaped from his mouth, he was humiliated by their lameness. This provoked no sympathy from Elisa. She thought he owed it to her to be someone she could respect. That meant not making bad jokes. It also meant being affectionate but not too affectionate, complimentary but not too complimentary, smart but not pedantically so, and a host of other things.

When Elisa felt that someone had wronged her, she was out-raged. Apparently, she was the only person in all of New York with any manners; everyone else behaved like an animal, especially to her, which was very hard for her to understand because—and this was news to Nate—she "bore no ill will toward anyone." She was furious if Nate didn't wholeheartedly support her in her indigna-tion toward such-and-such coworker, who had made a comment at lunch, which, though it seemed fairly innocuous when she repeated it to Nate, struck Elisa as unforgivably barbed. To suggest even the possibility of a misunderstanding, let alone an overreaction, was, as far as Elisa was concerned, to undermine her.

She seemed to have no internal sense of justice. When Nate got annoyed because she was late to meet him or because she seemed to him to be acting bored as he told her something he felt was important, he instinctively evaluated his irritation, tried to assess whether it was reasonable or fair, under the circumstances. (Perhaps she hadn't realized that what he was saying was important to him? Perhaps he hadn't been clear?) She, on the other hand, treated her emotional responses as infallible. His self-criticism, she seemed to perceive merely as a weakness to be exploited. "No," she'd say. "You really weren't clear."

Nate's only other serious girlfriend had been Kristen, who was, whatever else you might say about her, an extremely fair-minded person. Elisa was a bit baffling to him. But for a long time, none of her limitations mattered. Nate had grown up on the Old Testa-ment. He didn't expect his god to be reasonable or merciful. He may have privately grumbled about her demands, he may have tried to reason with her or cajole her, but Elisa's presence in his life, in his bed, her beauty (sometimes when he was with her he was simply overcome with the desire to touch her silky blonde hair or perfect doll face), the particular pains and pleasures of being with her: these had become, for him, existentially necessary.

Although Elisa was intelligent—and fluent in the things sophisticated people were supposed to be fluent in—Nate had realized fairly early on that her writing was often stilted and awkward. Her ideas tended toward strained attempts at a sort of academic profundity. There was also something brittle about her love of intellect and intellectualism and, more important, *intellectuals*, like Nate. This passion of hers had impressed him at first. But it was, he learned over time, a form of success mongering, a specialized form, but success mongering all the same. Long before he was ready to call it quits with her—long before even a seed of the thought had entered his mind—he began to assemble a picture of her much less flattering than his initial impression. Her taste, for example, was great—inasmuch as it was received, inasmuch as she absorbed what was fashionably highbrow. She really liked, say, Svevo—was able to see myriad virtues in Svevo—once she was primed to like Svevo, once she knew that Svevo was someone she was supposed to like. Once her father, the professor, or her boss, the Very Important Editor, had sung the praises of Svevo. But other times, railing against the "male literary establishment," she'd assert (to Nate, never to her coworkers) the value of some schmaltzy if well-meaning piece of middlebrow fiction about a girl and her mother, or a girl and her best friend, or a girl and the black woman who helped to raise her, who together combated predatory males and social injustice and ultimately learned the redemptive power of love. Those were the books she really liked, Nate realized after a while. The Svevo, the aging intellectuals of the *New York Review of Books*—all that, it turned out, was for show, even if she was putting on the show for herself as much as for anyone else.

Nate wished, for her sake, that she'd relax about it, realize it was okay not to be some kind of highbrow intellectual. She'd surely be happier at a different type of magazine, a less stuffy one, perhaps one of those Web sites for smart, independent women, where she wouldn't have to disguise her tastes and where, freed from the need to posture, her verbal cleverness, her knack for snappy aperçus, would come into play. (She was always criticizing him in the most *clever* and *imaginative* terms.) But, no, the high opinion of people like her father and her boss meant too much to her. She had to do something they valued, not something that she valued. Nate felt tenderness toward her when he saw her situation in those terms. Elisa was a beautiful, intelligent woman trying desperately to make herself into a slightly different kind of intelligent woman.

Incidentally, this was also the answer to the question that had so perplexed him initially: the matter of why she was with him. At that moment in her life, Elisa was, he realized, almost pathologically attracted not to status or money or good looks but to literary and intellectual potential. Nate possessed many of the same mental qualities as her father and her boss. And he had to admit that, no matter how much Elisa criticized his dress, manners, personality, and habits, her faith in his mind had been strong and constant.

She was a good influence on him in certain ways, compelling him to go to plays and concerts and gallery openings and well-reviewed restaurants in obscure corners of the city. His default had always been the neighborhood bar. In retrospect, though, Nate supposed that even when they'd been at their best, even as she'd clung to his arm sweetly when they walked from the subway to the pizza parlor in a once-Italian neighborhood in deep Brooklyn, even when they'd sat together drinking hot cocoa on a stone bench outside the Cloisters, staring across the Hudson at the red-brown New Jersey Palisades, even at those moments he had been on some level cataloging her inadequacies for future reference. By the time they'd been going out for seven or eight months, she'd become an increasingly frequent topic of conversation between

Nate and his friends. "Is it normal for your girlfriend to have what's basically a temper tantrum if you make plans for a Friday night without consulting her?" he would ask. "What does it mean that when she pronounces judgment on someone, my first instinct is to assume the opposite is true?"

After he and Elisa had been together for about a year, his dissatisfaction overwhelmed whatever it was—love? need? infatuation?—that had attached him to her. "When a friendship ceases to grow, it immediately begins to decline," said the amoral Madame Merle, and so it seemed to Nate. One day he found that Elisa's hold over him had loosened. He could contemplate her being mad at him without the thought triggering successive jolts of anxiety that inexorably, almost against his will, directed his energies toward effecting reconciliation.

Initially he treaded lightly—said no to more of her proposed outings, stayed at his place when he felt like it, made plans to go away with Jason and Mark one weekend without checking with her first. He brushed off her annoyance and waited to see if the old anxiety would reassert itself. It didn't. Elisa quickly sensed the change, with, it seemed, the same gut-level instinct that some animals sense an approaching storm. She became nicer, more accommodating. She suggested a barbecue restaurant, albeit a trendy one reviewed in the *Times*. She stifled her irritation when Nate told her he wouldn't spend a week at her parents' summerhouse because he wanted to work on his book. She slept with him more often and even bought lacy lingerie and garter belts and teddies with furry pom-poms over the breasts, and the sight of her thin, too-thin, body in these costumes touched him as much as it turned him on. "For me you did this?" he marveled, as she approached him in a red-and-black-striped corset that called to mind the costume of one of Zola's prostitutes. He had always enjoyed sex with Elisa. From the beginning, her aloofness, that bored, preoccupied quality she had, combined with the intensity of his attraction, had imbued it with a sense of quest, of contest; his satisfaction on those occasions when he'd succeeded, and she'd squealed beneath him, had been almost unparalleled in his erotic life. These occurrences became more frequent.

But except for sex, Nate's ardor did not appear to be coming back. The things that had bothered him most about Elisa—her selfishness, her criticism, her demands—were disappearing one by one, and still he felt no slackening in the pace with which indifference, even distaste, was overwhelming everything else he felt for her.

Then he ruptured his Achilles tendon and was on crutches. He stayed with her for a couple weeks because there were fewer stairs to climb to reach her apartment. She behaved beautifully, picking things up from his place, cooking for him, anticipating almost all of his needs. Nate returned to his apartment as soon as he possibly could. Being at Elisa's he had felt like a criminal harbored by the person he has wronged. He had by then almost entirely ceased to feel romantic interest. In its stead: a dispassionate appraisal of her merits and demerits that wasn't entirely to her credit. Even the sex, that blissful second honeymoon, had sputtered out. Increasingly conscious of his changed feelings, Nate couldn't escape the sense that he was taking advantage of her, taking something on false pretenses. He began to shrink from sleeping with her.

When finally he broke up with her, she was more upset than he'd expected. Although he pretended at sympathy, he felt it in only the shallowest sense: he saw her cry and in the moment felt bad. On another level, her tears gratified him: *So now you think I'm such hot shit? What about six months ago when you gave me crap the whole weekend we spent at my parents' house because they were too "shrill," and gave you a headache, and you had too little to talk about with them?* But he didn't say anything. He knew that if she said she was sorry, if she promised to change even more than she had already, it wouldn't matter.

She called him the next day, sounding alarmingly distressed. He agreed to meet her for coffee a few days later; this prospect calmed her down. Over coffee, he told her again that he was sorry but it was just too late, no, he didn't know why, it was nothing she did, he simply needed to focus on finishing his book and probably he wasn't fit to be in any relationship, maybe there was something wrong with him—anything to avoid the truth: that over time he had come to see her as overprivileged and underinteresting.

"It's just—" Elisa set her coffee cup in her saucer and looked at him with watery eyes. "I never really felt loved before. I thought this was it."

Something tugged at him. Back when he had been enamored with her, and incredulous that she had chosen him, hadn't he done a thousand little things to make her feel as fully, as wholly loved as possible? He had thought it would give him more of a hold on her.

But, then, he told himself, wasn't that just what happens in a relationship? It wasn't as if he had intentionally misled her.

They agreed, that day, to remain friends. But Nate soon found himself growing frustrated. Nearly every time they got together she brought up their failed relationship, insisting she just wanted to clear up a few things. When the conversation didn't go the way she wanted—and what she wanted sometimes seemed to be no less than for him to declare that he'd made a mistake in breaking up with her—she'd get upset. With tears came mawkishness and recrimination, unanswerable questions intended, it seemed to him, only to make him feel guilty. "You don't think I'm smart enough, do you?" "How am I ever supposed to trust anyone after I let myself trust you, after you *made* me trust you?" Meanwhile, he remembered with perfect clarity how little sympathy she'd had for him when she had been the one with more power.

Over time, though, another current of feeling began to build within him. No matter how much he told himself that he had done nothing wrong with regard to her, not according to the standards that he and everyone he knew lived by (if anything *she* was in the wrong in her clinginess and undignified hysteria), on some intuitive level, Nate began to feel culpable. A stentorian, Faulkner-like voice within him insisted on seeing the relationship in stark moralistic terms. He'd been drawn—this voice intoned—to Elisa because of her beauty, because she seemed first-rate, because of her well-known father and shining pedigree, and he, nerd, loser that he'd long been, had always suspected that people like her, people like Amy Perelman, with their good looks and popularity, had something he didn't, something impenetrable by intelligence alone, a sort of magic and grace, a wordless wisdom about how to live, and a corresponding access to unknown pleasures. Unlike with Kristen, to whom he'd felt a real kinship, Nate had glommed onto Elisa from reptilian ambition. And then, like a dog that sniffs at a foreign object before deciding it doesn't interest him, he trotted off, on to other attractions. Except his experiment hadn't been so painless for Elisa. Perhaps the strength of her attachment wasn't even as strange as it had once seemed to him. Before him, Elisa had dated a string of guys she seemed to have chosen on the basis of their good looks and propensity to treat her badly. Although he was less good-looking, Nate had apparently hit some sort of sweet spot, being both a nicer boyfriend *and* more desirable in terms of professional prospects than the parade of broad-shouldered sociopaths who'd preceded him. And as Elisa, not without basis, rated her claims to worldly admiration higher than she rated Nate's, it was easy to understand why she had felt secure in his affection.

If she was now sort of pathetic—shameless in her lack of pride and in her unreasonable anger—wasn't all that of a piece with everything he had long known of her? She had been spoiled by her good looks and good fortune; she lacked inner resources; she was petulant and childish when things didn't go her way. He had known all that since practically the first time they'd gone out. If he had wanted her when he knew she was immature, could he really use that as a reason to throw her over now, just because he no longer wanted what else she had on offer? Well, yes, he could, the answer was obviously yes—but still it made him feel bad.

Most of the time, Nate quieted the fundamentalist preacher's voice in his head. It was not to be trusted—it was simplistic, it was self-aggrandizing, according him a godlike power over others; it assumed, problematically, that he was smarter and stronger than Elisa and thus solely responsible for everything that happened between them. Yet his attitude did become more sympathetic toward her. He could always, in an effort to justify himself, list the ways in which she was lacking as a person (she was shallow and her concerns, even her disappointments, were narrow; her ill-concealed pride in her upper-class family was itself vulgar; she was acquisitive, not so much for money as for status and a "suitable"— i.e., alpha male—partner, et cetera), but what, really, did it signify? She may not be a particularly admirable or noble-minded person, but she was indisputably a person. She bled if you pricked her. Although he didn't buy Elisa's most histrionic claims as to the irreparable damage he had supposedly done her—all told they had only been together for a year and a half, they hadn't even lived together—Nate did come to acknowledge that he had hurt her badly. He promised to try, to really try, to be kinder to her, to help her if he could. Even though from his perspective the best possible thing would be to just drop out of each other's lives, he promised her he wouldn't "abandon" her.

But he messed up. He not infrequently found her maddening, particularly when she started in on her favorite/his least favorite topic of conversation: their relationship and all psychic wounds appertaining to it. He took too long to return her calls. The worst of it, though, was that he slept with her far too many times after they broke up, convincing himself that it was okay, that she "understood" the situation. Drunk, lonely, horny, feeling for her a tepid nostalgic affection, he'd contrive for a moment not to see what was obvious: that, apparently, he was willing to fuck with her head, to lead her on a little, because he wanted not just sex but to revel for a short while in the balm of her continued, perhaps even increased, affection. (She seemed to forget that for much of the time they'd actually been together, she'd found him lacking.) And for all he knew, she did understand the situation perfectly, better than he did. Maybe she had never for a single minute thought that this backsliding would amount to more than sex. Still, if she wasn't yet entirely over him, Nate knew he hadn't exactly helped. At least, he had stopped—that is, they had stopped sleeping together. They had agreed not to do it anymore.

This hadn't, of course, prevented her from coming on to him the night of her dinner party. But as she said, she'd been unhappy. A lot of that had nothing to do with him. Life had changed for Elisa since he and she had first met. Three and a half years was too long to be an assistant, even to the editor in chief of a Very Important Magazine. But her forays into writing for the magazine had been painful. Her pieces had been received by editors somewhat poorly and had been so extensively rewritten that she'd been stung. Nate tried to convince her that this was not unusual. Most people her age don't start off writing for magazines of this caliber. They work up to it over time. That was what he had done in his twenties. But Elisa had always been successful at whatever she'd undertaken; she wasn't emotionally prepared for failure of any sort. Without much in the way of humor or humility to put it in perspective, the crash of her expectations was crippling. She clung all the more tenaciously to her job: although she found it at times demeaning, she relied utterly on the prestige of the magazine, and of her boss, to feel important—that is, safe.

While she was still beautiful, she'd lost some of the freshness that she'd had when he first met her, when she was brand-new to the city and adult life and the literary scene, when she'd first entered their social universe as an unknown and nubile young commodity, whose good looks ensured a warm and enthusiastic welcome. Over time, the very quality that he had been drawn to, that indisputable first-rate-ness, had begun to diminish. She had become another attractive, unhappy single woman who could be seen at certain types of parties, complaining about her job and the men she'd been with. She was also known as his ex, which, accurate as it was, was not quite fair. He wasn't classified in the same condescending way as her ex.

Nate rubbed the back of his head.

What was the deal with him and Elisa? Hannah had asked. Sitting in the chair across from him, she smiled encouragingly as she waited for his answer.

She had told him about her ex. But his relationship with Elisa would be difficult to explain. There were things he wasn't proud of. Also, Hannah knew Elisa. He'd feel unchivalrous divulging certain unflattering facts about her to the woman he was currently sleeping with. Besides, he was suddenly very tired.

"We went out for a while," he said, standing up to signal he was ready to move to the bedroom. "It didn't work out. Now we're friends. I guess that's about it."

11

What had begun as an unusually cool summer by August turned into a very hazy, sticky one. Nate retrieved his clunky old air conditioner and installed it in his bedroom window as he began to work seriously on the magazine assignment that Jason had helped him get. Most days, he went for a run in the park, usually before eight, and then worked straight into the evening, rarely allowing even himself the pleasant distraction of Recess. Often he'd meet up with Hannah for a late dinner. Sometimes he felt he didn't have time for that, and she'd come over around eleven to spend the night. Though he occasionally regretted not having time to see his friends, he was happy during those weeks. He always felt most alive, most himself when he was immersed in a project.

When he turned in the piece at the end of the month, Hannah said she wanted to cook him a real dinner. "To celebrate the article," she said. Nate said that sounded nice.

In the meantime, he started in on a list of chores he'd put off while he was working on the piece: Buy birthday present for his mother. Renew driver's license. Switch banks to avoid punishing new fees recently imposed by current bank. Bills. Haircut. Laundry. Tedious stuff.

Perhaps that was why he wasn't in the greatest mood when he arrived at Hannah's for dinner. He couldn't think of any other reason.

She was stirring herbs into a pot of pasta.

He peered in. "Wow. Real clams. In their shells and everything."

She looked amused. "That's how they come. In shells."

Nate followed her to the table. She was wearing a dress he didn't remember having seen before, clingy and black.

As they began to eat, he complimented the pasta. She started talking about cooking and the "psychodrama of taste." Her mother and one of her sisters constantly got into these ridiculously heated squabbles about whose favorite cookbook was better or whether organic really was healthier. What was actually at stake, Hannah said, was the question of which of the two was more tasteful, classier—the mother with her white tablecloths and coq au vin or the sister with her butcher's block and Alice Waters–inspired recipes.

"Your sister wins," Nate said. "Definitely."

"You're not a neutral judge—you're her generation, more or less. And you've never tasted my mother's coq au vin."

Nate smiled, but it was a little forced. He didn't know if it was his imagination or if there was, tonight, some change in their dynamic, a diminution of the lively, crackling energy that usually infused their talk. Maybe he just didn't feel like talking. He turned back to the pasta. Not all the clams had opened. It was good, though. So was the salad she'd made to go with it.

When they finished eating, Nate began clearing dishes. As he returned from the kitchen, Hannah stood up to refill her wine glass. Then she reached over the table to refill his.

"That's okay."

She looked up, her mouth a surprised O.

"I don't really feel like it," he said, a note of apology finding its way into his voice as it occurred to him that she'd cooked him a nice meal and put on a dress. This, this dinner was a *thing*. In not drinking—in not getting into the spirit—he was failing to do his part.

Hannah clasped the wine bottle with both hands. A small crease appeared between her eyebrows. For an instant, Nate saw her in an unfamiliar light—vulnerable, needy. His guilt flickered into annoyance. Why a thing? Says who? Why should he be made to feel bad just because he wasn't in the mood to make a romantic fuss about a Tuesday night? He felt like reading. Or fooling around online. So what?

But just as quickly as it had appeared, the furrow in Hannah's brow disappeared.

"Okay," she said.

She shot him a quick smile as she pushed the cork back in the bottle. Nate, rocking on his heels, his thumbs hooked into the belt loops of his jeans, smiled back.

She turned and walked to the kitchen. Nate watched as she stood on her tiptoes and reached up to set the bottle on top of the refrigerator. Her black dress rode up her thighs. Her ass, in the clingy fabric, looked good.

A part of him wanted to feel it against his body, to get up behind her and whisper his thanks for the meal. But he was afraid that if he did, he'd raise expectations that, at the moment, he wasn't up to following through on.

"Do you mind if I check my e-mail?" he asked.

"Go ahead," Hannah said, walking back to the table. "I'll just hang out here." She lifted her glass. "With my wine."

The next morning, Nate put on running clothes and jogged toward the park. He was conscious of trying to evade, literally to outrun, a feeling of restlessness.

The night before had been sort of a drag. He'd sat by himself at Hannah's desk for a while, fiddling on her laptop, but he'd been uncomfortably conscious of her movements in the living room. He'd been glad when after about half an hour she came into the bedroom and asked if he wanted to watch a movie. He did. The film, an indie comedy that they watched in bed, on the laptop, cheered him. Temporarily. He'd woken up to the same feeling of dullness.

Yet everything was going well. Strong blurbs were coming in for his book. On the phone a few days before, his father had made an uncharacteristically approving remark about Nate's career choices. (His years of underpaid freelance work, previously seen as "bumming around," had been recast as evidence of "entrepreneurial spirit.") And he was getting laid.

When he went too long without sex, he invariably felt depressed. The pent-up sexual energy seemed to corrode his self-esteem. One-night stands mostly failed to satisfy. (Since the main criterion one selected for was willingness, perhaps this wasn't surprising.) Casual dating, he had learned, didn't work all that well either. Too many hurt feelings. What he had with Hannah—sex with a woman he liked—was better, clearly, than any of the other options.

Of course, it was a lot more than sex, what he had with Hannah.

The air, as he entered the park, was thick with humidity. When he stepped onto the running path, he glanced at his phone to check the time, then sped up.

Free-floating ennui wasn't something Nate experienced much until the past year. Before he'd sold his book, his adult life had been so circumscribed financially and so uncertain professionally—yet so charged with the beating pulse of his ambition—that he hadn't hungered for drama. Through no choice of his own, bohemianism, in the sense of not always knowing how he'd pay the rent, had been thrust upon him. The fear of failure had been real and constant. He supposed some part of him missed it, missed the urgency.

The running path, a utility road, really, curved through a wooded area. The foliage crowded out all signs of urban life. For a moment, Nate just listened to the sound of his footfalls on the asphalt.

A few days ago, he'd received a solicitation from the nonprofit that maintains the park. He'd felt a pang of guilt when he tossed the letter in the trash, but he had a tall stack of solicitations from various do-gooder outfits.

Once he would have thrown them all out unopened. It had seemed obvious they were intended for someone else. Someone who wasn't broke. Someone more like the rest of his Harvard class-mates. But though he was far from free of financial worry, Nate knew he no longer had quite the same excuse of poverty as he used to have. Yet he felt depressed whenever he thought about writing out a check to any of these worthy organizations, of then making a note of it for his accountant to get the tax deduction. He would have denied it, even to himself—deemed it a laughable affectation—but it seemed to him now that he had always secretly believed that in the way he lived (he refused to say his "life-style"), in his freelance, un-health-insured, sparsely thinged life, he was in a small way registering a rejection—of conformity, of middle-class convention, of not just acquisitiveness but enslave-ment to the idol of "security." Nevertheless, he'd wound up in the same place as everyone else. Was this—latte liberalism—his ines-capable fate? Surely it was. It was sheer vanity to pretend other-wise. What'd he think he was going to do, foment revolution with his precious essay about the commodification of conscience? Still, no matter how worthwhile the cause, no matter how many dissi-dents were spared torture or children saved from preventable disease, he never could send in his hundred dollars to this or that charitable organization without feeling like he'd crossed over and that something had been lost along the way.

Nate realized he'd slowed down. About a hundred feet in front of him, a blonde woman with a long ponytail was moving at a good clip. She had shapely legs and a long narrow waist. She reminded him a little of Kristen. He began using her as a pacesetter.

It was useless to lament what he'd lost—if he'd lost anything, if it weren't pure self-indulgence to think this way. He'd been extremely lucky. Sure, writing his book hadn't been entirely easy. To finish it, he'd eventually quit his biweekly book-reviewing gig, which had been the only claim to status he'd had in the eyes of the world. Even Elisa, who'd believed in the book, had wondered if giving it up was a mistake. "You never know what'll happen," she pointed out. But the reviews hadn't paid enough to justify the time and energy they required. He'd gone back to temping, which paid more, per hour, and required less mentally. He had proof-read. He had done what he had to—for the sake of something that existed only as a Microsoft Word document, a sprawling tale of a young immigrant family grappling with life in the American sub-urbs in the 1970s and 1980s, a work he'd been revising and rewrit-ing since he was in his midtwenties without ever having earned a penny from it. But writing his book—at least after a certain point, years in, when, by shifting its focus from the son to the parents, he'd finally seemed to find the thing's pulse and the novel began to take shape almost of its own accord—had also been the greatest pleasure of his life. That a publisher was then willing to pay him for it, pay him generously, was nothing to complain about. He'd do it again for free, in a minute. Many of those late nights, when he'd paced his apartment, his mind roaming the world he'd pains-takingly created and could finally inhabit—moving within it from character to character, feverishly distilling into words thoughts not his own but theirs—had been ecstasies of absorption and self-forgetfulness.

Of course, life couldn't always be lived at that pitch. Day-to-day life was bound, sometimes, to be mundane, full of workaday tasks and minor decisions. *Amnesty International or Doctors Without Borders? Dinner in or dinner out?* Some nights were bound to contain little more than a movie on Netflix.

As he emerged from the wooded part of the park, the heat began to wear on him. He started counting out his breaths.

The gap between him and the Kristen-like runner narrowed. He sped up even more, fighting his body's yearning toward comfort. As the path wound around the pond, the tall yellow grasses that lined its shore waved slightly in spite of the air's stillness. Nate overtook the blonde.

When he began to climb the last and longest hill of the running loop, thought was edged out by the need to focus on his breathing. All he could do was register in short, sensory bursts of intake the scene around him: leafy trees on his right, meadow on his left, an Asian chick in a Duke T-shirt running in the opposite direction, a swarm of passing bicyclists.

At the top of the hill, he was breathing hard. He forced himself to run faster. The last eighth of a mile, slightly downhill, was more tunnel-like, lined with trees on both sides. Each time his foot hit the pavement, he silently repeated the word *will*, as in *I will*, as in *willpower*, as in the thing that had made him get off his ass and write, night after night, when he'd been in his twenties, working those interminable temp jobs, long before writing the book had been fun, when all he'd wanted to do was get wasted, or at the very least do something passive, like read.

He reached the end of the loop and almost collapsed at the waist. Panting, he stumbled past a gaggle of Orthodox Jewish girls in long sleeves and long skirts. After a moment his breath became more regular. He checked his time on his phone. Twenty-seven minutes, twenty-two seconds. Not his best for 3.42 miles. The humidity had gotten to him.

Although he had come up with an idea for another book, he hadn't made any headway on it. He decided he needed more time to hash out the idea before he'd be ready to start writing. In the meantime, he yearned for something else to do. Because his review of the Israel book a couple months before had gone over well, he wrote to his editor at that publication and asked to review an upcoming novel by a prominent young British author. He was a little surprised not to get a response right away.

It came several days later. It wasn't the one he was looking for. Eugene Wu had been given the assignment. Nate couldn't believe it. He had done such a good job with the Israel book. (He thought he had anyway.) He had pretty much assumed this one was his for the asking. He couldn't believe he'd been turned down in favor of *Eugene*.

He and Hannah were having dinner with Aurit that night. On their way to the restaurant, Nate told Hannah about Eugene getting the assignment, but he downplayed his disappointment. He didn't want her pity. And it was embarrassing. He hated that being passed over in favor of Eugene bothered him as much as it did. It suggested a pettiness and an insecurity that he associated with mediocrity. It was not exactly the light in which he wanted Hannah, who was nobody's fool, to see him. Besides, between the two of them, he had always played the role of the more successful writer. He had been the one to champion *her* work, to build *her* up. For their roles to be reversed, even temporarily, would only add to his sense of indignity.

The restaurant they were meeting Aurit at had opened only recently. Aurit had chosen it. But the dinner had been his idea. He wanted Hannah and Aurit to get to know each other better. Although Aurit got on his nerves in a thousand different ways, he had never ceased to consider her one of the most intelligent and interesting women he'd ever met. Over the years, he had compared various women he'd dated to her, in terms of conversation. Until Hannah, the comparison had not tended to flatter the woman he was sleeping with.

While he and Hannah waited for Aurit to arrive, Nate scanned the menu and saw that the place was more expensive than he would have liked. He felt a twinge of irritation.

He had lately started to worry that he was spending too much, little by little letting his standard of living edge upward, as if his book advance money could never be depleted. As he'd just been reminded, freelance journalism assignments were unpredictable. And no matter how much he sometimes romanticized the past, he really didn't want to ever have to temp again.

"Hello! Sorry!" Aurit trilled a few minutes later as she sent semi-ironic air kisses at them.

A large leather purse and a pair of sunglasses and a set of headphones were peeled away and placed in a pile on the table. Once unencumbered, Aurit collapsed into the chair next to Nate's. "I've been on the phone with my mother," she said breathlessly. "Here's the thing about my mother . . ."

The story that followed dated back to childhood. Aurit's mother, in this telling, had long nursed an idea of herself as very sensible and self-sacrificing and unfrivolous. She propped up her self-image by constantly invoking a comparison between herself and these other women, "who've never had a job, who never, *ever* cook—they hire caterers whenever more than two people come over—who shop all the time, who resent their daughters' youth, who never read. As a kid, I bought the whole thing. It's only over time that I started to wonder where all these vapid, lazy, superficial women are. I've never encountered anyone quite so bad, let alone an army of such women, except maybe on *Dallas*. Then I realized the only place they exist is in her head, where they play a very important role. She can justify almost anything she does because she truly, deep-down believes she's more than entitled to have her 'modest' wishes granted, given the extreme and almost unparalleled excellence of her character, relative to other women."

Both Nate and Hannah were laughing.

Aurit shook her head. "It's like someone who surrounds himself with people who are less intelligent than he is so he can feel smart. Only she does it in her head. *So* fucked up."

"I know just what you mean," Hannah said.

It soon became evident to Nate that Hannah and Aurit liked each other. This had not been a given, particularly not on Aurit's end. Aurit was very picky and frequently evinced what seemed, to him, to be an arbitrary dislike for people he liked, especially women. But Aurit's approval didn't make him as happy as he'd hoped. Throughout the meal, he experienced a disorienting and rather emasculating feeling of being subsumed by a klatch of gabbing women. Aurit's and Hannah's combined selves created a stronger pull than either woman on her own. Instead of settling halfway between Nate's sensibility and Hannah's or Aurit's, the conversation was weighted toward the feminine. There was a giddily confidential, almost salacious quality to it. Moreover, Aurit and Hannah seemed to have decided beforehand to express only unequivocal agreement with whatever the other said. (When Hannah said she bought only cruelty-free chickens, did Aurit have to nod and coo quite so agreeably?—when, as Nate well knew, Aurit felt nothing but scorn for "Americans' childish sentimentality about animals.") Their enthusiastic supportiveness created a close, cloying atmosphere that made Nate clamor to get out.

"Did you have an okay time?" Hannah asked when the two of them were walking back to her place. "You seemed kind of quiet."

"It was fine."

He glanced through the open doorway of a restaurant kitchen. A white-smocked Hispanic man was stirring a steaming pot. "I just think Aurit sometimes dominates the conversation," he said. "Not to mention the way she pronounces judgment on everyone but herself. Does she really think she's above reproach?"

Hannah laughed. "She's, uhm, *your* friend."

"Yeah."

He and Hannah didn't speak much as they walked along quiet streets of brownstones. Nate knew there was a slight edge to his silence. His conscience told him he should say something to set Hannah's mind at ease—say he was tired or something. He didn't. Although his irritation was directed primarily at Aurit, it was sprawling enough to take in Hannah at its periphery. There had been, in her effort to be agreeable, something slightly insipid, a sort of relaxation of her usual quick, decisive judgment. She had gone along with Aurit, matching Aurit's girly, gossipy tone. She wasn't usually like that. But this criticism was so ungenerous that it made him feel guilty. Hannah had, after all, been gamely trying to get on with his friend while he had mostly been sullen and not much help.

As Hannah unlocked her door, it occurred to him that they had been spending a lot of nights at her place. He'd prefer if they alternated between his and hers. Tonight, her place made sense, because of the location of the restaurant, but still . . . he wasn't thrilled.

Inside, he checked the status of the package he'd sent his mother for her birthday. (It was, as it had been several hours earlier, in transit.) Then he checked the results of a baseball game and scanned the lead stories in the *Times*. When he finally got into bed, he and Hannah began fooling around. He wasn't really in the mood, but he went along from tact or inertia.

Soon Hannah was going down on him. It wasn't working. He started thinking about Eugene and the review. Then he thought about how he hadn't heard back from the editor he'd written to about his commodification-of-conscience essay. He remembered the day he'd gotten Hannah's first e-mail, when she'd quibbled with him about the idea. He'd thought to himself that sooner or later his dick was going to wind up in her mouth. Well, here it was.

He shut his eyes, trying to squeeze out all this unpleasant consciousness. He craved blankness, an absence of everything except for the sensation of Hannah's mouth on his cock. After a moment, he gave up. He guided Hannah away from him, pulling her face to his so he could kiss her.

Not long after, she drew back, tucking herself in like the letter *S*. "I . . . uhm . . ."

"Hmm?" he said.

"I was wondering . . . Is there maybe something you want me to do differently when I, you know, do that? I just wondered . . ."

She bit her lower lip.

"Oh!" Nate said.

As it happened, he had, more than once, felt slightly dissatisfied on this very score. It hadn't reached the level of "problem," but he had been fleetingly conscious of a small frustration. Strategically timed grunts and moans and gentle manual guidance he'd offered (by way of his hand on her head), intended to point the way toward some minor recalibration, had not been effective. But the complaint had always evaporated in the course of things, when they moved from one act to another. There is, after all, more than one way to skin a cat. Still.

"Uhm . . . ," he began.

He had always had a hard time talking about sex. That is, he had no problem discussing sex in general terms or sex as an intellectual or psychological or historical concept. When he was younger, he had enjoyed discussing various real or ideal women's bodies with his friends. But the other kind of sex talk, about what felt good and what didn't—this thing of *giving instructions*, saying, "touch me this way," "please do this, not that," even "faster" or "harder"—he found, had always found, excruciating. The prospect made him feel lecherous and animalistic and most of all unsexy, as if whatever small modicum of sexiness he possessed was derived from careful, curatorial self-presentation.

Typically, the only way he could do it, state aloud what he wanted, was to go all out, sort of become a different person—the kind who could tell, not ask, a woman to take him all the way in her mouth or to suck his balls or to get on her back and spread her legs. His voice, when he said these things, sounded different, hard and flat, stripped of its usual amiability. To get to this state, he had to drum up a certain amount of contempt for the woman (because he didn't speak to any human being this way, in any other context). He'd feel himself slip out of a more civilized, woman-respecting mind-set, as if this way of being weren't really of him but merely an acquired habit, like separating out bottles and cans for recycling.

It wasn't really a place he liked to go. It didn't matter that many women claimed to like being treated that way, to get off on it. In fact, that depressed him. After he came, he inevitably felt a bit disgusted, with himself and the situation, by which he meant, in large part, the woman he was with.

There had to be another way.

Hannah was sitting upright, naked, her eyes cast downward and her hair falling forward on her face.

Nate pulled the bedsheet up around his waist, covering himself. "I, uh . . ."

Their eyes met. Hannah's expression was meek and almost beatific in a kind of nervous desire to please.

Nate saw that it was hopeless. It had been a long day. He was tired. He didn't, just then, have it in him to look into those big, kind, cruelty-free-chicken-buying eyes and tell her he'd like her to suck his balls first and to please apply gentler but more consistent pressure with her mouth and to go deeper and, simultaneously, to flatten her tongue so it sort of cradled the seam as she moved up and down his shaft, and, finally, that it would also be great if she could caress the skin between his scrotum and his anus with her fingers.

"What you do is great," he said.

"Because you could tell me if . . ."

"There's nothing to tell."

From somewhere outside Hannah's apartment, a boom box whose insistent bass Nate had barely been conscious of was abruptly switched off.

He rolled onto his back and stared at the ceiling. He wanted to be outside, in the fresh air. He liked Hannah's apartment, but he'd never particularly liked her bedroom. She had one of those big, freestanding wooden mirrors, draped with scarves and belts and other feminine things, from which wafted all sorts of artificial floral vapors. The sight of it had always depressed him, recalling to him the fusty home of his childhood piano teacher, a Quakerly widow with a long gray braid down her back. Then there was Hannah's closet. Teeming with hanging clothes and stacks of blue jeans and sweaters crammed into every available space, with a brigade of boots and pumps and sneakers in clear plastic pouches bounding downward from racks attached to the doors, the closet haunted him even unseen. It almost too neatly embodied so much that was unattractive about women: mustiness, materialism, clutter.

He also realized that he disliked the corduroy throw pillows on her bed, one of which was currently wedged under his shoulder.

He wanted to get up, to walk through the cool night to his apartment, to get in his own bed, by himself, with a book, porn on his computer if he wanted it. *Why did she have to be so unsexy about it—so like a wounded dog? How the hell was that supposed to have made him feel?* But he knew if he tried to leave, he'd just implicate himself. The only guaranteed way to avoid a scene— "what's wrong? why are you upset?"—was to stay put, act normal. Cuddle. What did it matter anyway? Soon he'd be asleep, and then it would be morning.

He tossed the throw pillow from the bed and pulled Hannah close to him. "You smell good," he said. He wasn't sure who fell asleep first, which probably meant he did.

12

Ooh, kale," Cara said. "I never could find kale in Baltimore."

Nate and Hannah and Mark smiled in sympathy. They were seated in the backyard of a new and trendy farm-to-table-type restaurant. The night had been billed as a "double date."

It was a pleasant September evening. The restaurant's yard was lit up by hanging lanterns and furnished with splintery-looking wooden tables and benches. A waiter arrived and began expounding upon a variety of specials featuring early autumn vegetables. The young man's checkered shirt and high-waisted pants reminded Nate less of a farmer than a scarecrow.

When the waiter left, Nate tore off a piece of hard-crusted bread. "How's the job search?" he asked Cara.

She set down her menu. "Terrible. That's to be expected, I guess. Everyone I know who is my age is vastly overqualified for the jobs that are out there. I mean, answering phones?" She shook her head. "It's a real problem."

Nate murmured something that passed for assent.

"Cara's honors thesis on Baudrillard won the top prize in the comp lit department at Stanford," Mark said brightly.

"Is that right?"

When Nate met Hannah's eye, he was relieved to see from her expression that she found Cara as grating as he did. Under the table, he took Hannah's hand, pressing his fingers into her palm and running his thumb along her knuckles.

After their (non)conversation about blowjobs the week before, he had avoided her for several days, claiming to be busy or tired. He knew his annoyance wasn't fair, but he had wanted the awkward recollection, and the unfamiliar feeling of her apartment as stifling, to fade from his mind. It had—basically. Maybe they'd begun to see each other a little less than they once had, but surely that was to be expected as time wore on.

The waiter brought their drinks. Cara said something about video games. Their popularity portended badly for American society. She mentioned Europe and sighed in a way that suggested young men never played video games there.

"I don't know," Hannah said. "The people I know who play a lot of video games could be up to a lot worse. You know, doing actual harm to others. At least this keeps them occupied." She shrugged. "Maybe I just know some fucked-up people."

Nate chortled.

Cara was less amused. Her face was slow to change expression, like an old clock face behind which heavy wheels had to turn. It took a moment for the set of her eyebrows and lips to register perplexity.

"That's one way of looking at it, I guess," she said.

Mark jumped in to say that Hannah was onto something with the "distraction from worse" argument. "There's a lot of evidence to suggest that people are less violent than they used to be."

As soon as he realized that he'd basically taken up the opposing side, Mark looked nervously at Cara. Nate recognized the anxious solicitude of a guy who gets laid only when certain conditions are met. Poor Mark, Nate thought.

"I'm not saying that video games make people violent," Cara said a little pettishly.

Suddenly, Nate felt a bit sorry for *her*. She was pretty, self-possessed, and intelligent enough, but she was fresh out of school and repeating opinions that were no doubt fashionable there. In time, she would catch the tone of New York. Her schoolmarmishness was provincial. Here it was all about the counterintuitive. She'd learn. Besides, being pretty, self-possessed, and intelligent enough would go a long way, and if she wasn't well connected before she started dating Mark, she would be now.

Their waiter walked briskly past, foodless. Nate squelched a yawn. Time seemed to be moving very slowly. Even Mark was different in Cara's company. His sense of humor seemed blunted, as if he couldn't simultaneously exercise it and ensure Cara's minute-to-minute happiness.

Nate felt a stirring of appreciation for Hannah. He knew that if he had been single, had been eating dinner alone with Mark and Mark's new girlfriend, he would have gotten a little depressed. Cara would have seemed, however solipsistically, a stand-in for women in general—his future, more or less. He was glad to have met someone so . . . reasonable, so *not ridiculous*, someone he liked as much as he desired.

When, finally, they were dividing up the check, Nate happened to catch a sidelong glance at Cara. He was momentarily struck by just how good-looking she was. But then Mark had always been a very shallow guy, in terms of women. Then, it occurred to Nate that Mark could very well feel sorry for *him*, just because technically Cara was better-looking than Hannah (although Hannah was, as far as he was concerned, far more appealing). Still, it was a weird thought, and he pushed it aside. Sometimes he wished he could turn his brain off.

Back at his apartment, Hannah told him that her friend Susan was coming to town from Chicago that weekend.

She was sitting Indian-style on his bed, with her hair pulled into a ponytail and a weeks-old issue of the *New Yorker* in her lap. "Do you want to have brunch with us on Sunday?" she asked.

Nate was standing in the doorway. He combed a hand through his hair.

This invitation didn't do much for him. Hannah had described Susan as one of those people who sees her life as a long series of injustices perpetrated against her by various assholes. If you take issue with her account, you're one of the assholes. A real charmer, she sounded like.

Besides, he wasn't big on brunch as a social to-do. This one was easy to imagine: 11:00, wait in line with all the other yuppies at hip new restaurant, make tired conversation about whatever Susan does for a living and how New York compares to Chicago; 11:30, order a Bloody Mary, still standing outside, still waiting to be seated; 12:00, at the table, order inadvisable second Bloody Mary in attempt to stave off creeping boredom/existential despair; 12:30, split the check and silently regret blowing thirty dollars (the extra ten for the second Bloody Mary) when he would have been happier with the six-dollar Sunday Special (two eggs, bacon, home fries, and toast) at the nongentrified diner on his street.

Hannah had already taken out her contacts. She peered at him from above the rims of her glasses. Nate's glance flitted to the milk crate beside his bed. On it sat a stack of upcoming books that he wanted to go through with an eye to pitching reviews or essays. Reading in a leisurely, exploratory sort of way was just the kind of thing he enjoyed doing on a Saturday or Sunday, perhaps at home, perhaps at a sports bar with a game on in the background. He'd intended to spend last weekend this way, but it had gotten away from him. He wasn't entirely happy about that. When you're single, your weekend days are wide-open vistas that extend in every direction; in a relationship, they're like the sky over Manhattan: punctured, hemmed in, compressed.

Nate scratched the back of his head. "I don't know," he said. "I'm not sure what I'm doing."

He smiled nervously.

"Okay," Hannah said.

Nate couldn't read her expression, but instantly he felt apprehensive. Hannah turned back to the magazine. Almost unconsciously he remained where he was.

After a moment, Hannah looked up. "*What*?"

He stepped back. "Nothing!"

"God! I can't stand this!"

"Can't stand *what*?"

"You! Standing there, waiting for me to get mad at you because you don't want to get brunch." She made a face at him. "I don't care. I don't care if you come or not."

"Okay . . . ," Nate said slowly. "But you asked me if I wanted to come, so I just naturally assumed that you cared, at least a little bit?"

Hannah took off her glasses and held them in her hand. "It's like you want to make me out to be some kind of demanding, hysterical girlfriend," she said. "That's not who I am."

Nate was momentarily confused. He certainly hadn't expected her to be *this* angry. Then it sunk in what she was accusing him of. He heard his voice rise as he spoke. "Can you maybe tell me how exactly I made you out to be 'demanding and hysterical'? Was it something I said? Because I don't remember saying a damned thing."

"It's like . . . you just . . . ugh!"

Hannah stood up, and the magazine slid from her lap, landing in a heap on the floor. "It's just this vibe."

"A *vibe*?" Nate repeated, the word inflected with weeks of unspoken tension.

Hannah flushed.

Her discomposure had the effect of making Nate feel more composed.

"As far as I recall," he said coolly, "you asked me a question and I answered, and now you are mad at me for assuming, like a complete asshole, that you cared about my answer."

Hannah closed her eyes and inhaled through her nose. "What I mean is that it's not some test. I care like I care if we get Thai food or sushi whether you come or not."

"Great. Brunch. Not a test. Noted."

"Will you quit it with the sarcasm? *I get it*. It's not about brunch. It's how you've been acting. I feel you putting me into this box. I am not that person, and I resent you for making me out to be that person."

They were now standing head to head, with only about a foot of space between them. Nate felt energized—wholly awake.

"You realize I have no clue what you are talking about," he said. "What person am I making you out to be?"

She didn't blink. "The person forcing you to give up your freedom."

"Wait, am I the one in the box? Who's in the box? You or me?"

Nate felt himself shifting his weight from one leg to the other the way he did when he played football.

"Fuck you, Nate," Hannah said. "Just fuck you. You know what I mean. Or you would if you were being honest."

He threw up his hands in a pantomime of disbelief. "Excuse me for listening and trying to understand what you're saying."

"Fine." She shook her head. "Have it your way. I'm just being ridiculous."

Nate didn't contradict her. They stared at each other. "I'm going to brush my teeth," he said finally.

"Great."

The bathroom's fluorescent light was oppressively bright. A few of Hannah's long hairs were stuck to the grimy white porcelain of his sink. Nate felt a little shaky as he lingered over his teeth. He'd been mean, he knew he'd been mean, but she'd started it. There was no denying that. *Making her out to be demanding and hysterical?* He hadn't done *anything*.

He decided to floss. It occurred to him that maybe she'd have gotten up and gotten dressed. Maybe she'd pack up her things and leave. He approached the bedroom warily. Hannah was on the bed.

"I'm sorry," she said. Her voice was contrite but not otherwise emotional. "I'm sorry I blew up like that."

Nate was surprised to find himself disappointed. Not that she hadn't left—he hadn't really expected her to—but that she seemed normal again. When she'd been acting crazy, he'd had license to give vent to that pent-up tension, and yet to be also beautifully, effortlessly *right*. Something he'd learned with Elisa: it was not always unpleasant to deal with a hysterical woman. One feels so thoroughly righteous in comparison. Now he felt as if he were deflating. Although he hadn't been conscious of being turned on before—he'd been fairly disgusted by Hannah's hair in the sink—he felt his cock slackening, as if without his noticing it, he had been a bit hard.

"It's no big deal," he said. "Don't worry about it."

"I think we should talk about it."

"Everyone needs to blow off steam sometimes."

"I mean, the reason why."

Of course she did.

Nate sank into his desk chair, feeling dispirited, vanquished. He crossed his legs and then immediately uncrossed them.

"I'm sure it seemed to come out of nowhere to you," Hannah said in a fair and reasonable tone of voice, an aggravatingly fair and reasonable tone of voice. A voice that compelled him to be fair and reasonable too. "I think I reacted the way I did because I felt like you were waiting for me to burst into tears about brunch with Susan. It just seemed narcissistic or something. I don't know, it just pissed me off."

In spite of himself, Nate smiled.

She went on. "It's just that lately I've had this sense that some-thing is different. With you, or with us, and I keep waiting for you to say something . . . I don't want to be the kind of girlfriend who analyzes every little thing or makes us talk things to death—I really don't—but if something is up, I wish you'd just tell me. I don't expect things to be exactly like they were when we first started dating. But don't *oblige* me, like you're the put-upon boy-friend." Hannah sat up very straight; her tone became more insistent, almost defiant. "If you don't want this, fine. I'm not some girl who is dying to be in a relationship."

Nate leaned back in his desk chair so its two front wheels were raised off the ground. Pretty much every relationship conversation he had ever been party to included more or less the same caveats. Apparently, no woman in the early twenty-first century is the kind of woman who (a) wants a boyfriend or (b) wants to talk about her relationship, no matter how much she (a) wants a boy-friend and (b) wants to talk about her relationship.

As he rocked the chair back to face her, Nate cleared this un-nice thought from his mind.

"Hannah," he said gently, "I'm not 'obliging' you. I don't know what gave you that idea."

She tugged at her ponytail. "It's just—well, I hope you know that I don't think we have to spend every second together. I don't *want* to. But if you make excuses not to see me, as if you think I'm going to get mad at you, or if you skulk around and act guilty because you don't want to have brunch with my friend, it makes me feel like it's a bigger deal, like there's something else you're trying to tell me."

With his foot, Nate traced a circle on the floor. He said, "I thought you might be disappointed, that's all. I didn't mean any-thing by it."

Hannah nodded. "That's fair," she said. "I overreacted. I'm sorry."

She looked the way she sounded—sincere. An uncomfortable feeling had come over Nate. Now that he'd been accorded the full power to forgive, he didn't feel sure he deserved it. Even when they'd been fighting, he'd had some inkling of the box she'd been referring to. He might have feigned a bit more ignorance than he could honestly claim. But then the whole thing had happened so fast—he had just been defending himself.

"Don't worry about it," he said, feeling that the least he could do was be gracious. "I'm just glad you're not mad. And I'm sorry I was mean before. I guess I felt attacked."

"I can understand that," Hannah said. "And I'll drop this, I promise, but just to be clear . . . I don't care about Sunday. Susan isn't a close friend. But"—she paused and looked at him intently, her hazel eyes round and luminous in the light from his lamp—"if you *are* on some level unhappy, it would be better to say so now, before—"

"Hannah."

Nate rested a hand on each of her knees. Whatever mild dissatisfaction he had felt recently had been displaced by the fight, by Hannah's feistiness, by the moment's intensity.

"I like you. I want to be with you. The only thing I'm trying to tell you is that I don't want to have brunch with your friend Susan on Sunday. I hate to say it, but you didn't really make her sound all that appealing." He cocked his head. "You might want to work on your sales pitch next time."

"It's just that lately you sometimes seem a little—"

"I've been a little stressed," he cut in. "I thought by now I'd be well into another book, but I'm not. All I've got is an idea, and even that's vague. I feel as if I ought to be working night and day until I figure that out. I don't have a regular gig the way you do with the health news."

Hannah hugged her knees to her chest. "You want to do the health news?" she said. "Be my guest."

Nate sat down beside her on the bed. He could make out her nipples through the thin fabric of her T-shirt. "You know what I mean," he said.

The issue seemed, to him, to have been resolved, but they continued to talk for a while longer. This didn't really surprise him. In his experience, women, once they got started, exhibited a rather insatiable desire to confess, elaborate, iron out, reveal, and so on and so forth. Nate exerted himself to be patient. Hannah was generally an extremely easygoing girlfriend, more easygoing than anyone he'd dated since Kristen. He didn't begrudge her a little girlishness. They went to bed on good terms.

But she brought it up again the next time he saw her. They were on the subway, coming back from Manhattan.

"I feel kind of ridiculous about the other night," she said. "Getting so mad and then making us talk and talk. I hope you don't think I'm really . . . I don't know . . ."

The words trailed off, and she smiled helplessly as she waited for him to rescue her from her own sentence.

Nate's thoughts had been far removed from relationship issues, and he didn't feel like getting drawn into another of those conversations. He also didn't like being pressured to provide reassurances on demand, being made to perform his affection at someone else's bidding, like a trained seal. Besides, it seemed that in soliciting assurance—after everything that had been said the other night— Hannah was allowing herself to give in to a neurotic compulsion. That wasn't something he wanted to reward.

"It's *fine*," he said in the kind of cold, flat voice that only someone with serious Asperger's would take at face value.

Hannah's expression indicated to Nate that she did not suffer from Asperger's syndrome.

Nate looked away, a little repelled by the near panic he'd seen on her face. He was also afraid that if he looked at her, he'd feel bad and apologize, and he didn't want to feel bad or apologize. He didn't want to feel like the big bad wolf just because he wouldn't play this particular feminine parlor game.

He stared across the aisle at a little boy who slept with his head on his mother's shoulder. The boy's small calves were visible between the bottom of his pants and his socks.

After a minute, Nate's irritation faded, dissolving almost as quickly as it had come on. She'd been a little insecure; it wasn't the worst thing.

"Sorry," he said, turning to her. "I didn't mean to snap at you."

The panic had been wiped clean from her face. Her expression was blank, hard. But as she considered his apology, she seemed to relax a little.

"Don't worry about it," she said finally. "It's not a big deal."

Nothing more was said, and for the rest of the evening, they were resolutely light and cheerful.

13

Nate held his cordless phone to his ear with one hand as he half-heartedly sponged his kitchen counter with the other. He found his parents easier to talk to if he engaged simultaneously in other tasks.

He spoke first to his father, who was not actually that hard to deal with. All Nate had to do was be polite and impersonally pleasant, the way he would if he were talking to a well-meaning but nosy stranger, someone he met, say, in the line at the Department of Motor Vehicles.

"Did you get the next payment from your publisher yet?" his father asked. "You know that every day they hold on to that money, it's accruing interest that is rightfully yours."

"They made the payment, right on schedule," Nate assured him. "My agent has the money. She'll write me a check."

"Minus fifteen percent," his father said in a tone that suggested that this was a "Gotcha!" moment.

"Yes, dad. Minus fifteen percent."

"You know, Nathaniel . . . ," his father began. No argument could convince him that, as an aeronautical engineer, he might not have sufficient knowledge of the publishing industry to determine that the services of a literary agent were unnecessary.

Nate switched the phone from one ear to the other and rested it between his shoulder and his ear so both his hands were free. He began lifting up the grills of his stove and scrubbing the surfaces underneath with a Brillo pad.

"Have you given any thought to self-publishing the next one?" his father asked. "I've read that a number of established authors are starting to do that. Once they have a following, they don't need the publisher's name. This way, all the profits come to you. Eh?"

"I'll look into it."

Nate walked to the window and pulled up the blinds. Sunlight streamed into the kitchen.

His mother got on the line. She began telling him a story about the people at her work, how they were all moony about some television series "on HBO or Showtime or some such nonsense."

From a hundred and eighty miles away, Nate could feel her gathering energy, the satisfying torrent of contempt she was whipping herself into.

"They say that it's as good as a nineteenth-century novel," she said, her speech growing more rapid. "And these are supposed to be the 'smart' young people. They went to Georgetown and Columbia—practically Ivy League schools."

Through the window, the leaves on the trees' topmost branches were already beginning to fall off.

"Like Tolstoy!"

"That's nuts . . . ," Nate agreed.

But his tone was too mild. He felt rather than heard his mother's silence.

Unlike his father, his mother required that she and Nate be in vociferous accord. In colorful, overheated language, she framed life as a drama between "we" and the rest of the world, otherwise known as "those idiots." As a child, Nate had loved being on her side. Not only was she beautiful, with her long, honey-colored hair and tightly belted dresses, not only did her exotic French and Russian novels and aristocratic unhappiness appeal to his imagination, but her side was also so clearly the right one. It was the side of sensible governance: potholes filled in, corruption punished, Democrats elected, Israeli passenger planes and cruise ships not hijacked (the last position reiterated often after sixty-eight-year-old, wheelchair-bound Leon Klinghoffer was pushed overboard from the *Achille Lauro* when Nate was in the fourth grade). Hers was also the side of intelligence. (She had a moral disdain for stupidity and instinctively regarded Nate's classmates in the slow reading group with suspicion, as children of dubious character.) She stood for the appreciation of culture, especially literature, theater, and museums. When Nate got older, it was her smugness that bothered him. He was put off by the invocation of this all-thwarting "they," and the certain knowledge that all problems would be summarily solved if only "we" weren't obstructed at every turn. But if he questioned this presumption, his mother took it as an attack or clucked that he was too young and naive to understand. Their adult relationship was built on his willingness to humor her. Unless he was able to summon the energy and patience to appear to join her in this cloistered, airless "we," he—the son for whose sake she had left her home to start over in a new country—was rejecting her. With his dad, all he had to do was not argue.

Blinking into the sun as he gazed out the window, Nate knew he had failed. She'd sensed condescension in his tepid agreement. *He went to Harvard, and now he thinks he's too good for me.* She sucked in her breath sharply, as if it were her very soul she'd offered up to him and which she was now withdrawing. As clearly as if she were standing before him, he could see her nostrils flare once or twice.

It was too much, he knew—what his mother wanted of him. It wasn't fair or reasonable, his friends would tell him. But neither had her life been fair or reasonable. In Romania, she'd been denied all sorts of academic honors because she was Jewish. She wasn't even permitted to major in literature, as the humanities were almost entirely closed to Jews. She'd slept on a couch in the living room of her parents' one-bedroom apartment in a concrete tene- ment until the day she married Nate's father, whose family was a little better off. Then she'd come here and worked as a computer programmer—so that Nate could attend private school, so that he could go to a good college.

Nate leaned his forehead against the glass windowpane. "How have you been, Mom?"

"Fine." Her voice was tight and small.

He closed the blinds and shuffled back to the sink, sliding a little on the linoleum in his socks and tightening his grip on the phone. They were the reason he had this stupid cordless phone. His par- ents had insisted on a landline—"in case of an emergency." The only people who used it were the two of them and the telemarketers.

"You think I'm old-fashioned," his mother said after a moment. "Narrow-minded."

The sigh that punctuated this remark was a finely honed sym- phony of self-pity.

"*Mom*," Nate said. "I don't even *have* a TV. Of course I don't think you're narrow-minded."

She let out a small chuckle. "I guess we're both a little bit backward."

"I guess so."

There was another, less fraught silence.

"How's Hannah?" she asked finally. *Henna* was how it sounded from her lips.

Nate squeezed the water from his sponge.

"She's okay."

Several evenings later, he was sitting in Hannah's living room, reading Eugene's review of the British novelist's new book.

"Nate?"

The review was good—very good, Nate had to admit. Eugene was good.

"Nate?" Hannah said again.

Reluctantly, Nate laid the article down. Hannah was standing with her hands in her back pockets. "Yes?"

"What do you feel like doing tonight?"

Nate closed his eyes. What did he and Hannah usually do together? For a moment, he couldn't remember. Then he thought of the long nights of animated conversation they used to have, over the summer—nights when they'd never needed to "do" anything. He wasn't in the mood for that sort of . . . *communion* of togetherness. Certainly not.

He thought maybe he felt like watching baseball. The playoffs were approaching, and there was a game he was mildly interested in for its potential negative impact on the Yankees.

Hannah said sure, they could go to a sports bar.

They went to a place called Outpost, an unfortunate name, in Nate's opinion, for a newish establishment that appeared to be patronized almost exclusively by the white people who'd begun to move into the historically black neighborhood in which it was located.

The game hadn't started yet. When they sat down, Hannah told him she'd decided to take on some copyediting work for extra money. She started describing the exacting requirements of the publisher she was doing the work for.

Was this his life now? Nate wondered as she spoke. Sitting across from Hannah at various tables, in various restaurants and bars? Ad infinitum. Was this what he'd committed himself to the night they'd had that fight about brunch and he'd reassured her, told her that it was safe—that he was into this?

He tore off the slip of paper that kept his napkin rolled up and began toying with his knife and fork.

He tried to focus on what Hannah was saying—still about the copyediting job—but he found himself wondering how much she needed the money. At the rate she was going, she'd never finish her book proposal. Besides, her father was a corporate lawyer. He didn't doubt she could get money from him if she needed it. A nice luxury if you had it.

Though it was the last day of September, the evening was warm. Hannah had taken off her jacket. Underneath she was wearing a strappy tank top. It became her. She had nice shoulders. But when she moved her arms in emphasis of some point, Nate noticed that the skin underneath jiggled a little bit, like a much older woman's. It was odd because she was quite fit. He felt bad for noticing and worse for being a little repelled. And yet he was transfixed. The distaste he felt, in its crystalline purity, was perversely pleasurable. He kept waiting for her to wave her arms again.

When she finished her story, he just nodded.

He was hungry. Where was their food? he wanted to know. "Why do you think it's taking so long?" he said.

Hannah looked a little surprised by his vehemence. She raised her hands, her palms facing up. "No idea."

She asked him a few questions about what he'd been up to. His answers were short. He couldn't rouse himself to match her mood of cheerful pleasantry. If she were a stranger—a mere friend or acquaintance—it would be nothing, nothing at all, to fall into the rhythms of polite if banal conversation. But it was different with Hannah. Being with her had rarely entailed that kind of obligatory social performance; to start treating it that way now seemed like a defeat. Or a capitulation.

Hannah tried to fill the vacuum. As she flitted from topic to topic, Nate began to feel as if he were watching her from a remove, evaluating her. Even though she spoke with a fair amount of wit—she was telling a story about a friend's "almost aggressive tactfulness; she doesn't wait until you finish talking to start agreeing with you and supporting you"—something in her tone, an eagerness to please, a quality that was almost pleading, grated on him.

"Nate?" she asked finally.

"Yeah?"

"Is everything okay? You seem kind of . . . I don't know . . . *distracted*?"

"I'm fine," he said. He flashed a quick smile to compensate for what was unconvincing in his voice.

A moment later, Hannah got up to use the ladies' room. As he watched her walk away, he noticed that the jeans she was wearing made her bottom half look bigger than her top half, her hips and ass strangely wide and flat. He wondered why none of her girl-friends had told her this, about the jeans. Why hadn't she herself noticed? After all, a gigantic, full-length mirror took up most of her bedroom.

When she returned, she asked if he was mad at her.

As if she had done anything that would have entitled him to be mad at her. Why the fuck did women, no matter how smart, how *independent*, inevitably revert to this state of willed imbecil-ity? It wasn't as if he had the emotional register of a binary sys-tem, as if his only states of being were "happy" and "mad at her."

"No," he said. "I'm not *mad* at you."

She drew back.

Before anything more was said, the waiter brought their burgers. *Finally*. The game began. As he ate, Nate turned his attention to the television screen above the bar. He began to feel better.

"That really hit the spot," he said of his burger.

Hannah was doing something on her phone and didn't look up.

Nate pretended not to notice. "How's yours?"

She raised her gaze slowly and blinked several times, as if trying to determine by this means if he could really be such a moron. "You're asking me how my burger is?"

"*I'm sorry*," he said. "Sometimes I get grouchy when I'm hungry. It's no excuse, but I am sorry."

"Whatever."

"I should probably start carrying nuts in my pockets."

He saw the barest hint of a smile. She immediately suppressed it. But it was a start.

In the process of wheedling Hannah back into good humor, Nate, too, was revived. Having a project—getting back into Hannah's good graces—dispelled boredom and silenced that critical voice. He told her (because women love talking about personal life) about Aurit, who was flipping out because Hans was still balking about moving to New York.

"She treats his concern for his career like it's a transparent excuse. I've got to get her to quit that before she really pisses him off."

By the time their plates were cleared, all traces of Nate's former mood were gone. He appreciated that Hannah had gone along with his desire to watch baseball. He had a good time.

On the walk home, Hannah turned to him. "Nate?"

"Yeah?"

"What was the deal before?"

He tensed. He'd already said he was sorry. And what had he done, really? Spoken sharply to her? In fact, all he'd actually said was "I'm not mad at you." It could hardly be deemed a vicious comment. Maybe he'd been a *little* curt before. But. Come. On.

"I don't want to be overly dramatic," she said. "But . . . I don't want to be treated that way. If you're unhappy about something—"

"I'm not."

What was he supposed to say? That maybe she should do some tricep curls so her upper arms didn't jiggle? Buy some jeans that had been vetted from all angles? He sounded, even to himself, like some sick fetishist of female emaciation. He sounded like a real bastard.

He took her hand. "I don't know what came over me. I'm sorry."

"You know, Jason," Aurit said. "There's a certain type of man who likes to be with women he feels intellectually superior to."

"Who says models can't be smart?" Jason shot back, glancing at Nate for support.

The three of them were standing by an open window at their friend Andrew's new apartment. Andrew and his boyfriend were throwing a housewarming party. Jason was telling them about the Lithuanian model that the art director of his magazine had promised to set him up with.

"For your information," Jason said, "Brigita studied electrical engineering in Vilnius."

"It's like Lydgate in *Middlemarch*," said Aurit, apparently unimpressed by electrical engineering. " 'That distinction of mind which belonged to his intellectual ardor did not penetrate his feelings and judgment about furniture, or women.' " Aurit smiled sweetly at Jason. "Lydgate ends up with the dumb blonde, by the way. She ruins his life. His career, too."

Jason wrapped one of his long arms around Aurit's shoulders. "Aurit, darling, you're so cute when you get riled up. Like Mighty Mouse. But I've got to tell you, Lydgate's the best character in that book. Also"—he paused to take a sip of his beer—"*of course* George Eliot would think the way you do. She's not exactly unbiased. Smart women have a personal stake in vilifying men who fail to appreciate smart women. Trust me, men can do great things no matter who they marry."

"Jesus, Jase," Nate said.

"Think about it," Jason said. "If so-called companionate partnership between two intellectual peers were the measure of a man's worth, there'd be maybe two first-rate men in all of history— Eliot's own pseudo-husband and John fucking Adams."

Aurit had slipped out of Jason's grasp. She eyed Jason coolly. "Does the fact that you have no soul ever worry you, Jason?"

Nate snorted.

Their group broke up. Nate migrated from the window. The living room was packed. In the scrum of bodies, Nate spotted

Greer Cohen, looking rather fetching in tight jeans. Before he could wave hello, he felt a tap on his shoulder. It was Josh, a guy he played soccer with. Josh worked at a publishing house, and he congratulated Nate; he said he'd heard good things about his book, sensed growing excitement.

"Thanks, man," Nate said.

"It comes out in February, right?" Josh asked.

Nate nodded. Then he saw Eugene Wu. He told Eugene that he liked his review of the British author. Though he tried to conceal it, Eugene seemed pleased. After a bit, he and Nate got into a protracted argument about the relative proportion of women with breast implants in New York versus in red states. Nate realized he was having a good time. It occurred to him that he had more fun at parties when he had a girlfriend than when he didn't. Being in a relationship spared him from having to hit on girls, from getting into long, boring or boring-ish conversations with girls he barely liked in the hopes of getting laid. He was free to talk to the people he actually wanted to talk to.

As he left the party, he called Hannah. "Hey," he said into his cell phone when she picked up.

"Hi." She sounded as if she might have been sleeping.

"What are you up to?" he asked.

Although they hadn't had concrete plans to see each other, he had told her earlier in the day that he "might" call. He had contemplated asking if she wanted to join him at the party, but he hadn't. He didn't really know why. He just hadn't felt like it. Besides, she'd been the one who said, when they'd fought over brunch, that they didn't have to spend every minute together.

He paused in front of a subway entrance and asked her if she wanted him to come over. She hesitated. "I'll probably be in bed," she said. "But you're welcome to come. If you want."

The night air smelled pleasantly of burned leaves. It was starting to feel like fall. Nate decided to walk to Hannah's instead of taking the train. On his way, he stopped at a deli and bought her a Hershey bar because he knew she liked them, preferred them to fancier chocolates.

"I'm sorry I didn't call earlier," he said when he arrived. "I just got caught up in things."

She was wearing an oversized Kent State T-shirt, and her hair was loose, a little messy. "It's no big deal," she said. "I had a chance to do some reading."

Nate breathed in through his nose. He could tell she'd smoked a cigarette recently.

They sat on the chairs by her window and caught up a bit. He hadn't seen her for several days. She told him she'd been feeling a little down lately. She ran her fingers through her hair. She said she thought she needed to get back into her book proposal, something that she could really throw herself into. She hadn't been writing enough lately. Maybe it would cheer her. Nate felt a flicker of guilt. He suspected that he, that things between the two of them, might also have a role in her mood. He knew he'd been a little distant. But he agreed with her plan. "Work is always a big help for me," he said. "In terms of mood. That and sports, doing something physical."

She raised her eyebrows. "Do you know how many Pilates classes I do?"

Her tone was challenging. It reminded him of how she'd been on their early dates. Lately she'd been . . . more tentative, almost nervous.

He ran his eyes over her bare legs. "I know you look hot," he said. "C'mon." He took her hand, pulling her toward the bedroom.

In bed, he peeled off her T-shirt and underwear. The taste of cigarette in her mouth as they kissed wasn't ideal—over time her smoking had begun to bother him more—but it wasn't a big deal. He fondled her a little. Soon he was on top of her, sliding into her easily. At first, he felt great. But he was drunk and a little desensitized. He needed more. He began riffling through various mental images. He saw Hannah lying naked on his bed, one of the first times they'd slept together: an abandoned look on her face that he'd never forgotten, the way she'd arched her back as he approached, pushing up her breasts. This held his attention for a moment. Then he became conscious of a clock ticking and the whine of a bus outside. He turned his mind to Internet porn, a petite brunette who looked a little like Greer Cohen in a hiked-up businesswoman's suit getting it from behind on a big wooden desk.

Beneath him, Hannah's eyelids were crinkled shut. Then her eyes opened. For an instant, she and Nate looked directly at each other. She froze, as if she'd been caught. What he saw, before she masked it, was total vacancy, absence, as if she were a log floating down a river, as if she were scarcely conscious that he was fucking her.

Nate, leaning his weight on his elbows, looked away from her face, craning his neck and staring angrily at the wall behind her. If she wasn't having the best sex of her life, he couldn't help but feel it wasn't all his fault. She was too . . . merely acquiescent. Her bedroom persona was meek, pliable. Even her body, her pale flesh, had a soft, quivering quality—melting, enveloping, but lacking something . . . some plasticity, some pushback.

After a moment, he turned her over on her hands and knees. He felt a pang as he positioned her this way. It was one thing to do it doggie style when the sex was energetic and smutty, when it was in keeping with the joint mood. This wasn't that. This might as well be masturbation. It had nothing to do with her.

As her glowing white ass lurched back and forth, the loose flesh of her thighs flapping from his momentum, he couldn't help but think that there was something humiliating—to women— about doing it this way. But for him it was better, in terms of sensation. Besides, she was probably relieved that she didn't have to look at him. The expression on her face now was probably worse than absent. It was, no doubt, resigned.

He pounded harder. Hannah's hair, moist with sweat, parted in clumps on either side of her neck. Finally, he felt an orgasm build, and he reached underneath her to cup her breasts, thrusting a few last times as the waves of his climax coursed through him.

Afterward, he curled up against her. His orgasm had swept his irritation away. He felt a little bad for the way he'd pawed at her. He hadn't really done much to get her into it. *Next time* . . . He wrapped his arm around her in atonement, nuzzling his chin into the crook of her shoulder as he lay behind her. He felt spent and peaceful as he began to drift into sleep.

He only half woke up when he felt her wriggle from his embrace and slip out of bed. He heard the bedroom door close and opened one eye in time to see a yellow stripe appear underneath as she turned on the living room light. He fell back asleep. He woke up again when Hannah got back into bed. It seemed to him like a long time had passed.

"Is everything okay?" he asked.

"It's fine," she said. "Go back to sleep."

But there was something aggrieved in her voice, an unstated recrimination that, even in his half-asleep state, awakened a sense of dread. Tomorrow, he decided as he began to fade back into sleep, he'd call Jason or Eugene, see what they were up to. He was in a guy mood.

14

One night, Hannah told him she had slept around in high school. This was news to him. They were on their way back from a movie, and he'd made a comment about women in slutty Halloween get-ups. It was getting to be that time of year.

Hannah said that when she was a sophomore, she slept with a senior, a football player she felt sorry for because, though sweet, "he was so very stupid."

"I thought these probably *were* the best years of his life," she said. After that, various of his teammates wanted to go out with her. She went out with them, each of them, in turn. She shrugged as she told him this. "It seemed sexist and old-fashioned to act as if chastity really was a virtue like the born-agains thought."

She was a little tipsy—they both were—and her manner was flirtatious, but also defiant, as if she were daring him to be so prudish as to chastise or pity her. As if. Nate was titillated by this story, more turned on, in fact, than he'd been in a while.

When he'd been with Elisa, he had learned that contempt is very compatible with lust. Anger, even actual dislike and flashes of hatred, seemed to be a close enough approximation to sexual passion that the result was virtually the same. Guilt, on the other hand, is a very unsexy emotion. But now . . . It wasn't just that he found Hannah's blasé attitude toward her virginity sexy, the way atheism and Marxism and other antiestablishment, intellectual isms are sexy in an attractive woman. It was something far more corrupt. The image of those empty-headed, teenage douche bags fucking Hannah, passing her around from one to the next, of her *obliging* them because she was *nice*, turned him on like porn turned him on. Her dumb naïveté, that bovine, Marilyn Monroe–like credulity, transformed her from the Hannah he knew to a girl who allowed herself to be used and shared, a stupid chick who ought to be fucked. And that night Nate fucked her, fucked that other Hannah.

It was the hottest sex they'd had in a long time. From a certain perspective (say, a pornographer's), it may have been the hottest sex they'd ever had.

The next morning, Hannah woke up bright and cheerful. She suggested making eggs. Nate had to admit there was nothing obviously offensive in that. But as she sat there, with the sheet around her chest, her head cocked as she waited for his yea or nea, she struck him as cloying, overweening, as if there was nothing in the world she wanted to do more than make him goddamned breakfast. What she really wanted, he felt, was to have a cozy morning in—to bathe in post-coital togetherness.

"I *don't want eggs*," he said.

The happy expression—also much of the color—fled from Hannah's face.

"Okay . . . ," she said. "Well, I'm hungry. You want me to go and get bagels?"

"It's your house. You can do what you want."

She made a face and then shook her head quickly, so her hair fanned out. "Okay. *I'm* hungry. *I'm* going to get a bagel."

With her back to him, she began pulling jeans on.

"A whole-wheat everything with cream cheese and tomato . . ."

She turned around. She looked as if she might give him the finger. Nate smiled hopefully.

"Please, please? Take money from my wallet. Sorry to be testy. I didn't sleep well." He picked up one of the corduroy pillows on her bed and threw it across the room. "That thing was eating my face all night."

Hannah stared at him for a moment. "Fine."

When she was gone, Nate fell back into bed and gazed at the ceiling.

At moments Hannah seemed to trigger something sadistic in him. He could swear he didn't want to hurt her, but sometimes, when she looked at him in a certain way, or that eager note crept into her voice, a perverse obstinacy rose within him; to go along, to do what she wanted, felt treacly—intolerable.

The sheer white curtains on her window twisted in the cool October breeze. Nate stood up and looked outside. He felt ungainly, comically masculine, as the gauzy curtain grazed his bare chest.

He noticed the stack of books on Hannah's bedside table. *The Letters of Abelard and Heloise*, *A Sentimental Education*, *The Kreutzer Sonata*. Was he imagining it, or was there a theme? Books about lovelorn women, men whose feelings were shorter-lived. Maybe he was being paranoid. Maybe his girlfriend just had impressive taste in literature.

Nate heard the key turning in the lock, then Hannah's footsteps, quick and determined, as she moved through the apartment. He waited for her to come to the bedroom, intending to make up for his churlishness earlier.

After a minute, she pushed open the bedroom door. "Your bagel is on the table."

Before Nate could respond, she threw a clump of bills and coins at him. Then she turned around and slammed the door behind her.

As he collected his change from her sheets, Nate wondered if Hannah had intentionally echoed a john throwing money at a prostitute. He hoped so. It would reflect a certain malicious imagination that he couldn't help but admire, aesthetically.

He pulled on his undershirt and stepped tentatively out of the bedroom. On the table, he saw a white paper bag, bearing the words *La Bagel-Telle*. Hannah was nowhere in sight; after a moment, he heard the shower running in the bathroom. He sat down to eat his bagel. The irony was he really would have preferred eggs.

Elisa wanted his advice about an upcoming job interview, for a position at a weekly newsmagazine. When they met up, Nate wondered if excitement about the job was the whole difference. Because something was different.

"You seem good," he said. "Happy."

"Thanks."

Her face was tilted over her wine glass, and she looked up at him from the top of her eyes. Nate remembered her looking at him in just that way when she went down on him. He felt a fluttering belowdecks and automatically shifted in his seat.

As soon as he realized this, he blinked and rubbed his forehead. It had been a long time since he had reacted this way to Elisa.

She set her wine glass down and cocked her head. "How's Hannah?"

Nate shrugged as he took a sip of his whiskey. "Fine."

He paused, sucking on an ice cube. Elisa eyed him curiously. "Actually, things haven't been so great with us lately," he said finally.

"I'm sorry," Elisa said. But the crooked way she smiled suggested that this was just what she had hoped to hear. "Poor Hannah."

In spite of the bad character on display, Nate felt unusually fond of Elisa right then, protective and affectionate, feelings born of long familiarity. He leaned his elbow on the bar and smiled at her, resignedly as if to say, "What can you do?" Meanwhile, in the virtual reality chamber of his mind, he began to replay various scenes of fucking her. He had a large cache of raw material from which to draw.

They hung out for quite a while, until nearly midnight—bent over the bar, laughing a lot, gossiping about Elisa's coworkers and other mutual acquaintances, pulling apart not just their writing but their disordered personal lives, irritating habits, and personal unattractiveness. Nate allowed himself to slip out from Hannah's influence, the moral quality that would have made him ashamed to be this catty, this cruel in her presence. Her fairness, her lack of pettiness were things he liked about Hannah generally—he certainly respected her more than he respected Elisa—but the fun he was having felt deserved in light of the strain he'd been under in his relationship.

When he and Elisa said goodnight at the subway entrance, Nate felt a touch of wistfulness. He gave her a quick peck on the cheek.

"Good luck with the interview, E," he said. "You deserve it."

The following evening he met up with Hannah.

"Did you have fun last night?" she asked as they walked to a bar. "You were with Elisa, right?"

She didn't sound jealous, but Nate instinctively attributed that to savvy, not to an absence of jealousy. Immediately, he felt defensive—also a little annoyed to be put on the defensive when, thoughts aside, he had done nothing wrong.

"Yeah," he said, daring her with his tone to complain. "I did."

"Good," she said, just as coldly.

They were on their way to meet some of her friends from journalism school. At the bar, Nate's mood improved. Hannah's friends were by and large down-to-earth, hard-drinking reporters who spent a lot of time at City Hall or on the police beat or hanging out with Wall Street types. He soon lost sight of Hannah, but it was okay—they were a fun crowd. After a while, though, he got what Hannah had meant, back when they'd first started dating, when she'd said that she had felt a little bit isolated intellectually. He could see that there were aspects of her personality that she wouldn't be able to express with these friends. The thought made him feel tender toward her.

He spotted her talking to two women by a Ms. Pac-Man machine. He made his way to her and placed his hand on her hip. "Hi."

"Hey."

Her tone was clipped, almost hostile. After a moment, he realized she was drunk.

She started getting aggressive with him, treating his light remarks as criticisms and responding disproportionately, hitting him "playfully" but actually using a bit too much force. When she said she was going to get a drink, he suggested that maybe she didn't need another.

"Who are you to tell me what to do?"

He shrugged, and she went to the bar.

At his apartment later, she became downright belligerent, muttering hostile, not-quite-coherent reflections on him almost under her breath, as if to herself as much as to him. Her tone was false, full of a surly and world-weary and utterly put-on cynicism, a strange, unnatural bravado.

"You know that Irina and Jay and Melissa are *nice people*," she said. She spoke as if these were fighting words. Which, he supposed, they were. "That's what actually matters," she continued. "You know that the other stuff is all vanity, right? Writing, I mean."

She made a sarcastic comment about Nate's "artfully crafted sentences," which, she said, mimicked true feeling without knowing what it was. He imitated the stylistic devices of writers he admired without realizing that for those writers these weren't mere devices but means of expressing something true.

It was brutal stuff. Nate didn't take offense. She was obviously lashing out at him for the way things were between them. All he felt was mild disgust at her lack of control. Mostly he just wanted to go to sleep.

As they were getting into bed, she told him that he was treated like a big shot because he was a guy and had the arrogant sense of entitlement to ask for and expect to get everything he wanted, to think no honor too big for him. The funny thing was that Nate thought there was a great deal of truth in this. But he thought *she* could stand to ask for more. His main criticism of her, in terms of writing, was that too often she wasn't ambitious enough. She should treat each piece as if it mattered, instead of laughing off flaws proactively, defensively, citing a "rushed job" or an "editor who'd mess it up anyway," or referring to the insignificance of the publication ("How many people even read such-and-such magazine anymore?"). On top of it, she didn't seem to be writing much at all lately, aside from the routine stuff she did for money. In spite of what she'd said the night she told him she'd been feeling down, she didn't seem to be making progress on her book proposal. Still, he unreservedly thought she was extremely talented. She deserved more recognition than she'd gotten. It wasn't fair. He told her so now. Then he leaned over to turn out the light.

"That's nice of you to say," she said as the room went dark. "Every time I want to paint you as a total jerk, you go and say something nice. That's what kills me."

On the ceiling, dark shadows were indistinguishable from dust. Nate wondered for a moment if he should break up with her. But he liked her.

He turned onto his side. He was too tired to think about this right now. He'd think about it when his head was clear. Tomorrow. Later.

In early November, Peter came to town from Maine. Nate was sure Peter would like Hannah and looked forward to introducing them.

With women he didn't know well, Peter affected an exaggerated courtliness that some found off-putting and pretentious ("toolish," Aurit once said bluntly). But, over a dinner that also included Jason, Peter won Hannah over when he remarked that Flaubert had been responsible for untold numbers of men getting laid. "When Leon overcame Emma's last qualm with the remark that 'all the women in Paris do it,' he nailed it. Forget love, forget morality. Appeal to vanity . . ." Hannah laughed, delighted by this observation. That, in turn, delighted Peter.

At some point, they got to talking about the name Lindsay and how none of them had known any girls named Lindsay at Harvard or Yale, but apparently, according to one of Peter's academic friends, NYU was teeming with Lindsays, and could names possibly reflect such minute social distinctions? Nate glanced at Hannah, but she didn't appear to be outraged by their snobbery. She looked amused. When she spoke, there was just enough irony in her tone to chasten them but not so much as to seem humorless.

They ordered a couple bottles of wine and several rounds of cocktails. By midnight, Hannah was starting to get a little sloppy. Eager to let a good thing be, Nate corralled her into a cab. He was feeling happy and affectionate. As the taxi careened down Ninth Avenue, he leaned close to her and touched one of her eyebrows with his thumb. "You're so much fun," he said.

When they got back to her place, she disappeared into the bathroom. Nate got into bed. Several minutes later, she returned, wearing a tank top and high-cut underwear.

Then Nate looked at her face and saw that she'd been crying. She had tried to cover it up. No, that wasn't quite right. She looked as if she'd made a halfhearted attempt to cover it up but what she really wanted was for him to know that she was upset and ask what was wrong.

Although tears, even off-screen tears, were a new development, this didn't really surprise him—or rather his surprise was limited to the comparatively minor question of "why now?" when they'd had a really good night, when they might very well continue to have a really good night. As she searched for something in one of her over-stuffed drawers, her eyeliner smeared and her lips pursed, Nate felt not pity but exasperation. *You're hurting your own cause*, he wanted to shout to the crying, not-crying Hannah. *Can't you fucking see that?*

But her droopy vulnerability gave her the moral high ground. "Are you okay?" he asked.

"I'm fine."

"Why don't you come to bed?"

He spoke in the patient, patronizing tone of a person accustomed to dealing with the mentally feeble.

She swallowed and looked down, blinking as if in pain or embarrassment. Then—something happened. An idea or a mood seemed to take hold of her. Her face brightened, and her demeanor became less glum, more definite—animated.

"Come on," she said, her eyes glittering. "Let's go in the other room and have a drink."

Her voice had an inexplicable, almost lunatic pull. As he followed her into the living room Nate's irritation gave way to curiosity to see what would happen next.

Without turning on the light, she went and got the bourbon from on top of the refrigerator and then the two blue-rimmed glasses. Nate sat down by the window. The only sound in the apartment was the refrigerator's hum. Hannah returned from the kitchen and sat in the other upholstered chair, tucking her naked legs underneath her. She poured out the bourbon and handed him a glass.

He wasn't really in the mood to drink, hadn't been since the moment at the restaurant with Jason and Peter when he realized he needed to keep an eye on her drinking.

Hannah downed nearly half of hers in one gulp. She shuddered.

"It's so fucked up," she said. The words were clear and lucid, but her voice had a bitter, reckless quality. "I see it, but I can't do anything about it."

"See what, Hannah?"

She looked at the window. Their reflections in the glass were faded and translucent, crisscrossed by the slabs of brick on the apartment building across the street. She turned to face him, the liquid in her glass a luminous amber.

"I don't even smoke around you anymore. How great is that?"

"Do you want a cigarette? If you want one, go ahead and have one."

"Shut up! You're so patronizing. That's what I thought when I first met you. I thought you were so smarmy and self-satisfied and not that interes—I remember thinking, *How many times is he going to mention fucking Harvard?*" She laughed. "I never thought I'd—" She shook her head. "Oh, never mind."

Her voice had become singsong, as if she were speaking to a slightly daft elderly person.

When she spoke again, the pleasant quality was gone. "What was that tonight?" She fixed her eyes on him. "You were *so* affectionate."

Nate's grip on his glass tightened. Whatever was coming, he didn't want.

"Why?" Hannah continued. "Because your friend Peter liked me."

The pulsing of the blood in his temples felt like an aggressively ticking alarm clock.

"No offense," Hannah said. "But it kind of made me sick. I mean, what kind of person are you that your friends' opinions are so fucking important?"

"You're drunk, Hannah."

"And who am I that I go along with it? Perform for your friends so you'll . . ." She shivered as the words trailed off. "I'm ashamed of myself, too, just so you know."

Nate looked out the window, at the yellow crescent of light cast by a streetlamp.

"The thing is, the last guy I dated"—Hannah began to speak earnestly, as if they were in the middle of hashing out something important together—"he was a writer. You probably know him— not Steve—this was just someone I went out with a few times. But, see, he had a trust fund and a great apartment, and one day we were there, and he had these Hispanic guys doing some work on his roof deck, and I asked him if he ever felt weird, you know, because he sat around all day and half-worked on his writing while these guys were right outside his sliding glass door, in the heat and everything. And he said, 'Yeah, all the time,' but, like, because that's what he was supposed to say. Because then he went on and said that writing poetry was hard work, just like being a day laborer is hard work, and the guys on the roof wouldn't want to trade with him, any more than he'd want to trade with them. And that was it, that was how he talked himself out of feeling uncomfortable about all his advantages. So callow, you know?" She looked at Nate intently. "You're not like that. No, you're sort of decen—"

"That might have just been something he said in the moment, not the sum total of his life's thought on inequality," Nate suggested.

"Maybe," Hannah said. "He was kind of a callow guy, though."

Nate smiled. He knew who the guy was. And he was an asshole. A tall, good-looking asshole.

Hannah squinted at her empty glass and then reached for the bottle of bourbon. Nate nearly told her to cool it but at the last moment stopped himself. Did he want to be that guy? They weren't in the restaurant, in public, anymore. Why the hell shouldn't she drink? Why shouldn't he?

He swallowed the contents of his glass. "Pour me some, too, if you don't mind."

Hannah brightened. "Sure!"

"Can I ask you something?" she said after she set the bottle down.

"Sure."

"What happened?"

Then, as if she knew that Nate would be tempted to feign ignorance, she added. "With us, I mean."

Nate supposed he'd known all along—when he'd agreed to accompany her to the living room—that this was where things were going. This was what they'd come out here for. Yet he still felt an impulse to pretend he didn't know what she was talking about—to deflect or postpone this conversation.

"I don't understand," she said. "Did I *do* something?"

When Nate spoke, his voice came out raspy, more pained than he expected. "I don't think—no."

He wished he could blame it on her—assign a cause. But he knew it was him. Whatever had happened, it was him.

"No, you didn't do anything," he repeated.

He looked at her. She was pale. The expression on her face so precisely mirrored how he felt, the sense of helplessness that had come over him. Almost without being aware, he got up and walked to her chair, perching on its arm. His irritation had faded. He felt protective and tender toward her. He was glad. It made him feel human and humane.

She scooted over, and he slid down beside her on the seat of the chair.

"I think, maybe, I'm just not very good at relationships," he said.

"Maybe we should just admit it's not working," she said. "I mean, right? A month ago if someone told me what things would be like between us, I would have said, no, I'd never stand for that. But I keep negotiating down what I think is okay. I like you—my problem is that I do like you. There's something about you . . ." She stopped and then sat up straighter. She started again in a new, more decisive tone. "But this thing, this thing that we've become, is sapping something from me."

Nate turned to her bookshelf. He began trying to make out individual titles in the dark.

"You can't be happy either," Hannah said.

No. As he tore his eyes from the books to meet hers, he was, as a matter of fact, nearly overwhelmed by sadness. It gusted over him. He felt almost unbearably lonely. He wondered whether he was flawed on some deep level, whether—in spite of all the friends who seemed to think he was a good guy (and he *was* a pretty good friend), in spite of being a fairly decent son—there was something terribly wrong with him. Did romance reveal some truth, a fundamental lack, a coldness, that made him shrink back at just the moment when reciprocity was called for?

He shuddered. As he drew in his breath, he took in the scent of Hannah's hair. It smelled of coconut—of what he now knew to

be the cheap drugstore coconut shampoo she kept in her bathroom, the kind of shampoo that would make Aurit or Elisa curl
their lips in disdain.

He remembered how much fun he'd had with her in the beginning, their early dates, how she'd made him laugh, how she'd surprised him by being so . . . *interesting*. He thought of how she'd
been tonight, at the restaurant with Jason and Peter. (And it wasn't
because Peter liked her. It was because she had been herself, the
person he had fallen for.) Even the callow bit. He knew what she
meant. And that was the thing, actually. He usually knew what
she meant. And he felt that she usually knew what he meant. From
the beginning, he had felt at home with her.

He leaned his forehead against hers. "I'm sorry about how
things have been. But let's keep trying, okay? I can do better."

She stared into the dark, empty air of her apartment.

He traced her bottom lip with his thumb. "I like you a lot," he
said. "You know that, right?"

In fact, he felt right then that he loved her. *Of course* he loved
her. Had he merely been punishing her for some unknown crime?
For being nice to him?

She didn't respond right away, just continued to stare off. "I
need to feel like you're trying, too," she said finally. "I need to feel
like I'm not in this alone, the only one who cares about what's going
on here."

He held her chin with his thumb and looked into her eyes.
"You're not," he said. "You're not the only one."

He felt her relax. "Okay," she said, nodding. "Okay."

He pulled her to him. Her chest trembled as she released her
breath. He held her tighter. He felt close to her, perhaps closer to
her than he'd ever felt, as if they'd been through something together,
seen each other not just at their best but in some real capacity, and
they were still here. She—she hadn't given up on him. He buried his
face in her hair, mumbling something about love.

15

Nate was at the counter, asking Stuart—Beth wasn't working today—for a refill when Recess's glass door swung open. In walked Greer Cohen, an autumn breeze swirling around her. As the door clicked shut, the rustle in the air subsided. Greer remained at the center of a small whir of activity. A sweater and various bags, one containing a rolled-up yoga mat, swung from her shoulders. Wild locks of wavy hair spilled out from a loose bun.

"Nate!"

Her smile expressed such pleasure that Nate couldn't help but feel touched. "Greer," he said. "What brings you here?"

"Yoga. Down the street."

Stuart was waiting behind the cash register for his money. Other patrons were looking up from behind their laptops. Greer's fluttering energy and lilting, girlish voice ruffled the still air of the coffee shop.

Nate slid a bill to Stuart and then put a hand on Greer's upper arm to guide her out of Recess's central corridor. When he felt her small arm through her sweater, a tremor passed through him. Until that moment, he hadn't consciously noted that Greer had become a recurring figure in his fantasy life, a sort of marquee name among the myriad other pretty girls who wafted in and out of various scenarios.

As she allowed herself to be led backward, Greer smiled up at him with what felt—absurdly—like complicity.

Nate asked about her book. They began talking about the day-to-day process of writing at such length.

"So much staring at the screen," Greer said. "I'd shoot myself if it weren't for yoga."

The girlishness of Greer's smile did not at all offset its suggestiveness.

"I feel you," Nate said.

Over time, he had revised his opinion of Greer upward. She was warm, friendly. You had to give her that. And her book deal was not nothing. It took no small degree of skill, in terms of basic writing ability and self-presentation, to manage that. Such savvy wasn't the same thing as real talent, but it was something. About her writing itself he had nothing to say. It wasn't his kind of thing.

They continued to chat for a few minutes. "You're dating Hannah Leary, right?" she asked at one point.

Nate shifted his eyes. "Yeah."

Greer's smile merely altered around the edges, becoming more conspiratorial.

"We should get a drink sometime," she said as she was getting ready to go. "Talk about book writing."

There was a new flurry of activity as a business card was produced from one of her bags. Greer grabbed a Magic Marker from the bulletin board and began scrawling on the back of the card.

She handed it to Nate. On the front, it said "AMD Global Brand Management." "Ian Zellman, Senior Strategist" was printed below. Nate looked at Greer questioningly.

She shrugged. "Just some guy."

Nate turned the card over. Greer hadn't written her name, just the ten digits of her cell phone number. He put the card in his pocket, not without a feeling of satisfaction at having triumphed over Senior Strategist Ian Zellman.

When Greer was gone, Nate was left in a pleasant state of bewilderment. He didn't know why Greer was so flirtatious with him. Perhaps she was attracted to his supposed intellectual cachet? Greer had sold her book for more money than he'd sold his, and would probably sell more copies, but as a memoirist of adolescent promiscuity, she lacked a certain . . . respectability.

He went back to work on the review he was writing. He forgot about Greer until later that night.

He was out with Jason, who was talking about Maggie from work. Maggie was thinking about moving in with "that douche," the Web site designer.

Nate slipped his hand in his pocket. He found the card with Greer's number on it. He ran his fingers along its edges.

He had cheated before. On Kristen. They were living in Philadelphia at the time, but he had been in New York for the weekend. He'd gone to a party at an apartment in what had at the time seemed to be deep Brooklyn but was actually very close to where he now lived. The only person he knew was the guy he came with, who by midnight was nowhere to be seen. Jason, at whose place he was crashing, was supposed to show up at some point, but until then what was Nate supposed to do but talk to girls? Why would a guy want to talk to him? He flirted in the habitual, desultory manner of someone who expects it to come to nothing. He was on a beer run with a girl he'd been chatting with when she turned and fell into him, pushing him into the limestone wall of an apartment building. Nate felt, as he halfheartedly kissed her back, only a startled impulse not to hurt the girl's feelings, in part because she wasn't even that pretty. He broke away quickly. But back at the party, he found himself acutely aware of her, attuned to every instance when his arm or thigh brushed against her. When she went to speak to someone on the other side of the room, he followed her not just with his eyes but with some animal instinct. It was as if, in order to crowd out all thoughts of Kristen, he had to blow up his desire into something outsized, over-the-top, something that simply didn't allow for reflection. In fact, the girl was merely a cute-ish, chipmunk-cheeked, slightly neurotic, casually but not convincingly slutty aspiring film . . . whatever it was people who want to work in film aspire to be. All the same, Nate was pretty much in a blinding fury of desire when they took a cab back to the apartment she shared in Alphabet City. Not-Kristen had her tongue in his mouth, Not-Kristen was unfastening a cheap red bra that clasped in the front, Not-Kristen had a bumpy constellation of moles around her collarbones and a loosy-goosy tummy—all of it only contributed to her intoxicating unfamiliarity. At some point, when she had him in her mouth, she created so much suction that the phrase *menacing vise grip* had come to mind. Nate had had to gird himself to bear it manfully. When they fucked, her multisyllabic mewing sounds were stagy, meretricious, as perfectly timed to his thrusts as if they were playing Marco Polo. And yet it was thrilling.

The thrill was harder to fathom the following day. On the bus back to Philly, Nate stared out the tinted window at the traffic on the Garden State Parkway. The sky was dull and gray, his face in the glass wan and abject. Whatever frustration he'd felt in his relationship had vanished. His life with Kristen seemed full of fresh air and intelligence and promise. Her austere beauty, the crispness of it, seemed to mark her as one of the elect. Why had he done this thing that could fuck it all up?

The bus lurched. The smell of other people's fast food made him feel sick.

When Kristen pulled up to the bus station to pick him up, Nate began furiously adjusting the straps of his backpack. Although he told white lies with the same facility as anyone who is generally successful and liked, he had never been a skilled liar when any sort of personal gain was at stake. He'd speak the words as if they were in scare quotes, as if to distance himself from whatever he said.

He reminded himself, as he tossed his bag into the backseat, that he didn't really have to lie. He had only to omit certain pieces of information. In the car, he passed into a state of becalmed terror. In bed later, Kristen apologized for being tired—thankfully. Sex would have been one more, exhausting semi-lie, but he would have felt too guilty to say no if she had initiated.

A few days later, when they were driving out to a suburban shopping center, Kristen turned to him. "You stayed with Jason over the weekend, right?"

The back of Nate's neck grew rigid. "Yeah."

Kristen's brow was furrowed. Beads of sweat formed under Nate's T-shirt as he waited. And waited.

"That's what I thought," Kristen said, after she made her left onto Delaware Avenue. The clicking of the turn signal ceased. "But I thought you might have stayed at Will McDormand's. I'd love to know what Will's apartment is like. Probably he has, like, a fireplace and an Andrew Wyeth painting in his living room and a mirror on the ceiling of his bedroom."

Nate snorted. "That sounds right."

But his heart was still thumping.

The worst part, though, *wasn't* that it was hard. The worst part was that it wasn't hard enough. Nate felt guilty, yes, but the knowledge that what Kristen didn't know wouldn't hurt her made this easier to bear than even a much more minor offense, such as snapping at her when she interrupted his reading to ask some unimportant question, like whether they should go to Ikea that weekend or if he'd call the phone company about the erroneous bill they'd received. In those instances, the hurt was immediate and palpable and instantly made Nate feel bad. But after this far more serious infraction, Nate experienced much less internal fire-and-brimstone than he expected. He saw that cheating could easily become if not routine, then at least more doable. In spite of the self-loathing, in spite of what was a little bit disgusting about the girl, and what he imagined would be a little bit disgusting about most girls one was likely to cheat with, the fun of it, the variety of it, was enticing: to have what he had with Kristen *and*, every once in a while, a little bit of that—that crossing into the unknown and unfamiliar. Possibilities occurred to him. He thought of a Goth-looking waitress at a nearby bar who he'd long suspected was flirting with him.

What stopped him was the realization that it was a bad road to go down. It wasn't only that he'd grow comfortable lying. He would also have to justify his behavior to himself: caricature Kristen in his mind, exaggerate her limitations and "prudishness," repeat pop-psych mantras about the uncontainable nature of male sexuality, as certain middle-aged men did, men who tended to strike Nate as not only sleazy but pathetic and distinctly unattractive. He could see, too, that it would destroy the best thing he had with Kristen. While she might not be hurt by what she didn't know, the need to hide key facets of his private life would mean he'd have to be on guard, think before he spoke, lest he contradict himself or reveal something unwittingly. Besides, it was 1999, and the specter of Clinton loomed large: the accomplished statesman turned into a joke because he couldn't keep it in his pants. Nate had made a conscious decision not to do it again, not to cheat.

He put Greer's card back into his pocket and turned to Jason. "Why don't you just tell Maggie how you feel about her?"

Jason looked surprised. "Don't you know?"

Nate realized he didn't, not exactly. He'd chalked it up to Jason's general weirdness about women.

"Spell it out for me."

Jason's Adam's apple quavered as he took a long sip of beer. He set the glass down on the table and leaned forward. "It's Saturday morning," he began, sweeping his arm in front of him with oratorical flourish. "I open my eyes and push off a floral comforter. Sunlight is pouring through a window, reflecting off a gigantic Ansel Adams photograph hanging on the wall. Where am I? I wonder. Oh!"—he cupped his ear—"what's that I hear? A scampering little footstep? It's Maggie! She comes skipping into her bedroom, cute as a button, in her Sewanee T-shirt and flannel pajama bottoms, full of little teeny bumpy nubbins. In her hands, she's holding a plate full of fresh-baked banana muffins, and she smiles up at me"—Jason paused to flutter his eyelashes, which he did with unexpected skill—"her little-biddy button nose is sweetly pink-tipped, and her smile is so sweet, it breaks your heart. And you know what happens? My cock shrivels up so small, it's like a tiny, little pink shrimp, like a fucking toddler penis. All I want is to get the hell out of there as fast as I can, get the fuck to some dank club full of models and do some coke. And I hardly even like coke."

"How do you know, Jase? Seriously. How do you know you wouldn't be happy?"

Jason traced the rim of his glass with his finger before looking up at Nate. "Well, Miss Lonelyhearts, even if there's only an eighty percent chance that's what would happen, I couldn't do it. Maggie's a really good person. And it may be hard for you to believe— you think you're the only one women fall for, you vain fuck—but she really likes me."

Nate started to respond—to defend himself—but then shut his mouth. Jason's sensitive side, on the rare occasions when it emerged, seemed infinitely fragile, like glass so fine that even discordant notes of speech could cause it to shatter.

"No," Jason said, his voice returning to a more familiar register. "What I need is a model with a really good personality. Too bad Brigita turned out to be such a dud."

Nate grunted sympathetically. They turned back to the chips and guac they were sharing.

After a while, Jason asked how things were going with Hannah.

Nate glanced at the flapping chef's door between the bar and the kitchen. "Fine. Good."

Since the night he and Hannah had stayed up drinking bourbon, things had been better. She was resolutely unmopey. She called him less, would sometimes fail to return his calls until he became increasingly eager to see her. He had taken her out for her birthday, bought her a scarf that Aurit helped him choose. Things were fine. And yet he sometimes felt her eyes on him, watching too closely, trying to read his mood, clearly worried that he was growing bored or distant. When he was especially affectionate, he picked up on an anxious, guarded happiness that she tried but failed to conceal, as if he were a drug addict or a gambler and she the long-suffering wife who detected signs of reformation. This seemed humiliating, for both of them.

Nate suppressed a sigh as he stood up. "I'm going to the bar," he said. "You want another?"

"Yeah."

"What I wonder is whether fashion really has gotten more ironic," Hannah said over brunch a few days later. "I mean, the nerd glasses and mom jeans and the eighties-inspired clothes."

Nate nodded absently.

"Or does it just start to seem ironic as you get older, because you've seen all the trends come and go, and you can no longer take them seriously? You've watched the waistlines of jeans move up, up, up and then down, down, down and now up again. And the glasses! They got smaller and smaller until it seemed like you needed glasses just to see your glasses, and then, boom, one day they are all of a sudden big and owlish again? But maybe to twenty-year-olds, who haven't become jaded by this cycle, those big glasses just look cool? Not ironic, but just nice, the way people our age genuinely thought tapered jeans looked nice in the nineties?"

While Hannah was talking, an attractive woman had entered the restaurant. She had a long mane of light-brown hair, thick but smooth and shiny, the kind of hair that awakens a primitive appreciation for good health and breeding. Her face was nice, too. The hair's-breadth difference between the exact set of her features and classic beauty (her nose was a little wide, her chin too prominent) didn't make her any less attractive. She was wearing a blazer that gave her a cute, grad-student sort of look but was cinched at the waist and short enough so that her legs looked extremely long. When she passed their table, Nate saw that her jeans clung tenaciously to her ass, which appeared to have benefited from years of horseback riding and lacrosse.

He turned back to Hannah. She was staring at him with her mouth open.

Nate looked away, taking refuge in his coffee mug, where oily droplets clung to the surface like small, prismatic reflecting pools. He'd looked at another woman. Big fucking deal. He didn't have the energy right then to deal with this unbearable, this *boring* tension between the two of them.

He started talking about the cover of his book, about how he wanted a few minor changes made, to rearrange the order of some of the blurbs and make the font color of the jacket copy more vivid against the book's background.

Now Hannah seemed to be nodding absently, playing with a glass saltshaker, rolling it between her thumb and fingers. This struck Nate as rude. She was, supposedly, his *girlfriend*, and this— his book—was only the biggest thing in his life. It wasn't as if he were talking about fashion.

The waitress appeared. "French toast over here, and eggs Benedict for you. How are we doing otherwise? Do we need more coffee?" She nodded her head as she spoke as if to guide them to the correct answer. Then she picked up the little white jug of cream from their table, tilting it toward her so she could peer inside. "I'll get some more. Ketchup for your potatoes? You got it. Be right back!"

Nate resumed his narration about the book jacket. He was glad he'd rejected the first design. He had felt bad doing it—he didn't want to be troublesome—but he felt it looked old and stodgy. Oscar, the designer, had done a brilliant job in the end. The new cover conveyed seriousness but also freshness, hipness.

Nate was in the middle of making this last point when Hannah cut him off. "I can't do this, Nate."

"Do what?"

"Sit here and be your cheering section. I'm not in the mood to ooh and ah about your *big* book and all your little successes."

"That's a nice thing to say," Nate said. (In fact, he felt relieved that she'd given him an opening to vent his irritation.) "That's a really kind, considerate thing for your girlfriend to tell you as you try to discuss something that's just slightly important to you. Do you want to talk about fashion again? Would that be more inter-esting to you?"

Hannah swallowed and closed her eyes. When she opened them, they trained in on his with angry precision. "Why don't we talk about the woman you were checking out? She *was* very pretty."

"For Christ's—"

"Don't bother," Hannah said. "I know how this plays out. You're going to tell me—or better yet, not tell me, just *imply*—that I am being irrational, that I am neurotic and jealous and impossible. After all, don't all liberated people in the twenty-first century know that it's no big deal for men to check out women? It's just biology. Only some impossible, ridiculous woman would mind.

Nate glared at the table.

Hannah kept talking. "But we both know you weren't just checking her out. You were being incredibly, *spitefully* obvious about it. You were broadcasting your contempt for me, or your boredom, or whatever. Don't worry, I got the message."

From other tables, laughter, strands of animated conversation curled through the air. Nate felt sweaty, conspicuous, as if Hannah were making a scene, even though she wasn't speaking loudly. There was an intensity that marked out their conversation from the others. *Which of these pairs of diners enjoying high-end hipster comfort food doesn't fit in?*

"So now I'm stuck," Hannah was saying. "If I complain, I look ridiculous, but if I ignore it, am I really then supposed to sit here and act like I'm all gooey-eyed and happy for you because you are just so successful and your book is so exciting? That kind of makes me feel ridiculous, too. Either way, I'm screwed."

"Jesus! I—I—can we please just eat our food?"

"I have an idea," Hannah said. "I can play the game you're playing. See that guy over there?" She gestured toward a man in a leather jacket sipping coffee on a stool at the bar. "Isn't he good-looking? He's so *tall*. I think I'm going to chat him up."

Nate met her eye. "Go right ahead."

Hannah winced and then shook her head. They eyed each other for a long, languorous moment, reveling in the cool pleasure of open hostility. Then Hannah leaned her face down into her hands, covering her eyes with the tips of her long, tapered, cellist fingers. Her hair fell forward on her cheeks. When she looked up, Nate sensed her anger was spent. This frightened him.

"Never mind," she said. "I can't do this. I don't want to."

With his fork, Nate moved some egg around his plate.

"I've tried playing that game," Hannah continued. "Pretending I don't care. And you know what? It worked. You always responded to it."

Nate willed himself not to move a muscle in his face, not to let on that he had a pretty good idea as to what she was talking about. To admit it seemed intolerably humiliating, a too-open acknowledgment of the dinky little rinse-and-repeat melodrama their relationship had devolved into.

"But I don't want to do it anymore," she said. "You'll always win this game because I'm only playing at it, and you—well, you . . ." She dropped her knife and fork, which apparently she'd been holding for quite some time like some kind of ritualistic accoutrements. They clattered as they landed on her plate. "Well, I don't know what you're doing."

Her eyes shone.

Nate realized, with some surprise, that he'd never actually seen Hannah cry, not in all these months. The closest had been the time when he could tell she'd been crying.

"And by the way," she said, no longer on the verge of tears but with feeling. "I think it's stupid. The whole thing is stupid. It doesn't reflect well on you."

Nate had lost the will to fight. "No, certainly not," he said quietly. "Listen, why don't we get out of here?"

A few minutes later, they set out for the park in the center of Hannah's neighborhood. Without touching each other as they walked down the street—their hands were buried deep in the pockets of their jackets—they spoke pleasantly, about topics of no consequence.

Hannah nodded toward a kitchen store on the other side of the street. "That's new."

"It's convenient," Nate said. "Next time you need a frying pan or something."

He looked away when they passed the bar they had gone to on their first date.

The park felt barren, the grass a dull green and the trees skeletal, their leaves long since shed. He and Hannah walked to a bench on the crest of a hill. For a while, they were silent.

"I guess we both know this isn't working," Hannah said finally.

Her hands were still in her pockets, but her arms were extended on her lap, so her jacket was pulled forward and made a sort of tent in front of her. Nate nodded slowly, careful not to show too much eager assent.

"I don't know why," she said. "I've tried and tried to figure it out, but after a while, I guess the only thing we can say for sure is that it isn't working."

Her voice was even, unemotional, but her eyes, when she turned to face him, were so imploring that Nate had to look away. He felt sure that she wanted him to contradict her, as he had that night in her apartment. But he couldn't do it again. The intensity of feeling he'd experienced that night hadn't lasted. The facts had become too obvious. Relationships shouldn't be this hard. *Nobody* thought so. He'd have to be crazy. And the simple fact was he no longer wanted this.

Greer popped into his mind: the way she'd smiled at him at Recess, the way he'd *felt* when she smiled at him. That had to mean something—that real, spontaneous longing. The card with her number on it was sitting on his dresser. "Global brand management?" Hannah had remarked dryly, when she'd noticed it there, amid the bitten-up pens and the torn-off dry-cleaning tags. "Thinking about a career change?"

The thought of Greer made him feel guilty. Why should it, though? It wasn't as if he'd called her. Yet it did. As much as he was beginning to feel relieved—and indeed he felt an easing of a deep, almost muscular tension that he hadn't even known was there—Nate simultaneously began to feel, as if in exact counter-reaction, both sad and ashamed.

"I'm sorry," he said. He made out a faint and fleeting bit of condensation in his breath.

"I guess I haven't been exactly perfect either," Hannah said. She took her hands out of her pockets and hugged her body with her arms. "I'm not mad at you. I've been mad at you, but I don't think I am anymore. I don't see the point."

Nate shifted his position on the bench, feeling uncomfortably as if she did have reason to be mad at him, though he couldn't say what it was precisely. He knew he'd hurt her, yet he felt bound by twenty-first-century chivalry to pretend he didn't know it, lest he seem presumptuous or arrogant.

"You know I think you're great," he said.

She merely raised her eyebrows. He felt the triteness of his words.

"The thing that bothers me," she said after a moment, "is that in the beginning, *my god*, you couldn't have been more into it. But since then . . ." She turned to face him. "*Why?* Why did you start this if you didn't care enough to try and make it work?"

Nate tried not to sigh. *Start this?* Obviously, they'd both had a hand in starting it.

"I did try."

"*Really?* Did you ever spend three seconds thinking about what the problem was and whether there was anything you could do to make it better? It was like you had nothing at stake, like you were a passive bystander."

Nate wished he didn't have to have to listen to this. He felt he'd heard it, or some variant of it, a billion times.

"And you always had your book," Hannah continued. "Whatever happened between us was not going to affect you much one way or the other because the most important thing for you is that your book is coming out. It's hard to compete."

"Are you saying that's a bad thing? Caring about my book?"

"I—no! Of course not. There was a power imbalance, that's all I meant. It wasn't fun being on the wrong side of that."

Nate wondered if it would be patronizing to suggest that she might be better off if she cared about her book more. It could be difficult to stay motivated sometimes—he knew that—especially when you were unhappy. But he also knew that you had to push through. He had. He had written his book even on days when it was the last thing he felt like doing.

He decided it would be better not to say this.

He stared through the bald trees to the stalls of the farmer's market that assembled at the park each week. On this gray day, it looked like the threadbare marketplace of some bleak eastern European village. He could smell the diesel from the row of idling trucks that transported produce and workers from upstate. It reminded him of dreary Sunday afternoons as a child, driving back with his parents from visits to his cousins in New Jersey or to the houses of his parents' Romanian friends in the D.C. suburbs, of looking out the car window at drab, shabby landscapes and being crushed by a sadness caused at once by everything and nothing—a general sense of life as a bleak, lonely, rather hopeless affair.

He thought of his immediate future, of being single. He remembered the night he and Mark had hit on Cara, the feeling of dullness that had come over him when he had contemplated his single life, the incessant, relentless flirting, its underside of loneliness and cynicism.

"Sometimes I think I've lost something," he said to Hannah. "Some capacity to be with another person, something I used to have." He laughed mirthlessly. "I feel pretty fucked, to tell the truth."

Hannah looked incredulous. "I don't know what to say to that. What am I supposed to say?"

Nate was stung by her tone. "Never mind," he said. "I'm feeling sorry for myself. It's stupid."

Hannah shut her eyes. When she opened them, she spoke slowly. "I feel like you want to think what you're feeling is really deep, like some seriously profound existential shit. But to me, it looks like the most tired, the most average thing in the world, the guy who is all interested in a woman until the very moment when it dawns on him that he has her. Wanting only what you can't have. The affliction of shallow morons everywhere."

"Jesus! If you're going to—"

"I'm sorry," Hannah said. "I'm being harsh, but give me a break. If what you say is true, if you just have some 'problem,' it kind of sucks for me, too. I can't sit here and try to make you feel better. It's like the robber asking his victim to sympathize with his uncontrollable compulsion to rob people." She squinted up into the pale sky. "Give me a few years, until you're on your deathbed or something."

Nate made a chortling sound. So did Hannah. Their eyes met. Her smile was strangely companionable, as if they were old war buddies.

He knew with near-perfect certainty that there would come a time when he would be feeling down and lonely and crave more than anything Hannah's company, her warmth, her intelligence, her humor, her ability to understand him. On that night, as he returned home to his empty apartment, he'd regret this day. But he also knew that on all the other nights—the, say, forty-nine out of fifty nights when he wasn't unhappy in that particular way— he'd be glad to be free of this, of the heavy, unfun yoke of it. This thought made him feel bad all over again.

"I'm sure a lot of it *is* my fault," he said. He smiled ruefully. "And by a lot, I mean all."

"Ah, the self-deprecating dude routine," Hannah said. "'What a lovable fuck-up I am.' The annoying thing is that it makes you look good, but it doesn't get *me* anything."

The return of bitterness in her voice took Nate by surprise. Each time he thought they'd moved beyond reproaches, she turned angry again. He foresaw a potentially endless loop. He was also getting hungry—he hadn't eaten much at breakfast—and it was growing chillier outside.

"I guess we should get going," he said.

Hannah turned her face away from his. A wall of straight reddish brown hair moved up and down as she nodded slowly. "Yeah."

He pretended not to notice as she wiped her cheek with the back of her hand. The truth was he felt a flash of resentment. It seemed manipulative.

16

Nate had a long and intimate relationship with guilt.

He felt guilty when he passed by the neighborhood homeless guy, a bespectacled, middle-aged man with a salt-and-pepper Afro whose lilting refrain—"Can you spare a dollar, bro?"—echoed as you walked away, like an effect on a dance remix. He felt guilty when, in a Manhattan office building, he saw an elderly janitor stooped over a mop, joints creaking, jowls hanging over his collar. He felt guilty when a blank-faced Hispanic or Asian man refilled his water glass at a restaurant. He thought of ten- and twelve-hour shifts, of returning to squalid apartments shared with a dozen others. He felt guilty on the subway, when, as the train moved deeper into Brooklyn, more and more white people got off. Eventually almost everyone who remained was black—and tired. Overworked, underpaid. He felt guilty when circumstances forced him to get up early on a frigid winter morning, and, hurrying along wind-swept streets, he saw Southeast Asian vendors blowing on their hands as they set up their coffee carts. What had he done to deserve his easier—his easy—fate?

His intelligence was just something he'd been born with. Luck of the draw, like being beautiful. It was a rationalization to say that he'd worked hard. It was like being given a fine knife and taking the trouble to polish and sharpen it: it's great that you make the effort, but someone had to give you the knife. And it wasn't just intelligence. Nate felt guilty when he thought about his grandparents and great-grandparents in eastern Europe—shtetls and pogroms and worse.

In such a context, the small-scale romantic disappointments of privileged single women in New York City did not even remotely make the cut. Yet the day after he and Hannah broke up, Nate was riled by a strong sense of guilt.

At the park, he'd been so—well, he hadn't been able to see beyond a great cloud of irritation, which had seemed not only to justify his actual behavior but much worse behavior as well. He'd felt that he behaved remarkably well, that, in an effort to extricate himself from such a subtle and uncomfortable snare, he could have been much meaner. There had been times with Hannah, in the past month or two, when he had found himself feeling so harassed that it had seemed an act of heroism that he hadn't told her exactly what he was thinking in the bluntest possible terms. And yesterday, at brunch and after, he'd been at moments so aggravated that his endurance of the whole breakup scene had seemed, on the whole, a display of magnanimity. He hadn't said "enough" and taken off, as many guys would have. Many guys would have told her she needed to chill out—implied she was obsessive, fucked-up.

Yet, now, as he wandered around his apartment, shuffling list-lessly from room to room, Nate didn't feel so hot. He felt guilty about various things. Checking out that woman at the restaurant, for one. For the way he'd been in general.

He was also baffled. So many times, as their relationship had begun to deteriorate, he had gone from being irritated by Hannah to feeling remorse once his irritation passed. He'd always thought that in the aftermath, when he felt bad, he was clearheaded, see-ing the situation for what it was. Only now it seemed to him that he'd been in some kind of fugue state the whole time, going back and forth from one mood to the other, without ever stopping to consider what was driving the insane back-and-forth. Instead, he'd just avoided her for stretches.

At the park, he had thought Hannah was unreasonable when she accused him of not trying, but now he wondered if he had, at some point, stacked the deck against her—decided he didn't want her and then set things up so she'd justify his slackening interest. Because he knew—of course he knew, he wasn't stupid—that his behavior had contributed to, if not entirely caused, her insecurity. And of course her insecurity (*Are you mad at me? Can I please, please make you breakfast?*) just made her more annoying. But it had felt as if he couldn't help the way he behaved. When he had behaved badly—snapped at her, checked out that woman, whatever—he had been acting from some overpowering compulsion. And yet he had once liked her quite a bit.

He stopped pacing and stood by the window, blinking at the paper-white sky. The truth was he hadn't stopped liking her. Even now. That was what had been, what continued to be, so confusing.

The stentorian voice inside his head told him he'd been a jerk. He'd known his behavior had confused her. He'd watched her diminish, grow nervous and sad, become in certain ways someone he didn't recognize. Whenever he'd felt bad about it, he told himself that he wasn't forcing her to stay with him. She could break up with him any time she wanted.

But now he thought of something Aurit had said—written, actually, in a truly excellent piece of expository writing. She'd described her parents' fucked-up dynamic, how her father's response to any criticism was "if you don't like it, leave." Aurit argued that for the person with more power in a relationship to refuse to take seriously the unhappiness of the other, simply because nothing is forcing them to, is the ultimate dick move: "It's like if the United States in the 1950s said, 'Sorry, black people in the South, but if you don't like the way you're being treated, you can go back to Africa.'"

On the other hand, Hannah *wasn't* a disenfranchised minority,

Nate thought, leaving the window and padding from the bedroom to the kitchen. Why should he have had more power? He didn't ask for it. When he remembered that, he began to resent her, for her meek willingness to put up with his bad behavior. For her willingness to be his victim. Sure, she'd snapped back, gotten pissy, but these had been empty little torrents, the indignant flailing of a small animal caught in a trap. By and large, she'd put herself at his disposal, made it easy for him to hurt her. And now he had to be his own judge and jury. But he had his own feelings to worry about. It wasn't fair to make him responsible for both of them.

That made him feel a bit better, for a little while. Then it occurred to him that she'd put up with him because he had wanted her to. Until he didn't. He had always stopped being a dick to her as soon as he sensed he'd crossed the line and she might actually walk away. She'd allowed him to torment her in this way because *she liked him*. Maybe she even loved him.

The thought made him wince.

Because, come on, was he ever going to find someone with no annoying tics or physical imperfections? What real criticism did he have of her? That she sometimes drank too much? So did he. That she seemed not serious enough about her writing? The truth was that before their downward-spiraling relationship seemed to consume her, she had struck him as quite serious. That she was sometimes insecure? *All* women were sometimes insecure. The ones who claimed they weren't were craziest of all.

He pictured Hannah, at Francesca Whatshername's rooftop party. He remembered how she'd held her own against Jason. He remembered how, well, *happy* he'd been that night.

He decided to call Kristen. If a person as upstanding as Kristen, a person who also happened to be a very strong and intelligent woman—*a pediatric oncologist*—a woman who had lived with him on intimate terms for more than three years, thought highly of him, he couldn't be quite so awful a person as he felt like now.

Kristen picked up on the second ring. Her voice was warm and rich—and deeply familiar, still. It moved him even after all this time. "Nate!" she said. "It's nice to hear from you."

One of her dogs barked in the background. "Corky—our newest," she told him. "He's only a year—German shepherd mix. A real handful."

Kristen lived in Boulder with her husband, an MD/PhD who did something very laudable and impressive, Nate forgot exactly what, through the university. (Ran some kind of innovative and also highly compassionate clinic?)

Kristen said she and David were fine. Great, in fact. The new house was also great, although they'd barely unpacked. "No time."

But she found time to rescue and care for three dogs?

"I guess," she admitted.

"And run?"

"I did the Denver marathon in September," she said, a little sheepishly.

Nate laughed fondly. "You don't change, Kris."

He heard David calling her name. "Just a sec," she said to Nate. Away from the mouthpiece, she began talking to David, her voice garbled and indistinct. While he waited, Nate pictured dinner at Kristen and David's: candles on the table, the dogs sprawled on plaid cushions, boxes piled up on the hardwood floors.

"Tell me how you are," she said when she got back on the line.

Nate stood by the window, drawing circles in the condensation. Outside, twilight was descending on the angular, postindustrial Brooklyn landscape—a choppy sea of billboards and cranes and squat, gray tenements.

"I've been better."

He told Kristen he'd broken up with yet another nice girl. "Really nice. Nicer than most actually."

But it just stopped working. He had felt—it was hard to explain. Things had gotten "heavy." He'd been conscious of not living up to some expectation. Not being into it enough, into her enough, he supposed. He'd felt, after a while, as if he were constantly letting her down, as if she were always mad at him. It was no fun. By the end, the relationship had been suffocating. That had to mean something, right?

"Nate!" Kristen said. "Of course it means something. Suffocating is not good."

"Right!"

"I'm sure there was a reason you didn't want to move forward with this, uhm, Hannah, even if it's not clear to you now what it was."

Something in Kristen's pinched tone—he could picture her nose slightly wrinkled—told Nate that she assumed Hannah was, well, sort of awful in some way that would be obvious to anyone but him.

But what if—and he couldn't say this, not to *Kristen*—there was nothing wrong with Hannah? What if the problem was just that she didn't do it for him anymore, at least not enough? Perhaps the reason his relationship with Hannah had dragged on as long as it had, so much longer than his other recent attachments, was that usually his attraction waned in tandem with his interest in the girl herself. Women usually began to grate on him at around the same time he found himself losing interest in sleeping with them. This confluence had filled him with a pleasing sense of his own lack of shallowness. The problem with Hannah, he now felt, was that the drop-off in his attraction, in his excitement about her, had not corresponded to his feelings about her as a person. It had showed him up, to himself.

To Kristen, he just said, "What if the reason I felt so conflicted is because I'm, I don't know, just messed up somehow?"

"You're not messed up, Nate."

Right. Nate had forgotten that in Kristen's world, being messed up meant you were a six-year-old kid with a tumor the size of a grapefruit. And when he realized this, he once again (this always happened at some point when he spoke to Kristen) couldn't get past the knowledge that to her, his problems were that of a decadent New Yorker who whiles away his time on self-indulgent personal drama. He felt he could hear the way Kristen would summarize this conversation to David when they sat down for their candle-lit dinner. Good old Nate, single New York guy, can't seem to settle down. Smart, right? David might ask. Yes. But very, well, you know, neurotic, self-involved. Nate would be cast as an amusing counterpoint to their virtuous, community-oriented lifestyle, his problems, his unhappiness, reaffirming the rightness of their way of life.

This was not helpful. Nate turned so he was leaning with his back against the window.

"I also feel kind of guilty," he said, the glass cool through his T-shirt. "I couldn't make up my mind." He thought of the night he and Hannah stayed up drinking bourbon at her apartment. "Or rather I kept changing my mind. I think I was kind of a jerk."

"Isn't that what dating is?" Kristen asked. "Trying to make up your mind?"

"I guess."

"Nate," Kristen said emphatically. "You dated her for, what, four months? Five? You get a pass for being unsure about the person for the first few months. Be more careful next time. But give yourself a break. It's not as if you led her on for years and now she's too old to have children."

"Yeah."

Kristen, Nate realized, didn't have much sympathy for the romantic travails of women. Although she was good, so very good, the sphere of her sympathy was a bit circumscribed. She had always lacked a certain kind of imagination. She was so sensible and self-disciplined; the only indulgence she allowed herself was contempt for those who didn't manage their lives as competently—or as shrewdly—as she managed hers. (He thought of her string of boyfriends, each lined up almost before the old one was cut loose, a trend that continued right up to David.)

Having to her satisfaction dispatched with the subject of Hannah, Kristen began describing Corky's latest shenanigans, which involved a garden hose and a neighbor's gargoyle. (A *gargoyle*? Where the hell did they live, anyway?) As he half-listened,

Nate supposed he, too, was not sympathetic to Hannah's plight in theory. It was just that, theory aside, he actually *felt* bad.

After they got off the phone, Nate continued to wander through the gloom of his darkening apartment, choosing not to turn on the overhead lights, as if to keep his external reality in tune with his internal one. He remembered the first night Hannah had come here. They'd stayed up late, talking. They'd fucked. More than once. The second time, it must have been three or four in the morning, and they'd been talking for hours. He'd started kissing her, and then he was on top of her. He couldn't believe he initiated sex. He was exhausted. His cock had spoken against the judgment of his brain, which was afraid that he wouldn't be able to do it or that it would feel like work. But it didn't. It was good—really good, actually.

In the kitchen, he opened his refrigerator, then stared into it, listening to its hiss.

On one of the metal racks, there was a bunch of limp celery Hannah had bought for him. She thought he might like it as a snack with peanut—no, almond—butter. She didn't realize that when he was hungry he didn't have the patience even to clean and cut celery. But he liked the almond butter. It *was* better than peanut butter. He shut the refrigerator door.

It wasn't all guilt, what he was feeling.

"I always thought she was . . . well, kind of . . ."

Nate leaned in. "Yeah?"

"Well . . ."

"What?"

"Weird."

"*Weird*?"

Jason's forehead was scrunched up in thought. When, finally, he spoke, his voice had a strained quality, as if he were trying to distill very complicated, highly abstract ideas into mere words.

"Don't get me wrong. I like Hannah. But I just didn't see you with her. You guys seemed on edge together. Like, her voice would get sort of squeaky when she was talking to you. Sometimes, she seemed nervous around you. I don't know. It just struck me as weird. I didn't see you two being happy together. You didn't really *seem* happy."

Nate and Jason were sitting in a windowed alcove at a bar near Jason's apartment.

"But maybe it's me?" Nate said.

"What do you mean?"

"Maybe it's my fault I wasn't happy. Maybe I—I don't know— stopped trying."

Jason sat back in his chair and rubbed the side of his head, rumpling a section of his hair so it stood up like bristling fur. "Say you did 'stop trying,'" he said. "It was probably *because* you weren't happy. Right? It's not as if you're a masochist." He kneaded his hands together. "Trust me, you're not a masochist. You're pretty good at looking out for your interests."

Nate began picking at some masking tape that had been applied to the armrest of his chair. He listened to the pelt of rain on the windowpane. He felt defensive on Hannah's behalf, as if Jason were letting her down. (*Weird?* Nate had thought Jason liked her—genuinely liked her.) He remembered how Jason had said long ago that he didn't think Hannah was his type. What was it Jason had said? That he tended to like girls who were "girly and high-maintenance." The recollection sparked a sour suspicion that Jason was pleased to have his prediction bear out.

Nate would have preferred to talk to Aurit, but she was in Germany. After getting off the phone with Kristen, he'd also considered calling Peter in Maine, but there seemed to be something kind of girly about calling everyone he knew to discuss his breakup. Also, he would have had a hard time talking to Peter about this. Peter, in the arid expanse of his own romantic life, came at these things with different assumptions. Peter took for granted that if a woman was cool and attractive and liked you, you'd want to be in a relationship with her. So had he, once.

What Nate wanted now was to change the subject. Which was easy enough. Soon Jason was outlining his next essay. A hit piece—on meritocracy.

Nate pressed his palms against the tabletop. "You aren't arguing that the problem is that we don't really have one—but that meritocracy itself is bad?"

Jason nodded enthusiastically. "Fairness in a meritocracy is just homage to exceptional talent. For the unexceptional—by definition, the bulk of people—meritocracy is a crueler system than what it replaced—"

"Than slavery? Feudalism?"

"For every Jude the Obscure," Jason continued over him, "prevented by a hereditary class system from going to Oxford, there are a thousand other stonemasons who lack Jude's intelligence. Meritocracy is great for guys like Jude, who had talent. For the others, it's bad news."

"Wait," Nate said. "How are the other masons injured if Jude gets to go to Oxford? Is this like how straight marriage is injured by allowing gay marriage? Because I don't get that either."

"They're exposed as lacking. Duh." Jason shook his head. "If everyone remains in the station he's born to, there's no shame in it, but if it's in one's power to rise, the failure to do so becomes a personal failure."

"Oh, I see," Nate said, relaxing into the pleasant contours of impersonal argument. "It's better for everyone, but especially for the poor themselves, to know and accept their places. I think I've heard this argument before. From all sort of apologists for aristocracy. Queen Victoria, maybe?"

Jason exhaled loudly. "The difference—and this should be obvious—between me and some clenched-ass Tory is that the Tory denies Jude's existence, refusing to believe that there is any outsize talent in the 'lower orders.' Or, if he acknowledges it, is hostile toward that talent. See upper-class anti-Semitism."

"Still," Nate said. "You'd keep Jude down—to prevent other

blue-collar workers from feeling bad about themselves. Maybe you should spare the people your lack of hostility."

Jason shrugged good-naturedly. "We all have our own way of showing love."

Nate got the next round. This bar had the distinction of being patronized in about equal numbers by both black and white residents of Jason's neighborhood. Jason came here often, something Nate had been reminded of earlier in the evening when he witnessed the bartender greet him. For a moment, Nate had seen Jason as the bartender must have—as a good-looking, well-dressed, gregarious guy, a well-liked regular.

Nate walked back to their chairs slowly, carefully holding their two full beers.

After a while, the conversation came back around to relationships.

"As a rule, men want a reason to end a relationship, while women want a reason to keep it going," Jason declared, waving his glass. "That's why, after the fact, men look to all the things that were wrong with the relationship, to confirm the rightness of ending it. Women, on the other hand, go back and search for what might have been different, what might have made it work."

Foam was dripping down the side of Jason's glass. Nate felt a wave of affection for his friend, who without making reference to it was staying out too late, drinking too much, on a work night because Nate needed the company.

"Men and women on relationships are like men and women on orgasms, except in reverse," Jason continued boisterously. "Women crave relationships the way men crave orgasm. Their whole being bends to its imperative. Men, in contrast, want relationships the way women want orgasm: sometimes, under the right circumstances."

By the time they left the bar, Nate was in a much better mood.

Walking home in the rain, he thought of what Jason said and remembered a disagreement he and Aurit once had. She was railing about a guy who had broken up with her. She felt he was mistaken about what he wanted. She said that men and women both need relationships just as badly; men just don't know it. They misattribute their unhappiness to other causes, which is frustrating for women, who watch men make choices that harm both of them. Nate had argued that the word *need* loses its meaning if you define it that way. If you think you don't want to be in a relationship, and find happiness in other things like friends or work, how can anyone claim that you're suffering from a deep-seated longing to be in a relationship?

Nate had arrived at his building. He climbed up the stairs and unlocked his door, fumbling a little with the keys. When the door opened, he felt a wave of fondness for his humble apartment and for the simple pleasure of being in it, alone.

No, he certainly didn't *need* to be in a relationship.

The next morning he woke up fairly early, paid his electric, cell phone, and Internet bills, and bought his bus ticket to Baltimore for the Christmas holidays. Then he had coffee with the editor of a literary journal who was eager to publish his commodification-of-conscience piece. On the way home, he stopped at the grocery store. When he returned to his apartment, his fingers were red from the twisted straps of the various plastic bags he was carrying (he always forgot to bring a canvas bag—partly on purpose, because it was a little wussy). The day was clear, and his apartment was bathed in a flattering golden light. The shrill voices that had assailed him yesterday had mostly packed up and gone home.

On his computer, he found an e-mail from Aurit, from Hamburg. He'd written to her the day before. "I'm in a hurry," she wrote, "but wanted to say that I'm really sorry to hear about you & H. Maybe sorrier than you. I wish we'd talked beforehand. I feel as if you might not have spent enough time thinking about what might have caused the 'bad dynamic' you described. Is it worth thinking about? Or is it too late? Either way, I hope you don't mind if I write to her. I feel bad for her. Talk soon, A."

Sorrier than you? What the hell was that supposed to mean? Goddamn Aurit. He deleted the message, lest it disturb his rapidly improving spirits.

He picked up Ian Zellman's card from where it was lodged in his sheets. The night before, after he got home from the bar, he'd drunkenly taken it off the dresser and carried it to bed with him, contemplating calling Greer right then and luckily not actually doing it. Now he sat on his bed with his phone in his hand. Rays of sunlight cut stripes through the bedroom air. Greer picked up on the second ring. Her phone voice was girlish and cute, yet somehow sultry, too. Her laughter thrilled him. As they spoke, his chin was pressed bashfully against his shoulder; he ran his hand through his hair and smiled broadly.

A couple days later, in Manhattan for a meeting with his book editor, Nate ran into Amy Perelman, from his high school. He hadn't seen her for five or six years, since soon after she got her MBA. Now she worked for an investment bank. She told Nate she was in M&A, which seemed "really unsexy a few years ago when everybody was making big money in derivatives and other things that no one understood," but in retrospect she was glad not to have "gotten into that whole game." She shook her head sadly as she told him that bonuses were still down. It took Nate a moment to realize that she wasn't speaking ironically, pretending to be a tone-deaf investment banker.

She said she was engaged. The simpering way she held her hand so he could see her ring struck Nate as uncouth, sort of provincial. He was not in the habit of being offended by flirting, but he couldn't help but feel that there was something aggressively condescending about the way Amy halfheartedly flirted with him. She behaved not as if she were attracted to him but as if she were still the most popular girl at school and he the adoring acolyte, as if with her every small smile she were throwing pennies that he'd scramble to pick up off the ground. Besides, while she was still technically quite pretty, she really didn't do that much for him anymore. With her too-heavy makeup and the artificial tint of her blonde hair, she looked older than many of the artier, noncorporate women Nate knew in Brooklyn who were the same age.

It didn't help that she failed to pick up on his relative success in life. When he'd seen Amy last, he was a struggling freelance writer who lived in a tiny garret in Brooklyn. "Not much has changed," he told her now, although, he added quietly, he did have a book coming out shortly. She responded as if she didn't really get it, a bland "That's great." Maybe she thought he was self-publishing or something? So he maneuvered to mention that he'd written something for a particularly prestigious magazine. "That's cool," she said, but he could tell it didn't mean much to her. Nate knew she didn't intend to be disparaging. (She did say that she'd "heard Brooklyn had gotten really nice.") The things that made him feel successful in his own circle simply had little resonance outside that circle. It bothered him that Amy's inability to see him the way he wanted her to—as a success, as her equal—got to him. Why should it matter?

Nate marveled at this encounter most of the way home. He never thought there would come a day when Amy Perelman, whose yellow-and-white scrunchy might very well still be sitting in a box in his parents' condo, would be so unattractive to him. What made it even more striking was that not long ago, he'd happened to run into another girl from his high school. He was at a reading near Columbia when he saw Michelle Goldstein, the frizzy-haired, theater-loving girl he'd rolled his eyes at back then, Michelle Goldstein, of *pas de deux* and *coup d'état*.

At his apartment, as he flipped through his mail, he laughed. Not at Michelle's expense, but at the general idiocy and affectation of youth. Because Michelle, all these years later, had been really *nice*. She was a labor lawyer. She seemed very earnest and left-wing, like an old-school Upper West Sider. Which is where she lived, with her husband and son. The husband, she told him, was an actor. ("Not quite aspiring—he's very talented and does a lot of really wonderful off- and off-off-Broadway work—but let's just say, we don't need a full-time nanny. Which is good, because we can't afford one.") They lived in an old rent-stabilized place on 104th and Riverside that her husband had been in for years, previously with roommates. She complained about how "rich" the neighborhood had gotten. Michelle's hair, casually pulled back, was still a little bit frizzy, and her jeans were kind of mommish, but she was appealing, far more appealing than Amy Perelman.

Nate was still thinking about this when he walked to his computer and scanned his in-box. There was a message from Hannah. Without pausing to think about what it might contain, he clicked on it. A new window appeared. He sat down.

Dear Nate,

At the park the other day, I told you I wasn't mad. I don't think I was lying. I think I was numb.

Later I got mad. The first thing that pissed me off was the way, when I said this isn't working, you *nodded*. What the fuck? What did it mean to you a few weeks ago when I told you that the only way I wanted to stay with you is if you promised you were in this too? I for one meant that I didn't want to be in a relationship with someone who was going to fucking nod when I proposed breaking up with him. (I also get angry when I think of that night at my apartment. Why did you persuade me to stay with you if you didn't really want it? Were you playing some kind of game?)

So, yeah, I've been angry. At you—but also at myself. Because I never thought I'd let myself be treated this way. I know I deserve a lot better and frankly I've gotten a lot better from other guys.

I didn't expect to feel this way about you. Before we got together, I'd heard things about the way you treat women. And at first, I thought you were really full of yourself. I thought you took for granted that I was dying to go out with you because you think you're such hot shit. I hated that.

I bring this up because later, when things started to suck, I kept thinking about that time, before I'd fallen for you too hard to get out so easily. It was as if I hoped the fact that I hadn't put myself totally in your power from day one might somehow protect me from getting hurt later. It didn't, obviously. Eventually I let go. I trusted you. The way I feel right now, I wish I hadn't.

I don't mean to be melodramatic. I know that relationships often don't work out. But I remember how things were, not that long ago. They were pretty great. At least, I thought so. I felt like there was something real between us—like I really knew you and got you. Is that really stupid of me? I can't help wondering, did I do something wrong? Was I too difficult? Not difficult enough? Should I have called you out on it as soon as I felt like you were, I don't know . . . changing— instead of taking you at your word when you said everything was fine? I can't stop wondering, and yet I know it's messed up that I'm thinking this way, as if it were my job to make it work, as if I was supposed to figure out what you wanted and adjust accordingly.

The only thing I know is that when I tried to talk about what was going on with us, it felt like you always wanted to shoot it down. I began to get nervous about irritating you—I felt you pulling away and I didn't want to alienate you even more, so I didn't push us to talk more. In retrospect I regret that. It was obvious something was wrong for a while. Looking back, it seems stupid that most of the time we just ignored the elephant in the room.

I wonder—had we talked, really talked, would things have been better? Sometimes I think of things that are so obvious to me, and I hate that they aren't, or weren't, obvious to you. Such as, why do you think it was that we had a good time when we hung out with Jason and Peter? It was because they were nice to me—they acted like they actually wanted to hear what I had to say, which you barely did at that point. (Thank you for that, by the way—for the way you've treated me lately.)

But then I think of how sad you looked at the park when you said that you worry you no longer have the ability to be in a relationship. And it makes me wonder if you are as upset and confused about this as I am. If so, maybe we should talk now, try and figure what happened. Maybe it's not too late to deal with this honestly and openly.

Part of me thinks I shouldn't send this, that I've already been burned enough. But I'd rather not become that scared of being honest.

H

There were a number of things Nate felt like doing when he finished reading this e-mail. One was slamming the metallic top of his computer shut and throwing the thing against the wall. Another was running hard for about ten miles, uphill. A third was reading some very bracing, very austere, very *masculine* philosopher. Say Schopenhauer. One thing it decidedly did *not* make him want to do was get back together with Hannah.

Nate hadn't been attentive to every sentence; he wasn't able to be. Reading the e-mail was so unpleasant that he found himself skimming. He felt as if doing so were a courtesy to her, as if he had caught her in an embarrassing posture and were politely averting his eyes. (The part where she mentioned other guys? He shuddered for her—it sounded so . . . *desperate*.) But he'd read enough, more than enough. He got it. The letter—its conclusion, the thing about "talking more," "dealing with this honestly and openly"— struck him as willfully deceived. Anyone could see that they'd given their relationship any number of chances and that their conversation at the park had been decisive. The e-mail was confused, disordered, veering back and forth between anger and a wild, almost desperate compulsion to pull the arm of the slot machine yet again and hope for a different outcome, based on what? Because he'd said he worried he might be incapable of being in a relationship? When he told her that, he'd been speaking truthfully, but, come on, it was a fear that seized him every once in a while and then passed almost entirely from his mind. It wasn't worrying him at all right now. And it certainly didn't make him want to keep at a relationship that was so clearly dead.

Besides, the e-mail was a visceral reminder, as if he needed one, of the reasons he didn't want to be with her. Reading it brought back all the feelings of guilt and dread and discomfort he'd come to associate with her.

But the letter conferred an obligation. She was clearly upset. He owed it to her to do something. In the next several days, Nate debated writing back, but he saw almost immediately there was no way he could produce an e-mail of equal length, and a few lines of text from him, with her message hanging below, in its grand textual abundance, would look so paltry, so meager, an insulting little pellet atop her voluminousness. It wasn't only that he didn't have the patience to write at anywhere close to equal length. The truth—and this scared him a little—was that he didn't know what he would say. There was a certain moral vanity in her implicit assumption that everyone could sit down and whip out something like her letter, as if everyone's feelings were so known and upstanding. He couldn't have produced such a letter no matter how hard he tried. Even after all the hours he'd spent pacing his apartment the other day, he didn't really know what he thought or felt, and what he did know was confused and, frankly, somewhat upsetting. What he had learned, in the subsequent few days, was that his unhappiness was eminently containable, if managed correctly. That meant not dwelling. It meant moving forward.

Since writing was out, Nate figured he should call her. On a number of occasions, he was about to do it. But he kept putting it off. He couldn't decide if they should have it out on the phone or if he should propose coffee. Probably the latter, but then a part of him wondered if maybe that wasn't a good idea. Coffee would run longer than a phone call. She'd want him to say a lot of things he didn't much want to say. Not just for his own sake. He didn't want to be forced to say things that would hurt her feelings. The only really honest thing that he had any desire to tell her was, he suspected, the last thing she wanted to hear. He wanted to say that he was sorry for not having broken up with her sooner, for not having seen sooner that it wasn't working and wasn't going to work. He shouldn't have nodded at the park. She was right about that. He shouldn't have been with her at all at that point. In retrospect, he felt he'd had a failure of nerve that night at her apartment; they should have broken up then. But he didn't think she'd appreciate hearing this. And other than that, he didn't know what he'd say. Besides, the endless stream of postbreakup conversations he'd had with Elisa was an object lesson in the way these things could backfire. He didn't want to get into another drawn-out and in the end unhealthy dialogue. And Hannah wasn't Elisa. She was more mature, one expected more of her.

Maybe a phone conversation, short and sweet, was better?

Each time he made up his mind to do one or the other, phone call or coffee date, he couldn't quite bring himself to pull the trigger, and he told himself he'd decide for sure later; he'd do it—one or the other—later.

A week after Hannah sent the e-mail, he came strolling back from Greer's on a lovely, sunny Friday morning. He was in a good mood—it had been a good night, a very good night. He saw another e-mail from Hannah. He knew immediately he'd fucked up. He should have done *something*. The subject line was blank. Nate clicked on the message.

> God, I can't believe I am such a moron. I can't believe I wrote you that e-mail in some moment of god knows what. I just wanted to say I take it back. You're a bigger asshole than I ever imagined. I can't believe you couldn't even be bothered to respond. Anyway, there's just one other thing I wanted to tell you. You're really bad in bed.

17

So you're dating Greer now?"

Nate and Aurit were walking along Fifth Avenue in Park Slope, their scarves flapping in the wind as they squinted against the midday sun. Aurit had just gotten back from her trip, a week in Israel and two in Germany.

It wasn't just disapproval Nate picked up in her voice. He knew she'd disapprove of Greer. She thought Greer was shallow and twitty. So had he, before. What bothered him more was something withering in the way she pronounced the word *you*, as in "so *you*'re dating Greer now."

"Greer's really smart," he said as they approached their destination. He regretted the words as soon as they were out of his mouth.

"I don't doubt it," Aurit said. She pulled open the restaurant's glass door. "I mean, she's been so successful in her career. Remind me, how much did she get for her sex book?"

Then they were enveloped in the restaurant's warm air, rife with the scent of maple syrup. A hostess with an Australian accent directed them through a narrow aisle to a table in the back. By the time they sat down, that particular strand of conversation was lost. After Aurit's long trip, there was much to be discussed. Hans was finally going to move to New York.

"That's fantastic," Nate said.

Aurit told him how this had come to pass, the conversations she and Hans had had, the plans they'd made.

Later, she asked if he'd spoken to Hannah.

"You haven't talked to her?" Nate asked.

"I asked you first."

Nate poured sugar into his coffee. "Don't be like that."

"Fine," Aurit said. "She and I have e-mailed. Briefly. She didn't say much."

"Well . . . ," Nate said. "I think she may be a bit nuts."

The table wobbled when Aurit set her mug down. "Don't go there, Nate. It's ugly. Especially because *she* was so classy about it. She didn't say anything bad about you." She looked at him pointedly, jutting her chin out. "What happened?"

"She basically told me I'm the biggest jerk who ever lived." Nate ran a hand through his hair. He tried for a casual "What can you do?" smile. In fact, the way things with Hannah had so quickly devolved made him intensely uncomfortable.

Aurit cocked her head. "What'd you do, Nate?"

"Nothing."

"Don't be an unreliable narrator. What'd you do to piss her off?"

"Literally, I did nothing. That was the problem."

"Uh huh . . ."

"I didn't respond to an e-mail she wrote."

"Did you apologize?"

"You didn't see the e-mail she wrote me in response to my nonresponse. I think we've gone past the point of apologies."

Aurit shook her head. "Nice."

Nate considered making a joke about how lying in wait for him on the streets of New York was an army of hostile women, with Juliet at its head. Even Elisa, who pretended to be his friend, was half in the enemy camp. Now Hannah, too, had joined its ranks. Meanwhile, on the other side, there was still only one Nate. He didn't make the joke, though. He did not in fact feel jokey about it. He felt bad. When he thought about it. He tried not to think about it.

"In her e-mail, Hannah tried to be low-key," Aurit said. "But I got the feeling she was pretty upset. Honestly, I'm surprised you're so cavalier about it." She studied Nate with curiosity. "You guys were together for, what, five, almost six, months?"

"Five," Nate mumbled.

"And you seemed to really like her. Like, a lot."

Nate looked at the place on the table where his plate had been. "It probably won't last long with Greer," he said suddenly, surprising himself. "It's probably just a short-term thing."

He and Greer had slept together on their first date. Because Greer had been extremely flirtatious the whole night, this hadn't surprised Nate. What had surprised him was that she burst into tears immediately after. He'd felt confused and concerned and also, strangely, fascinated—by her mutability, the way she moved seamlessly and unselfconsciously from a sort of tarty affect to that of a naïf. It had been like watching a reptile shed its skin; it held him transfixed. The night had an otherworldly quality, veering back and forth from one mood to another. When Nate left in the morning, he felt as if he'd lived through a whole lifetime.

When he came to pick her up for their third date—Greer inspired in him old-fashioned gestures of chivalry, which was odd because in another sense he felt as if he were coming almost entirely because he wanted to sleep with her again—he found her not yet dressed to go out. Her hair was askew. She'd been crying again. The combined force of a comment from her editor, an incident on the bus in which an overweight woman had accused Greer of shoving her, and a conversation with her sister had "annihilated" her.

For an instant, Nate was uncomfortably reminded of Elisa— that never-ending river of tears. He felt an impulse to flee. He didn't flee. He didn't even really want to. His most vivid impression

of that night was from much later, well after Greer had been con-
soled: the glint of her belly-button ring in the moonlit bedroom as
her body rose and fell on top of his.

The fling stretched into a longer and longer fling.

Nate had been wrong about the nature of Greer's interest in
him. She hadn't been drawn to his "intellectual cachet." She had,
she told him, felt some kind of powerful, "almost kinetic," physical attraction to him. Nate, unaccustomed to seeing himself as an
object of erotic fascination, was incredibly turned on by this. He
was also inclined to believe her. A memoirist, Greer was a skilled
narrator of her own emotions. And what she said dovetailed so
neatly with what he'd felt, the attraction to her he'd nursed for
quite a while, before they got together.

Long ago, he had placed Greer into the category of people who
had gleaned amazingly little actual knowledge in four years at
Sarah Lawrence or Vassar or Gallatin or whichever fancy progressive school they'd attended, where that much-heralded goal of
modern pedagogy, to teach students "how to think," was considered better achieved without the interference of actual facts. Her
ignorance of things that had happened—certain illustrious sack-
ings, schisms, famines, et cetera—was almost touching. She was
equally unfamiliar with many books and ideas widely deemed to
be of world-historical import. But Greer had ideas of her own, all
sorts of them. They just weren't rooted in any context beyond
that of pop culture and a certain strand of women's literature. She
had also perfected an imperturbable irreverence, an earnest and
sincere belief in her superiority over stuffed shirts. Like Nate.
Greer was no phony. Unlike Elisa, she didn't pretend. Greer stared
you in the face and said, "Really? You're asking if I've read *War and
Peace*? Do you really not know the answer?"

As he had told Aurit, Greer was smart. Like a finely honed
sports car, her mind wasn't weighted down with unnecessary
encumbrances, but she was naturally gifted in the dialectical
mode of argument, quick to point out the holes in your logic and

to come back with counterarguments. When dialectic failed her, she had at her disposal another powerful tool: tears. This rhetorical device she considered perfectly legitimate: tears fell under the rubric of sincerity.

If Greer wasn't rigorous or self-critical, she was impassioned and empathetic, with great reservoirs of feeling about the issues she cared about. Her personality, like her writing, was lilting and engaging. And what Nate had once taken to be a certain artificiality on her part, he came to see as theatricality, which was different and was part of what made being with her so vivid. He soon found himself charmed by her quirky interests—her unpredictable enthusiasms for, say, piñatas this week, or tiny little postcards that fit only one sentence the next. He noticed, too, how other people responded to her. She had a way about her—a charisma, a storytelling verve, an effortless cool in dress that was as fashionable as Elisa's chic but far less fussy, an instinctive social ease that she used benevolently, lavishing attention upon the shyest and most awkward members of a group. One night she played the guitar for him. Her hair was in a messy ponytail; a thin strap of her tank top had fallen on her upper arm. She was, as she sang a Liz Phair song—her voice small, unschooled, but achingly pretty—about the sexiest, most touching thing he'd ever seen. Sweet and tough and sad and hot all at once.

Not only was she unimpressed by it, Greer was inclined to think Nate's "intellectual whatever" was kind of a bore, a sort of masturbatory exercise that she tolerated with pretty much the same condescension that he tolerated what he was apt to describe, in his mind, as the "puerile, self-indulgent navel-gazing" that characterized her work. Every once in a while these attitudes toward each other's writing slipped out in stray remarks, usually during fights, which they began to have nearly as soon as they grew more serious.

Although she prided herself on being honest, Greer wasn't always, strictly speaking, truthful. She didn't invent wholesale so much as scramble and rearrange to suit her current purpose, facts reconfiguring themselves like marbles in a tipped bowl. She was hardly aware she was doing it. In the moment, she believed what she was saying wholeheartedly. For her, that was enough. She also slid easily into manipulation when backed into a corner. She felt no qualms about that either. So it was that a minor argument about his being late or failing to do some small thing she thought he ought to—say, pick up his cell phone when she called—would escalate. She'd make all sorts of outlandish claims; he'd become so enraged at her "dishonesty" or "manipulation" or simply her "triviality," that he felt entirely justified dispensing with tact. All sorts of pent-up criticisms came pouring out, many of which had nothing to do with the ostensible subject of the fight. Once he uttered aloud the phrase *puerile, self-indulgent navel-gazing*. It bothered her more than the words *stupid* and *cunt*, both of which had also found their way out of his mouth. (For Nate, those moments had been, frankly, thrilling, the words accompanied by a frisson of illicit pleasure. It was liberating, the idea that you could talk to a woman this way and nothing worse would happen than that she'd yell back that you were a "fucking piece of shit asshole.")

Somewhat to his surprise he and Greer came out of these fights scarred but also purged. In between exaggerating her flaws, accusing her of a much greater degree of dishonesty et al. than she was in fact guilty of, things slipped out. He told her, for example, that it was the most annoying thing in the fucking world when she asked, *in that voice*, "Are you mad at me?" In turn, Greer told him about fifty other, much worse things that he did. Apparently, he was a real asshole. He had innumerable ways of belittling her and women in general. He bullied her when they argued, which is why she sometimes started to cry. She was not, she explained, trying to evade the issue. She was merely frustrated, and if her tears made him stop bullying, made him *stop and listen to himself*, so much the better. It wasn't so much that she convinced him—

Greer's feminism often struck him as conveniently self-justifying and inconsistently applied (that is, reliably applied in instances where it bolstered her position and otherwise ignored)—but the fear of setting her off did exert a strong pull on him to modify his behavior. Invariably, their fights ended, for Nate, in relief at realizing that Greer was not in fact nearly as unscrupulous or unintelligent as in anger he had painted her. Also, predictably enough, hot sex. Not even make-up sex so much as making up by way of sex. A moment would come when Nate would simply realize the absurdity of what they were fighting about; his anger would just *turn*. By that point, Greer—perhaps because she too was tired of fighting, or perhaps because she was turned on by how hot he had become for her—could usually be brought around pretty quickly.

Greer was needy—that is, she needed an audience—but it was not always clear to Nate why she needed him in particular. Sometimes, he'd glance at her, see anew how sexy, how charming she was. Anxiety would creep over him. Wouldn't she rather be with a guy who was better looking and more fun, someone less ponderous and academic? After a couple months, he asked her, why him? Yes, he remembered what she'd said about attraction, but why— why was she attracted to *him* instead of someone else? She picked up one of his hands in hers and ran a finger along his palm and up and down his fingers. She told him that his helplessness and incompetence in maneuvering objects in the physical world were endearing. "Sometimes, I look at your big, clumsy hands—these fingers . . ." She smiled and kissed the tip of his index finger. "Your hands remind me of bear paws . . . I watch you chop vegetables or button your shirt, and, I don't know, I'm just filled with affection." What she said was sweet, but Nate was still partly unsatisfied. It felt exogenous to him, to the real him.

But he knew what she meant about being touched by vulnerability. Greer's littleness appealed to him. He enjoyed beyond reason being able to encircle her so thoroughly in his arms. He felt protective, especially in her darker moods, when she cried after sex or was rendered helpless by some minor setback. In these moments, the world ceased to be filled with innocent amusements (teeny tiny postcards! piñatas!) and became a sinister X-rated carnival of rapacious, leering men vying constantly to fuck her: "It makes me sick!" And they'd sit on the floor, her knees pulled into her chest, as Nate held her, stroking her small, hunched-over back with his big hands.

In February, his book was published. Although Nate had privately nursed fantasies of being single when this happened, it turned out to be better to have a girlfriend for that. At the parties on his (brief) book tour, he tried to remember the names of people he hadn't seen for years or had just met a few minutes before. He felt inadequate when he couldn't or when he wasn't enthusiastic enough in his chatter. The whole process was exhausting and unnerving—he often felt embarrassed or ridiculous—and he was glad to have someone to call afterward, or better yet to curl up with at the hotel with a movie on. He felt closer to Greer, even grateful to her, after being together through this.

A certain twee quality to her mental landscape, a histrionic, self-dramatizing tendency that occasionally grated, the goddamned manipulative tears—all these bothered him at times. But Greer was nice, sweet-natured, especially when all was going well, when she felt liked, not just by Nate but in general. She was as sensitive as an exotic plant transported from its natural ecosystem, but when she got what she needed, she was radiant. Day-to-day, they were happy. Nate was rarely bored. With Greer, there was always some distraction, a crisis or a fight or some fantastic scheme of hers. Such as wanting him to watch her fuck a woman.

What Greer lacked in strict rectitude, she made up for in more feminine virtues, such as warmth and compassion. Like Hannah, she was lively and fun to be around. Unlike Elisa, she was willing to do things he enjoyed. She also had a strong caring impulse. She liked to cook for him and to generally see to it that he was well taken care of. Initially, he found this surprising in a girl who was so wild in bed (though the whole sex-between-Greer-and-another-woman didn't happen, and as time wore on, and their dynamic changed, it grew increasingly unlikely ever to happen).

Greer had met his parents briefly at his book party, but in the spring he took her to Maryland to spend time with them. He was struck by how much nicer to them she was than Elisa had been. They didn't, on the whole, like her, he could tell. Or, rather, his father liked her okay, and his mother, who was critical of all the women he dated, hardly bothered to conceal, underneath an imperiously cordial bearing, a sniffy personal distaste. Nate, full of tenderness and gratitude for how hard Greer tried, attempted to paper over his mother's coolness.

Although that kernel of uncertainty kept him keenly awake to his feeling for her—he couldn't help fearing that Greer's inexplicable attachment to him would turn off as suddenly and as mysteriously as it had turned on—he was also, over time, afflicted from the other end, by her jealousy. Whether he liked it or not, this was a fact of life, part and parcel of being with Greer. The fear of a jealous fit imposed limitations on not only his behavior but his conversation. Nate toned down his praise of other women, even of their writing. Aurit became a sore subject. ("I've never been attracted to her!" Nate insisted. But Greer, he finally realized, was astute enough to know that. She was jealous not of Aurit's sexual appeal but of the respect he had for her, grudging and qualified though it seemed to him. "You treat whatever Aurit says as if it has special weight because she said it," Greer said once. "If I say the same thing as she did, you act like her agreeing with me gives what I said legitimacy.")

Greer was always on the lookout for ways she was being belittled or denied her due. Never would Nate have checked out another woman when he was sitting across from her. He didn't know if she'd wave her steak knife in the vicinity of his heart or start crying, but it didn't matter because it never happened.

They celebrated their six-month anniversary. "I guess you don't have a problem with relationships after all," Aurit remarked one day, on one of the ever-rarer occasions that she and Nate got together, just the two of them. "I guess you just hadn't met the right person."

Although Aurit had mostly come around on Greer—had come to respect her feminism and emotional insight, even if the two of them hadn't really hit it off as friends—something in her tone irritated Nate. "Maybe it was just the right time," he said, largely to contradict her.

Aurit narrowed her eyes. "Do you know that you often subtly undermine Greer when she's not around?"

"Well, I can't very well do it when she is around, now can I?"

Aurit didn't look especially amused.

"Relax, I was kidding," he said. "I just think timing has something to do with it. Don't you?"

"I wouldn't know," Aurit said. "For women, it's almost always the right time." She spoke rather edgily. Hans was just then considering going back to Germany because he still hadn't found a job in New York. "The thing that I think sucks," she added after a moment, "is that whenever you—men, I mean—decide that it is the right time, there's always someone available for you to take up with."

"I don't think that's true," Nate said. "What about Peter? Or Eugene?"

"Eugene has a toxic chip on his shoulder. And Peter lives in Buttfuck, Maine."

Despite what he'd said to Aurit, Nate did feel that he'd simply found the right person. After the first few months—which, between the sex, her moods, and their fights, had been for him a dizzying adventure—he and Greer began to fight less. Over time, ground was ceded, claims granted. Now he always took Greer's calls when he was out. He was supportive in certain required ways. (He had learned, for example, that it was *not* ridiculous for her to want him to come over in the middle of the night because a friend of a friend had been mugged the evening before and she felt scared.) If sometimes he felt frustrated by her demands, he felt something else, too: his very exasperation contained the suprisingly pleasant reassurance that he was reasonable, far more reasonable than she was. Besides, he had come to accept that he was happier, more productive, less distracted by loneliness and horniness with a girlfriend than without. If that meant he had to make certain compromises for the sake of the relationship, so be it.

There were times when he was embarrassed by Greer, when he cringed a little inside. She could be too much—too cutesy and childish, too likely to proudly proclaim a poorly thought-out and poorly informed opinion, too self-enamored to see that she some- times betrayed a glib superficiality that at its worst bordered on vulgarity. But these were just isolated moments, flashes of feeling that passed quickly. And who was he to judge? He—bookish, moody, work-focused as he was—certainly wasn't perfect. Per- haps what disturbed him more was an occasional feeling of loneli- ness. Sometimes Greer, in perfect innocence, would say something that devastated him, a remark that in its substance or even in its mere elisions expressed volumes of casual, reflexive indifference to, even derision toward, many of the things he cared about most. Certain aspects of who he was were simply incomprehensible to her. It was all just "intellectual whatever." For Greer, writing was a way of monetizing her charisma. It allowed her to spend her time thinking about what she most liked thinking about: herself, her feelings. It was impossible for him to explain to her what it was for him, what certain books, and a certain type of thinking, were to him. He didn't really try. It'd probably come out sounding wrong anyway—hollow. Pretentious.

Such talk wasn't really what their relationship was about anyway. Their conversations were flirty and cheering, a change of pace, especially after a day of work. With her, Nate went into Greer mode, which was lighter, more indulgent, sillier than his normal way of being. This granted him a certain amount of privacy. He retained a separate self, distinct from his Greer self, which was untouched, free, no matter how obliged his physical person was to, say, come to Greer's aid when she got scared. And the truth was, even then, when he trekked out to her apartment in the middle of the night, he was almost always glad to see her. Even after the passage of so much time, the particular way that Greer was pretty called out to him deeply. There was about her, in her smile, her sweet little laugh, her light, birdlike touch, her very littleness, something that didn't just turn him on but made him positively feel—well, something he'd never felt before.

One day Greer asked if he'd broken up with Hannah for her. Nate made the mistake of saying not really. "It was on its last legs anyway."

"So am I, like, your rebound thing?" she snapped. "I know you think she's *so* smart."

"Greer! I was never even serious about Hannah. You and I have already been going out for longer than she and I went out for."

Nate learned a few days later that Hannah had sold her book proposal. Greer had probably heard that, too; it was probably what set her off. Privately, Nate was glad for Hannah. He had a fondness for her that was not really changed by the way things had broken down at the end. He thought of her sometimes, thought of things he'd like to tell her, observations she'd appreciate, and felt a pang of disappointment when he realized that was impossible. Sometimes he thought of the good times they'd had together, but more often, those memories were drowned out by the recollection of his unhappiness toward the end.

He felt guilty when he thought of various women in his past (although he was pleased, and somewhat egotistically relieved, to hear, from both Jason and Aurit, that Juliet's wedding announcement was in the *Times* one Sunday). When he thought of Hannah, he felt something else as well. He and Hannah had related on levels that he and Greer didn't. This was not, for Nate, a comfortable thought. His relationship with Hannah had shown him things about himself that he wasn't entirely proud of, about what he really valued in a woman and what he claimed to value but in fact could live without.

When he and Greer had been together for a little over a year, they decided to move in together. It seemed to make sense. Things were going well with them. His lease was up. Even he had to admit his apartment left something to be desired. Greer's wasn't great, either.

In the midst of packing, he took a break to go to Cara's birthday party. Over time, Cara had grown on him some. She was a nice person. Nate had even, at Mark's request, helped her get a job, putting in a good word for her with a magazine editor who needed an assistant. The important thing was that she and Mark were happy (although, out of her hearing, Mark did spend an awful lot of time riffing about how "women" lack humor).

Before the party, Nate was to have dinner with Jason and Aurit and Hans, who had decided to stick it out in New York after all, and Peter, who was in town, and Peter's new girlfriend. He'd actually met someone up in Maine. She was nice, Peter's new girlfriend, an archivist in Portland. Cute, too, if a little out of place in New York, in her ponytail and fleece jacket.

Greer had texted him earlier in the day to say she wouldn't be joining them. Nate felt a little guilty that he was relieved. When Greer hung out with his friends, she invariably wound up feeling bad. She thought they didn't think she was smart enough for them, or for him. There was no way for Nate to explain that that wasn't it. It was a matter of conversational style. Greer liked to charm and entertain with her Greerness, to regale the group with tales of her latest quirky hobby or comic misadventure—her half-ironic interest in astrology and consequent visit to a psychic, her run-in with a neighbor who complained about the garlic smell emanating from her apartment when she cooked. Maybe a pet theory about reality television or 1990s teen movies. The kind of impersonal argument, aggressive back-and-forth, and different brand of humor that he and Jason and Aurit and Peter engaged in made Greer feel left out, even rebuffed. But contrary to what Greer thought, his friends liked her fine. They were happy to pay tribute to her charm for five minutes in the beginning of the evening and at interstices throughout, between conversations, but the bulk of the time, they simply wanted to talk normally—that is, in the way that was normal for them. There was no way for Nate to explain this to Greer without hurting her feelings.

Over dinner, Jason told him that Elisa had been promoted at the newsmagazine where she now worked.

At Greer's request, Nate had ceased to be in touch with Elisa. This turned out to be for the best. Elisa derived satisfaction from the fact that Greer found her so threatening that she forbade Nate from seeing or speaking to her. From Jason, Nate learned that Elisa remarked on this whenever the opportunity arose. Nate didn't doubt that the triumph of that was more than adequate compensation for giving up what even Elisa must have known was a pretty dysfunctional friendship. (Besides, she had been a lot happier since taking the new job; she'd started dating a reporter there.) Nate, for his part, was mostly relieved to be free of the burden of Elisa, without having had to make the decision to drop her himself. And Greer, naturally, enjoyed this proof of her power to effect speedy sacrifice.

Once they ordered, Nate told his friends that his book had been long-listed for a fairly prestigious award. He tried to downplay it, but he was in fact extremely pleased. To celebrate, they made him drink a glass of a dessert wine that Hans insisted was considered good luck in Germany.

They walked from the restaurant to the party. Nate didn't intend to stay long. He had a lot of packing to do.

He'd been at the party for only a little while when he saw Hannah on the far side of Cara's living room. He made her out just in time to see her see him. She flinched and immediately turned away. When Nate looked back, she was gone.

He went into the kitchen to get a drink. Hannah was by the refrigerator. He had hoped to find her. "Hi," he said.

"Hi."

Her voice was cool, her expression unreadable. He said it was good to see her. She smiled blandly and looked as if she wished he wasn't there.

Nate held a beer in one hand. In his pocket, the fingers of the other coiled and uncoiled against his thigh. He realized he wanted to tell Hannah he was sorry. Or something. But he was afraid it would come out wrong. Patronizing. He decided to do it anyway. Greer told him he overthought these sorts of things, and she was often right.

He took a breath and plunged ahead. "I wanted to say that I'm sorry. About a lot of things. Really. I was an ass."

Hannah's expression became a little less guarded. She said yeah, he kind of was. But she said it a little wryly, more amused than angry. After a moment, she started to apologize, too. "I shouldn't have written what I—" She blushed.

He realized what she was referring to. Perhaps he colored as well. "Don't worry about it," he said.

She looked away from him. But there was something arch in the way she sucked in her lips. Nate shrugged and rolled his eyes conspiratorially. She met his glance. Nate felt, more than saw, some kind of recognition of camaraderie. For an instant, the embarrassments—the disappointments—of the past were a grim joke that they alone shared.

He noticed that her hair was subtly different, still straight and falling past her shoulders but a little more fashionably cut. She was wearing more makeup than he remembered as typical for her. She had on a shortish skirt. She looked good.

Not long ago, Aurit had told him that Hannah was seeing a documentary filmmaker. Naturally, this had bothered him a little. Documentary filmmakers were the most pretentious people in the world. He'd always thought so. The thought of some jackass filmmaker enjoying Hannah's intelligence, her humor, her maturity irritated him. He felt that only he, Nate, was smart enough to fully appreciate the value of her special merits. Which was insane.

He wondered now if she was still seeing the filmmaker. It would probably be weird to ask.

"I heard about your book," he said instead. "Congratulations."

"Thanks."

"I know it'll be terrific."

"That's nice of you to say."

Then silence—amiable enough, but soon a bit anxiety-provoking.

"So . . ." Nate began. There was something he wanted to say, but he didn't know what it was. For lack of anything else, he asked if she'd seen Peter. She shook her head. "He's here for the weekend," Nate said. "He'll be happy to see you."

He thought she blushed again. He wondered if that had been the wrong thing to say. But why? Perhaps it had just reminded her of things. Then he too remembered the night she'd met Peter. The restaurant, the conversation, her apartment after. He'd held her and he'd felt—he'd felt something so strong and so sad. Had he told her he loved her that night? He had loved her that night.

Suddenly, he was lightheaded. He gripped his plastic cup too tightly, and it began to crumple in his hand. Beer overflowed onto his shoe.

"Careful," Hannah said, smiling. Then, unexpectedly—he

thought they were just getting started—she said she should get going. "My, uh, friend is in the other room. We've actually got to take off. Tell Peter I said hello. I wish I'd seen him."

Nate left soon after. On the subway home, memories poured forth: long nights spent talking in the chairs by her window, in his bed, a lot of laughter, the easy but deep rapport, sex that at its best was full of such feeling, such intensity. He felt a sense of loss, the force of which surprised him as much as the fact of it. He'd thought about Hannah so infrequently since they'd broken up.

At home, he was met with a dry papery smell. The moving boxes, stacked in shadowy piles along the walls.

He began to pace. *Of course* Hannah never seemed more appealing than she did now, when she was out of reach, when he was about to move in with Greer. And yet he felt sure it was more than that, what he was feeling. The affection he felt for Hannah was real and spontaneous and familiar. It was what he had felt when they were together—at their best moments.

But he had been unhappy with her. That was why they'd broken up.

He retrieved a half-filled box from the ground and placed it on his desk, intending to pack up his file cabinet. He didn't. After a moment, he walked to the window. When he opened it, a blast of cold air rushed in. He let it wash over him, making the hairs on his arms stand up.

Even now, it was hard for him to say why he'd been unhappy with Hannah.

After a moment, he closed the window. He sat down at his computer. When he turned off the light and got into bed, it was nearly three. He still had trouble falling asleep.

At least, he thought as he turned over yet again, he'd be busy tomorrow. Maybe Greer would come help him pack. Clearly he wasn't very efficient on his own. Yes, that would be nice. Greer would fill the apartment with light cheer as she laughed at his pitiful progress and at the little messes that were constantly unearthed as he dug into the backs of his closets and moved items of furniture that had been rooted in place for years.

With this thought, Nate began to feel better. And then he knew. This thing he was feeling now—this sense of loss, of longing—would fade, pass from him like any other mood. As it should. What he and Greer had was pretty fucking good. Moreover, he liked his life, his friends. He was pleased with his progress on the new book; perhaps that was, for him, more important than anything else. He was, whether or not he deserved to be, happy.

In a few days, it would be as if this night never happened, the only evidence of it an unsent e-mail automatically saved to his drafts folder. ("Dear Hannah . . .") He'd no more remember the pain—or the pleasure—of this moment than he would remember, once he moved into the new apartment, the exact scent of the air from his bedroom window at dawn, after he'd been up all night working.

Acknowledgments

I was lucky to have incredibly supportive early readers. I am indebted to Melissa Flashman and Ryan Ruby, who read the book chapter by chapter as it was being written. Ryan, your line edits were terrific, and I'm grateful for the many conversations we had about Nate. Mel, your early enthusiasm helped me believe in the book. I'll always be incredibly grateful to you for that.

I'd also like to thank Stacey Vanek Smith, for her support not only of this novel but of previous attempts. Stacey, I will always think fondly on our long phone calls about Isabel and Abby and Tom, before Nate was a glimmer in anyone's eye. Carlin Flora also read more drafts than any person should have had to. Carlin, I have benefitted in both fiction and life from your sensitivity and insight into character and relationships.

Michelle Orange, Meline Toumani and Gary Sernovitz were also generous enough to read and respond very thoughtfully. Megan Hustad also provided excellent feedback.

I'd also like to thank Anthony Madrid, whose response to my first draft helped to shape the second. Also thank you for years and years of the most wonderful friendship and conversation imaginable. You taught me so much. I wouldn't recognize the person I'd be if I hadn't met you in Tucson all those years ago.

Thanks also to Dan Ray, Lou Rouse, Matt Bonds, and Myles Perkins for letting me listen in on years of guy talk.

I am very grateful to my literary agent, Elyse Cheney, who pushed me to make the novel as strong as it could be and who read it far too many times to count. In addition, Sarah Rainone is a sensitive, insightful, and creative editor, and I am indebted to her wonderful editorial skills. Thanks also to Alex Jacobs, who worked tirelessly on behalf of this novel, and read and responded to drafts at various crucial moments, and to Tania Strauss, who offered a refreshing new perspective.

I'd been told that editors don't really edit these days, but that couldn't be more false when it comes to Barbara Jones, my wonderfully sensitive and astute editor at Henry Holt. Thank you also to Joanna Levine, Kenn Russell, James Meader, Vicki Hare, David Shoemaker, and everyone else at Holt, with additional heartfelt thanks to the person who had to input my obsessive markings on the text. Also, I'm so grateful to Tom Avery, whose enthusiasm has meant so much, and to everyone at William Heinemann and especially Suzanne Dean. Speaking of Britain, thanks also to Natasha Fairweather.

I also want to thank my brothers, Zev and Steve Waldman. Zev, your line edits were terrific. Steve, I couldn't have had a more consistent and kind champion than you've been for so many years. My amazing and adored cousin Wilhelmina Waldman has also been a huge support over the years.

And of course a huge thank-you to my parents, who never once suggested that I get a "real" job and who have always been incredibly kind and supportive. Your love and patience have seen me through too many crises to count.

Finally, thanks to my amazing husband, Evan Hughes, from whom I have learned so much, about writing and everything else. Evan always treated my fiction writing as the most important thing I could be doing. He is a brilliant editor and a wonderful observer of people and has endured endless conversations about Nate and company. Evan, to say I couldn't have written this book without you is true—and beside the point. I can't begin to imagine my life without you.